HER LAST SUMMER

A Veronica Lee Thriller: Book One

Melinda Woodhall

Melinda Woodhall
Visit my website at www.melindawoodhall.com

Printed in the United States of America

First Printing: March 2020
Creative Magnolia

CHAPTER ONE

Portia Hart's four-inch heels clicked against polished marble as she entered the hotel suite's foyer, dropped her bag on the floor, and pressed a switch on the wall. Recessed lighting illuminated the luxurious suite's elegantly appointed sitting room. She didn't notice the man standing in the shadows as she crossed to the big window and looked down at the dark river below.

Catching sight of her reflection in the glass, she pushed back a strand of silky blond hair and inhaled deeply, then smiled and turned her head.

"I know you're here," Portia called out in a playful voice. "I can smell your cologne. It's the one I picked out for you in St. Barts, so you can stop playing around. I've been on my feet for hours and…"

Her voice faltered as Xavier Greyson appeared in the bedroom doorway. Folding leanly muscled arms over his smooth, bare chest, he rested against the doorjamb and let his lips curl into a wicked smile.

"I thought I'd surprise you and come early," he said, raising an eyebrow, "but if you'd rather I leave and come back *tomorrow*-"

"Oh no, you're here now and I'm not letting you go anywhere." Portia stepped forward, lifting her face to his. "I thought I'd have to spend the whole night up here all alone."

Melinda Woodhall

Allowing her to pull his head down for a lingering kiss, Xavier raised a hand and entwined it in her long, blonde hair. He tugged her head back and gazed down into her adoring eyes.

She really is a beautiful woman. And so very trusting.

He bestowed a gentle kiss on her forehead and released his grip. Ignoring her cry of protest, he moved back into the bedroom.

"First things first, my dear." His voice was soft but firm. "As you were saying, you've been on your feet for hours. You need a warm bath and a stiff drink."

Portia followed him through the bedroom into the suite's opulent bathroom where a crystal chandelier hung over a massive, freestanding tub. She gasped in pleasure; the tub was already full of hot water. Puffs of steam drifted up, turning the room into a warm, dreamy haze.

"That water looks divine." She turned to him and raised a perfectly arched eyebrow. "And the tub's deep enough for two."

Her whispered words sent a ripple of regret down his spine. For a split second, he was tempted to delay his plan and join her in the tub.

What harm will another hour do?

He dismissed the thought as quickly as it had come. He couldn't afford a further delay. The book signing had lasted longer than he'd anticipated, and the hardest part was yet to come.

No, the plan is in motion. There's no turning back now.

"I think you just might be right." Xavier reached out and untied the silk sash of her dress with a practiced hand. "So, why don't I go ahead and pour us some wine while you slip out of those clothes."

Leaving Portia to undress, Xavier padded back into the living room and crossed to the bar. An open bottle of the hotel's most expensive Merlot sat beside two crystal wine glasses. He reached into the pocket of his jeans, extracted a tiny plastic bag, and considered the fine white powder within.

This will make it all a bit easier. For both of us.

He shook the powder into the bottom of one glass then stuffed the bag back into his pocket.

"I was getting lonely in there."

Portia's voice startled him, and he jumped as her arms circled his waist. Her bare feet had made no sound on the marble floor.

Pouring a long splash of wine on top of the powder, Xavier exhaled and turned to peer down into Portia's eager face. He noticed that she'd changed into one of the hotel's bulky cotton robes.

"I ordered the best Merlot they had," he murmured, trying to gauge the look in her eyes as he handed her the wine, "to celebrate your book hitting the bestseller list *again*."

Portia shrugged her shoulders as if to say the achievement was no big deal, but a blush of happiness stained her cheeks. Xavier filled the other glass and lifted it to clink against hers. He wondered if she had noticed the slight tremor in his hand.

His heart faltered as he saw the smattering of white powder on the rim of her glass, but Portia seemed oblivious; she brought the glass to her lips and drank deeply.

"Now, let's see about that bath," she said, carrying her drink out of the room. "The water's getting cold."

Looking around the living room one last time, Xavier reviewed his plan. He didn't feel good about the delay, but he had no choice. He'd just have to get the next step over quickly and move on.

Relieved to see the robe discarded on the floor, a genuine smile played around his mouth as he took in Portia's long, slender figure reclining in the luxurious tub.

She is an exquisite woman. One of my better finds, I have to admit.

He shook his head to clear it.

"I'm feeling a little dizzy." Portia's words were slurred as she squinted up at him. "I think the water's too...hot."

Xavier took a deep breath and moved forward, steeling himself for what had to come next. The uneasy sensation was back. Something didn't feel right, but what could it be? Had he forgotten something? Or was he just getting weak and soft?

"You're just tired," he said, circling the tub and placing his well-manicured hands on Portia's shoulders. "I'll scrub your back."

"No, I really...don't feel well. I want to get out. I don't-"

A gush of hot water stopped her words as he forced her shoulders down, triggering a sudden flash of panic. She flailed her arms and kicked her feet, sending a wave of water over the side of the tub.

Anger flooded through Xavier as he struggled to hold Portia down, feeling the scalding water soak through his jeans.

The bitch got my jeans wet. How am I supposed to get out of here now?

He gripped her shoulders with mounting frustration. A black t-shirt and hoodie were hanging safely in the closet, but all his other clothes were packed and waiting for him in the car.

He hadn't planned on leaving the hotel looking like a drowned rat. His appearance would definitely raise questions. Especially since the after-dinner crowd had likely dispersed by now. A lone man walking out in soaking wet jeans would be noticed.

A stinging pain brought his attention back to the woman struggling under the water. Portia had stuck up one desperate hand to claw at his wrist, while her other hand now gripped the edge of the tub. Xavier grimaced as her long fingernails dug into his skin.

Stifling the curse that hovered on his lips, he tightened his aching hands in frustration and pushed Portia lower in the water.

I should've waited for her to pass out. I should've followed the plan.

Her eyes bulged and widened in fear in the water below him, and he looked away with distaste, knowing from experience that her face would soon darken into a revolting shade of blue. Xavier kept his cold eyes averted as Portia convulsed beneath him, refusing to give in to his rising panic.

Everything is going to be all right. I'll find another way out and no one will ever know I was here. I'll be long gone before she's even discovered.

4

Finally, after what seemed to Xavier like hours, her body went limp and sank heavily to the bottom. One last feeble gush of water spilled over the side as the struggle ended.

Xavier's heavy breathing was the only sound in the room as he gazed down at Portia's lifeless body with grim satisfaction. The job was almost done.

A high-pitched ring filled the silence of the room, and Xavier jumped in alarm as Portia's cell phone vibrated against the marble countertop. He looked over at the phone with narrowed eyes.

Crossing to silence the call, he recognized the face that flashed on the screen. It was Jane Bishop, Portia's literary agent. He pushed the button to send the call to voicemail, and the display went dark again. But Jane Bishop's meddlesome face had heightened his anxiety.

It'll only be a matter of time before the old bat sends out the calvary.

Xavier knew he'd better hurry. He'd gotten through the hardest part of the plan already. It was time to move on to the next stage. He turned to survey the room. Puddles of water surrounded the tub, and the cotton robe rested in a sodden heap several feet away. Splotches of blood made a trail from the tub to where he stood by the sink.

He looked down to see two bloody scratches on his forearm.

"Shit!"

Grabbing a plush hand towel, he wrapped it around his arm and tried to think. He'd screwed up, but he still had a chance. He'd always managed to find a way out before. This time would be no different. He just needed to keep his head straight and act fast. Pulling more towels off the rack, he fell to his knees and began wiping up the water.

✳ ✳ ✳

Xavier gave one last look around the room and sighed. He'd done what he could to correct his mistakes. The floor was relatively clean, his wine glass had been rinsed and dried, the empty pill bottle was on the counter, and Portia's body was motionless in the cooling water.

Now he needed to focus on his escape. The whole ordeal had taken much longer than he'd planned, and the hotel was bound to be quiet and deserted by now. Small towns like Willow Bay never had much of a nightlife, even if it was a Friday. His plan of mingling in with the crowd that was leaving the event would no longer be feasible.

By now the only one hanging around will be a bored security guard.

No, he'd have to move on to plan B, and he'd need to do it fast. The longer he hung around, the more likely he'd encounter a witness. Or make another mistake.

Zipping his jacket, Xavier felt the right pocket to reassure himself that the thick roll of cash and Cartier watch were still safely inside. He pulled his hood up to cover his head and opened the door.

The suite was located at the end of the hall just as he'd recommended to Portia, telling her it would protect her privacy and shield their relationship from the prying eyes of the public and press.

If she'd suspected he had wanted to avoid the cameras positioned on each floor by the elevator, she had never mentioned it. She'd trusted him after all.

Head down, Xavier stepped into the corridor and hurried toward the stairs at the end. A red *EXIT* sign glowed overhead as he slowly pushed the metal door open.

Half expecting to hear the wailing of an alarm, he relaxed his shoulders and stepped into the hot, dimly lit stairwell. A faint *click, click, click* made him look down.

Drops of water fell from his still-soggy jeans and splashed onto the concrete floor. But was that what he'd heard? Shaking away a feeling of unease, he began to hurry down the stairs. Fourteen flights of stairs and he'd be outside and home free.

But the clicking started again, and this time Xavier recognized the sound of high heels descending the stairs a few flights below him. Startled, he leaned over the rail and looked down into the upturned face of an equally startled young woman with long, bright pink hair. Her eyes, rimmed with heavy black liner, widened at the rage etched on his face, then dropped to take in the hoody and wet jeans.

Knowing he had only seconds to act, Xavier hurled himself forward, banging down the stairs toward the only person that had seen his face. The only person that would be able to place him at the hotel. He had to stop her before she got away. He had to make sure she didn't have a chance to tell anyone what he'd done.

CHAPTER TWO

V eronica Lee emptied the remains of her breakfast into the trash and rinsed her plate in the sink. She wasn't expected at the Channel Ten news station for another hour. That left just enough time for a quick run. Opening the front door, she stepped out into the blazing hot Florida morning, narrowly missing Winston's fluffy orange tail.

"What are you doing out here, boy?" She bent and stroked the big tabby's thick fur. "You must be baking out here with that coat on."

Winston blinked up at her with blatant disinterest, then plopped his head back onto his paws, as if the ongoing heatwave had drained all his energy. Veronica continued down the porch steps, but the buzzing of her phone stopped her halfway down the walk.

As soon as she saw Hunter Hadley's number she turned and trudged back up the stairs. The station manager wouldn't call unless something big was going on. Her run would have to wait.

Her boss didn't waste any words on a greeting.

"Portia Hart was found dead in her suite at the Riverview Hotel this morning. I'm heading to the van now. I'll meet you there."

"You're going to the scene? What about Gustavo?"

"Gustavo *texted in* his notice last night." Hunter's voice dripped with disdain. "He's going to Channel Six. Actually, he's already gone, so I'll run the camera. Now *go*."

Veronica closed the door behind her and headed upstairs to change into camera-ready clothes. Pulling out a navy-blue dress and matching heels, she considered adding a tailored jacket.

No, definitely too hot for that. I'd just end up sweating on camera.

Brushing her long dark hair into a high ponytail, she surveyed the effect in the full-length mirror behind her door.

"I look like I'm about twelve," she complained to her reflection as she applied two coats of black mascara, swiped on a classic red lipstick, and added a rosy blush to her cheeks.

"There...that's a little better."

She turned away from the mirror with a sigh and headed down the hall, trying to tread as quietly as possible past her mother's closed door. It was a Saturday, and Ling Lee would want to sleep in. Her job as Willow Bay High School's principal meant she had a six o'clock wake-up each weekday, even during the summer school schedule, and she would get irritable if she didn't have a few extra hours of sleep on the weekends.

And, of course, it would make it much easier for Veronica to leave the house if her mother wasn't aware she'd been called to report on an active scene.

Ling Lee had always been an overprotective mother, but she'd grown increasingly paranoid after Veronica had been taken hostage by the Willow Bay Stalker only months before. Although Veronica had escaped without serious injury, both mother and daughter had been traumatized by the ordeal.

And while Veronica had thrown herself into her work to try to forget that she'd almost been the victim of a serial killer, her mother hadn't been able to move on quite so easily. Ling's constant worrying had grown worse, and Veronica could rarely leave the house without listening to a litany of dire predictions. She had heard them so often that they played over and over in her mind even when Ling wasn't around.

"I warned you to take care, Veronica. You can't trust anyone. Especially strange men like that Boyd Faraday. Next time you might not be so lucky."

Shaking her head to clear out her mother's warnings, Veronica opened the front door and scooped up Winston. The hefty cat had been a welcome source of comfort during the last difficult months, and she hugged him to her as she carried him to the kitchen.

"It's way too hot out there for you to be running around, Winston," she said, pouring fresh water and kibble into his bowls. "You better stay inside...where it's safe."

She smiled as the tabby lowered his head to the bowl, dismissing her concerns with a swish of his tail. She was beginning to sound just like her mother.

* * *

Veronica parked her big red Jeep in the Riverview Hotel garage and stepped out into the blinding glare of the July sun. As her eyes adjusted, she took in the crowd of reporters, gawkers, and officials gathered outside the hotel's main lobby. She marveled that they seemed oblivious to the intense heat radiating off the pavement.

Or maybe after a month of record-breaking temperatures and record-low rainfall, we're all just getting used to it.

The police had cordoned off a press area. Veronica noted with dismay that the Channel Six news crew had already claimed the prime spot between the hotel's drop-off lane and the busy boardwalk that led down to the river. It looked like they were preparing to shoot a live feed.

Nick Sargent acknowledged Veronica with a brisk wave. The poplar Channel Six reporter's even features, close-cropped hair, and smoothly-shaven jaw had earned him a clean-cut image that worked well with his viewers. Veronica was tempted to wave back before she caught sight of Gustavo Perez standing behind Nick's tall frame.

The cameraman caught her eye and shrugged his skinny shoulders, then offered Veronica a toothy smile. She glared and turned away as he lifted his camera toward Nick.

Her gaze fell on a uniformed officer that stood guard in front of the hotel's employees-only side entrance. He looked familiar.

"Officer Eddings?" Veronica held up her press credentials as she approached. "Remember me? I'm Veronica Lee...with Channel Ten."

Officer Eddings' boyish face lit up.

"Sure, I remember you. You were in that special report on the Willow Bay Stalker. That was good work, Ms. Lee."

"Just doing my job." Veronica suppressed a pleased smile. "I'm wondering if you can tell me what happened to Portia Hart?"

A guarded look replaced the smile.

"I wish I could help you, Ms. Lee, but I've been given strict orders not to make any statements to the press." Looking around as if he feared being overheard, he lowered his voice. "Our new media relations officer was pretty adamant about that."

Hiding her disappointment, Veronica nodded and shrugged.

"Well, orders are orders, Officer. Thanks anyway."

She started to turn away, but Eddings reached out a hand.

"I can't make an official statement," he said, clearing his throat. "but unofficially I can tell you that the cleaner who found the body had already been talking to your competitor when we arrived."

"My competitor?" Veronica asked, her eyes flicking around the scene. "You mean Nick Sargent with Channel Six has already spoken to a witness?"

Before Eddings could reply, Hunter Hadley appeared beside her with a camera in hand.

"As I said...our media relations officer, Ms. Frost, will be making an official statement as soon as information becomes available," Eddings blurted, eyeing Hunter with suspicion. "That's all I can say."

So much for me getting the inside story now.

Veronica turned her frustrated eyes on Hunter, who leaned in close as if to tell her a secret. She forced herself to ignore the jolt of excitement that shot through her at his nearness, and instead tried to focus on his words.

"Slimy Nick Sargent has scooped us again," Hunter muttered, giving Gustavo a dirty look. "And he's stolen our cameraman."

"What's so slimy about Nick Sargent?" Veronica kept her voice low as she gave the Channel Six crew a sideways glance. "He seems nice enough to me."

"Sure, he puts on a good act, but I've dealt with enough lowlifes in my time to see through his nice-guy routine. You will, too...*eventually.*"

Bristling at his patronizing tone, Veronica watched her boss stride back toward the news van. He stopped to greet someone in the crowd, lifting a hand to brush a dark curl off his forehead. She felt her eyes lingering on his broad shoulders and his strong, tan forearms.

"I got a family to feed."

Veronica jumped as Gustavo Perez suddenly appeared beside her.

"Gotta go where the money is, you know. And from what I hear Channel Ten is pretty much bankrupt. She's going down and I didn't want to go with her."

Veronica frowned at him in confusion.

Is Channel Ten in financial trouble? How would Gustavo know?

She pushed the disturbing thought away when she saw Nessa Ainsley's unmistakable red curls approaching through the crowd. Willow Bay's new chief of police was walking beside the town's medical examiner, Iris Nguyen.

"Nessa? Do you have an update for us?" Veronica called, trying to catch the police chief's eye. "Have you established cause of death?"

Nessa stopped in front of Veronica and shook her head.

"All I can confirm is that the body of a woman was found this morning in a guestroom at the Riverview Hotel. The woman's identification and the details surrounding her death have to be withheld pending the notification of next of kin."

Hunter Hadley approached with the camera lowered by his side.

"I hate to break it to you, Chief Ainsley, but Channel Six already broadcast the name of the woman as Portia Hart. Are you disputing the Channel Six report?"

"No, dammit, I'm not, but-"

"Well, Portia Hart is...was...a celebrity," Hunter said. "So, I'd assume there's no putting the genie back into the bottle now."

Nessa ignored the comment. She stormed past the circle of people gathered around Nick Sargent's tall, athletic figure as he spoke to the camera in a grave voice that perfectly matched the somber expression on his face.

"...an anonymous source on the hotel staff shared the shocking details behind the woman's death."

Nick kept his dark eyes fixed on the lens as Gustavo operated the big camera.

"We can now reveal that Portia Hart, the author of the runaway bestseller, *Simply Portia*, and a social media sensation, was discovered dead in the bathtub of her hotel suite this morning."

A gasp of shock and dismay rippled through the crowd. Nessa uttered a low curse as she heard Nick's next dramatic statement.

"Sources have also indicated that Portia Hart's tragic death may have been drug-related. Stayed tuned for further details as the story develops. This is Nick Sargent with Channel Six News, reporting live outside the Riverview Hotel in downtown Willow Bay."

"He's just speculating," Hunter muttered in her ear. "Trying to sensationalize the story to raise his ratings, as usual."

Shocked into momentary silence by the disconcerting idea that Portia Hart, the poster girl for clean, simple living, had died of a drug overdose, Veronica followed Hunter back to the Channel Ten van. They still needed to shoot their segment, even if they didn't have much information to share.

Nick Sargent may have beaten them to the scene, but he was risking his reputation, and that of the entire Channel Six station, by reporting on rumors and conjecture. Veronica wondered what he was trying to do. Were ratings really more important than the truth?

Maybe Hunter's right. Maybe Nick Sargent really is a slimy lowlife.

Reviewing her notes one last time, Veronica took a long, calming breath and kept her eyes on Hunter's fingers as he counted her down.

Five, four, three, two, one...

"This is Veronica Lee with a Channel Ten breaking news report brought to you live from the Riverview Hotel."

She ignored the trickle of sweat making its way down her back.

"Portia Hart, bestselling author, and daughter of the late billionaire Remington Hart is dead. As her many fans and followers begin to mourn, the authorities in Willow Bay are now working to determine a cause of death..."

CHAPTER THREE

Nessa Ainsley followed Iris Nguyen off the elevator and down the long hall. She winced as they stopped in the open doorway of Suite 1408, recognizing the sickly smell that hung in the air. The stench of death and decay never got any easier to take.

Pulling on the protective mask, gloves, and booties that Iris had provided, Nessa followed the ME into the suite and looked around.

"Nice view," she murmured, gesturing toward the large window while trying to ignore the queasiness that had settled in her stomach.

"We're in here, Nessa," a deep voice called from beyond the door leading into the bedroom. "Is Iris with you?"

"Yep, I'm here." Iris stuck her head into the bathroom and studied the room through protective goggles before stepping inside. "And Wesley will come up with the gurney once he parks the van."

Moving into the room behind Iris, Nessa waved at Detective Tucker Vanzinger, then forced herself to look toward the tub. She dreaded what she was about to see but knew she didn't have a choice.

When she'd been promoted to chief of police earlier in the year, Nessa had promised herself she would stay actively involved in the department's efforts to keep Willow Bay safe. She couldn't do that by sitting behind a big desk and barking orders, no mattered how much that idea appealed to her at the present moment.

The body in the tub looked nothing like the broken, decomposing bodies Nessa had often witnessed at other scenes. Portia Hart's pink, unblemished limbs floated under the surface, completely submerged in the clear water. Her head slumped down at an awkward angle and her face was hidden behind a tangle of long, blonde hair. The ends drifted in the water around her narrow shoulders.

Reaching out a gloved hand, Iris shifted a sodden strand of hair away from Portia's face, revealing a gruesome patch of bloated, discolored skin. Pulling the hair back even further, Iris pointed to the white froth that had bubbled out of Portia's nose and mouth.

"The froth could mean the deceased inhaled liquid into her lungs," Iris murmured, "although it could also be a sign of a drug overdose or even a cardiac event."

Nessa tried not to show her revulsion, but her stomach heaved as the putrid stench grew stronger, and she was forced to turn away.

"What's your initial take on this, Vanzinger? Accidental overdose? Suicide?" she asked in a tight voice. "Any signs of foul play?"

"I wouldn't rule anything out yet." Vanzinger rubbed the stubble on his cheek with a big hand, as if to soothe himself. "I took a look around and have some questions."

Nessa raised her eyebrows and waited.

"For one thing, there's an empty pill bottle on the sink. The patient name's been scratched off, so that got my attention."

"Of course, we can't say for sure she took whatever was in it." He cocked his head and looked over at Iris. "We'll need the autopsy results to know what she ingested and if it killed her."

"Okay, what else?" Nessa asked, sensing Vanzinger's unease.

"Well, I noticed that there aren't any towels in here. Like...none."

Looking around, Nessa saw that the silver towel racks were empty.

"I mean, a fancy room like this is bound to have a whole stack of plush towels, and I wondered what happened to them," Vanzinger continued. "Turns out there's a pile of them in the bedroom closet. A big, wet pile. Seems weird."

A loud rap on the doorframe announced the arrival of Wesley Knox. The brawny forensic technician carried a big bag over one muscular shoulder. A camera hung from a strap around his neck.

"We'll photograph the body in situ first, Wesley," Iris instructed. "I also want to take samples of the water before we move her."

Nessa stepped back, giving Iris and Wesley room to move around the tub as they photographed the body from every angle. Her eyes fell on the empty pill bottle. She bent to read the label, not wanting to disturb the bottle until Iris had a chance to photograph and bag it. The top of the label had been scraped off, although a thin strip remained. Nessa could make out a long string of numbers.

"Jankowski said I could take lead on this one," Vanzinger said over her shoulder. "If that's okay with you."

"Sure, that's a good idea," Nessa agreed, glancing back at the figure in the tub. "He'll probably find this scene...*difficult*. It hasn't been that long since he found Gabby's body."

They both fell silent at the mention of Vanzinger's partner. Detective Simon Jankowski's ex-wife had been Willow Bay's media relations officer before she'd met an untimely end at the hands of the Willow Bay Stalker. Although Jankowski had ultimately helped bring the killer to justice, he was still trying to heal and come to terms with everything that had happened.

"Nessa, I think you'll want to see this," Iris called out.

The diminutive medical examiner was leaning over the tub, looking through the camera lens into the water. She motioned for Nessa to stand beside her.

"There's slight bruising on her shoulders as if someone was gripping them." Iris moved back to give Nessa more room. "And two of the fingernails on her right hand are broken. See there?"

Staring into the water, Nessa saw Portia's right hand resting on the bottom of the tub. The fingernails on her index and middle fingers were cracked, leaving angry red lines where the tips used to be.

"We'll need to look for the rest of the nails," Vanzinger muttered. "See if she broke them while she was here in the room."

"Looks like they've been torn off to me," Wesley said, his voice hesitant, "like maybe she was defending herself."

Iris moved to the other side of the tub and took a few more shots of Portia's hand at various angles before looking up.

"Let's not jump to any conclusions, Wesley. Fingernails get broken all the time. If the deceased was taking medication she may have passed out or fallen, which could also explain the bruises. We won't know for sure what happened until we're done with our exam and the autopsy."

Meeting Vanzinger's eyes over the tub, Nessa wondered what they were going to tell the press outside.

If I tell the reporters out there that we don't have the foggiest clue how or why Porta Hart died, they'll call for my badge...or my head.

"You think somebody set this whole thing up? That somebody killed Portia Hart and then tried to make it look like an accident?"

Vanzinger's suggestion set Nessa's nerves on edge. Could Portia Hart have been murdered? If so, who would want to kill a woman that had helped millions of people get their lives back on track?

"Maybe she did this to herself," Nessa mused out loud. "Maybe the whole celebrity thing became too much for her."

"Yeah, it seems like lots of famous people turn to drugs to deal with the pressure," Vanzinger conceded. "Maybe Portia Hart had a secret habit that she couldn't handle anymore."

Nessa wondered if the fabulously rich and beautiful Portia Hart would have really wanted to kill herself.

And addicted to pills? I'd never have guessed.

The whole phenomenon around Portia's hugely successful book, *Simply Portia*, had centered on Portia's revelation that living a simple life of gratitude had brought her greater happiness than living the jet setting life of luxury and wealth she'd been born into.

Everyday people had been fascinated to read that the glamorous daughter of the late billionaire Remington Hart had found true happiness by giving up many of the things most people could only dream of attaining.

Even Nessa had a copy of Portia's book waiting to be read on her bedside table. She'd been hoping it contained the secret to making her own life a little simpler and a little happier.

The admission made her feel extremely ungrateful, especially since she was finally where she wanted to be both personally and professionally. After years of hard work, she was the police chief of a town that she loved, and after a decade of marriage, she and Jerry were still going strong.

So, why can't I just relax and enjoy what I've got?

The answer to that question was what Nessa and millions of other women in similar situations had hoped to find in Portia Hart's book. But looking at the empty pill bottle, Nessa now wondered if the author had secretly been an addict who had used a façade of happiness to sell her book.

Was everything she said in her book just a lie?

The thought depressed her. If Portia Hart had been miserable enough to kill herself, intentionally or not, could any regular woman hope to find simple happiness?

Nessa turned to see Vanzinger looking even more downhearted than she felt. The idea of anyone taking their own life would depress the most optimistic of souls, but Vanzinger's miserable expression told Nessa that something more personal was bothering him. All of a sudden, she realized what it must be.

"I'm thinking of calling Riley Odell," she said, trying to sound casual. "If there's even a chance this is a homicide, we're going to need all the help we can get right from the start."

Vanzinger frowned.

"What good's the state prosecutor going to be if we don't even have a suspect? Hell, we don't even know if a crime's been committed."

"Well, she can help us prepare the case for one thing, and make sure the media doesn't taint any future jury pool."

Avoiding Vanzinger's skeptical gaze, Nessa moved toward the door. She wanted to get Riley Odell's take on the situation. And just maybe Vanzinger and Riley would patch things up if they worked together on a case. It was worth a try.

Taking out her phone, Nessa tapped in a number she'd come to know pretty well over the last few months. Of course, it was Saturday and Riley might have turned her phone off, but if the town's new prosecutor was half as driven as Nessa suspected, she figured Riley would be working, and that she'd want to know about the potentially high-profile case as soon as possible.

CHAPTER FOUR

R iley Odell sat up straight and stretched her aching back, grateful it was the weekend, and City Hall was closed to the public; the normally busy halls were blissfully cool and quiet. She surveyed the stack of files on her desk and sighed. It seemed the stack was always expanding, no matter how many late nights and weekends she worked.

While Willow Bay was one of the smaller communities within Riley's assigned judicial circuit, the little town had eaten up most of her time and attention during the last few months due to the Willow Bay Stalker trial. But now that Boyd Faraday was safely locked away, she needed to focus on the pending cases waiting for her attention.

Her phone buzzed just as she reached for the top file on the stack. The caller's name on the display prompted another sigh.

"Nessa? What's up?"

"Portia Hart's been found dead in her suite at the Riverview Hotel." The police chief's familiar southern drawl sounded strained.

Riley frowned.

"Portia Hart? Am I supposed to know who that is?"

Nessa snorted.

"I thought you were part of the connected social media generation. You should know these things. Portia Hart is Remington Hart's daughter. You know him, right?"

Riley didn't bother answering. Everyone knew the billionaire financier and his wife who had died in a horrific plane crash years before. The name was as well-known as Rockefeller or Vanderbilt. He'd been American royalty.

"Well, his daughter Portia wrote a book that's sold about a gazillion copies," Nessa continued. "She was in Willow Bay on a book tour. Stayed at the Riverview Hotel last night. The cleaner found her this morning floating in the bathtub."

"Oh...that's terrible." Riley's initial surprise was followed by a sinking suspicion. "And you're calling *me*, so it must have been a homicide. How exactly did she die?"

"Well, we aren't sure yet. Could be a suicide or an accidental overdose, but there are signs that someone else may have been in the room with her...that there may have been a struggle."

Riley sat up straighter in her chair.

"So, her death is suspicious?"

"Well, yeah," Nessa conceded. "Of course, Iris Nguyen can't make an official determination until the autopsy and death investigation are complete, and the press is already outside the hotel running live reports and circling like vultures."

Stomach sinking, Riley pictured the media circus that was sure to follow. Press coverage of any high-profile victim's death was always intense, but if Remington Hart's daughter had been murdered, it would be especially brutal. They'd all need to be prepared for the onslaught.

"I just thought you'd like a heads up," Nessa added. "If we open up a homicide investigation the press will be all over us looking for answers. They'll want someone charged; we'll be on the hot seat until we have a suspect."

Hearing a deep voice in the background, Riley realized that Detective Tucker Vanzinger must be working the case.

"Are you calling from the scene?" she asked, already on her feet.

"Yep, but Iris will be transporting the body over to the ME's office pretty soon. Of course, if we call this a suspicious death, we'll need to have Alma and her team come in and do a full search of the scene."

Riley heard the hesitation in Nessa's voice. The new chief of police was about to open a can of worms, and she was smart enough to be worried about it.

"I'll be right over," Riley found herself saying. "We'll need to work together closely on this. Present a united front to the press and the community."

Riley didn't wait for Nessa's response. She ended the call and headed out into the stifling heat.

* * *

It wasn't quite noon when Riley arrived at the Riverview Hotel, her glossy black hair already wilting. She glared at the sun, angered by its relentless assault on the sweltering town, but that only caused her eyes to water.

"Any chance of rain today, Officer?" she called out as she approached the cordoned-off security entrance where Andy Ford stood guard. "Or would that be asking too much?"

Andy grinned at her and shrugged.

"I wouldn't count on it, Ms. Odell," he replied as he waved her through. "From what I hear we won't see any rain until next week."

Stepping into the air-conditioned lobby, Riley breathed a sigh of relief and looked around for Nessa.

A middle-aged man stood by the elevator in a shiny suit. His nametag identified him as *Dennis Robinson, Hotel Manager*. He kept anxious eyes trained on Riley as she approached.

"I'm looking for Chief Ainsley with the WBPD."

Riley kept her voice crisp and authoritative.

"She's on the fourteenth floor." The manager gestured toward the elevator with a curt wave. "Along with a whole heap of other people."

The elevator doors were just about to close behind Riley when Dennis Robinson stuck out a hand to stop them.

"You wouldn't know how long this is gonna take, would you? I don't wanna sound heartless, but it's bad for business, you know?"

"What I know, Mr. Robinson, is that a woman's dead and we need to find out why." Riley's voice was ice cold. "But I can assure you that it'll take less time if you stop asking inane questions and let us do our job."

Watching the shocked hotel manager's face disappear behind the closing doors, Riley felt a stirring of guilt.

The poor man is just trying to run his business. He has a right to know what's going on.

Riley knew if she were ever going to fit into the small town, she would need to learn how to play nice. Willow Bay wasn't like Miami or Tampa. It wasn't a busy city bustling with strangers that you might never see again.

She stepped off the elevator on the fourteenth floor and saw Tucker Vanzinger's red crew cut and broad shoulders at the end of the hall. Her intention to play nice evaporated, replaced by a grim resolve. She wouldn't let herself be fooled by the big detective again. She was older now, and wiser. An expert in the art of self-preservation.

"Hey, Riley, how are you?"

Responding to Vanzinger's greeting with a curt nod, Riley strode to meet him halfway down the hall.

"Nessa already filled me in on the basics." She opened a notepad and took the cap off her pen. "Has the ME given you a preliminary cause of death yet? Or time of death?"

"Iris is just talking to Nessa now." Vanzinger studied Riley's face with a hurt expression. "They're getting ready to move the body. That should throw the media into a frenzy."

She thought of the reporters gathering outside. More news crews from around the state, maybe even around the country, would be arriving as the news spread. The demand for all the gory details would grow. Tenley Frost would need to make a statement soon.

"What about her next of kin?"

The change of subject seemed to throw Vanzinger.

"Oh, well, I guess Iris will make the official notification, and then we'll set up time for an interview. I-"

"Where are the security tapes?"

Vanzinger stiffened at her sharp tone.

"Why are you involved already, Riley?" he asked, crossing his thick arms over his chest. "Shouldn't you just sit back in that big office of yours and wait for us to identify a suspect?"

Regarding him with cool, indifferent eyes, Riley shook her head.

"Things have changed in Willow Bay since we first worked together, Detective Vanzinger. It's no longer *business as usual* on my watch."

Vanzinger remained silent and cocked his head as if waiting for her to continue. She obliged, trying to sound detached even as her blood boiled. He should know better than anyone else that the WBPD needed to change the way it operated. And Nessa couldn't do that single-handedly.

"If the WBPD determines the scene is in fact a homicide, then having the prosecutor involved from the start can only be a help."

She paused as frustration flooded Vanzinger's face.

"Is there a problem, Detective?"

Shrugging, Vanzinger motioned to the door.

"Just wondering if you're done now. Cause I got a dead woman in there and I gotta figure out what or who killed her."

He didn't wait for her answer, just spun on his heel and marched back down the hall. Riley followed close behind him, indignant at his rebuke but determined to keep her calm. She couldn't let him see the effect he had on her.

The smell seeping out of Room 1408 made her eyes water, and she stopped at the door, glad that crime scene protocol prevented her from entering.

Determined not to gag, she looked through the living room into the open bedroom door just as Wesley Knox and Iris Nguyen emerged pushing a gurney. Riley's stomach clenched as she caught a glimpse of Portia Hart's discolored face.

Seeing Riley's stricken expression, Iris pulled up a crisp white sheet, covering everything but one tangled strand of blonde hair that had escaped. As she stepped out of the way to let the gurney pass, Riley caught sight of her own pale, strained face in the mirror across the room. She almost didn't recognize herself.

Is that what I've become? A miserable, uptight stranger?

Once again, she questioned her real motivation in pushing for the assignment in Willow Bay. What had she been trying to accomplish by coming back to the place that had almost broken her? And what was she doing now by thrusting herself into Vanzinger's case?

What am I trying to prove?

Forcing her focus back to the situation at hand, Riley cleared her mind. There was no room for self-doubt. She was good at her job and there was a suspicious death to resolve. She couldn't let anything get in the way.

Iris and Wesley rolled the body down the long hall toward the wide service elevator used by the hotel staff. Riley watched as the elevator doors closed behind the gurney, then turned to see Nessa behind her.

"Looks like we're gonna have to treat this as a possible homicide." Nessa pulled down her face mask and exhaled heavily. "Iris suspects

Portia drowned, and that she may have been forcibly held underwater."

Nessa continued before Riley could ask any questions.

"There are bruises on Portia Hart's arms and shoulders, and she has several broken fingernails."

"And those pile of wet towels didn't get there by themselves," Vanzinger chimed in. "I mean, why would Portia have dried up the floor, stashed the towels in the room, and then gone back to the tub? It just doesn't add up."

Riley opened her mouth to argue that there were other possibilities and other scenarios, then closed it again. This wasn't the time or place to get into a disagreement with Tucker Vanzinger. Sensing the friction between Riley and Vanzinger, Nessa held up a placating hand.

"Okay, then it's settled," she said. "Let's get Alma and the crime scene team down here right away. They can perform a thorough search and collect any evidence."

Vanzinger frowned at Nessa's words and cleared his throat. Riley saw a blush of color work its way up his neck.

"Um, I actually called Alma as soon as I saw the broken fingernails," he admitted, then nodded toward Riley. "And I thought you agreed it was suspicious, Nessa. Why else would you ask the state prosecutor to come down here? I guess I should have waited-"

"No, you did the right thing, Vanzinger. This is your case and your scene. I'm just here to lend a hand and offer guidance."

But Vanzinger's frown didn't fade. Riley could see something else was bothering him.

"What's wrong, Detective?"

"Well, the press got wind of all this and spread the news before we could notify this woman's family. She may have been some kind of famous author, but I think her family still deserves to hear the news officially."

Both Nessa and Riley stared at Vanzinger in surprise. Nessa pushed back a red curl and sighed.

"I have to agree. Vanzinger, why don't you go on over to the ME's office and work with Iris on the next of kin notification? Between the two of you, I'm sure you can handle it."

A frowned flashed between Vanzinger's eyes, but he only nodded.

"I'll join you shortly," Nessa continued. "And if we're lucky, Iris will agree to perform the autopsy this afternoon."

Riley watched with mixed emotions as Vanzinger hurried toward the elevator. She'd learned the hard way that some men couldn't be trusted, no matter how nice they seemed. No matter how badly you wanted to believe that their nice-guy routine wasn't just an act.

But she'd allowed Tucker Vanzinger to lure her in before, and he'd let her down in the worst possible way. It had taken her a long time to get over his abrupt departure from her life. Now, a decade later, she was stronger and smarter. Too strong to let him see how much he'd hurt her, and too smart to fall for the same game twice.

CHAPTER FIVE

Lexi Marsh rolled onto her side and pulled the thin sheet up to her neck, but she still couldn't seem to find a comfortable position in the lumpy double bed. The late-night encounter in the stairwell had spooked her, and she hadn't been able to sleep at all after she'd raced back to her apartment at half-past midnight.

Every time she tried to close her eyes, she saw the man's enraged face framed by the dark hood and heard the ominous sound of his shoes pounding down the stairs after her.

Giving up all hope of sleep, Lexi sat on the edge of the bed and reached for her purse. She dug around in the little bag until her fingers found the plastic pill bottle. Her stomach dropped at the hollow sound of the last two pills rattling against each other.

This bottle was supposed to last a fucking week. Molly's gonna go apeshit if I go back to her asking for more so soon.

She shook out the pills and stared at them, wondering if she should just take one and save the other one for later. Her hands trembled slightly, making the pills jitter in her palm. She impulsively popped them both in her mouth before she could stop herself.

Picking up a half-empty soda can on the bedside table, she washed down the pills and forced herself up and off the bed. She wanted to get out of the suffocating room.

I need to eat something. Or maybe have a smoke. Just one...that'll be it.

Lexi hadn't smoked a cigarette for more than a week, but the insidious thought played over and over, stuck in her mind like the random line from a song that wouldn't go away.

No, I have to quit...otherwise I'll end up getting lung cancer like Granny.

Stumbling out to the living room, she tried not to think of all the other things she needed to quit. Smoking was only one of the vices she had that threatened her health and safety on a daily basis.

The living room window was shuttered, and Lexi glanced toward the shadowy corners of the little room as if the man from last night might be standing there waiting for her. Flipping on the light, she noted with relief that the only thing in the corner was a dusty pair of running shoes. The relief turned to guilt as she tried to remember the last time she'd had the energy to go for a run.

Sinking onto the sofa with the television remote in hand, Lexi felt the pills beginning to take effect; all thoughts of exercise and guilt floated away. She just needed a little time to relax. Maybe a dose of reality television would help.

She pressed the *ON* button, leaned back, and exhaled. Everything was going to be all right. Sure, she'd had a scare, but that was to be expected in her line of work. It came with the job.

Lexi gazed at the screen, her mind wandering as the Channel Ten noon broadcast started. Suddenly registering what the reporter was saying, she sat up straight and read the headline, squinting to make sure it was real. That it wasn't just the pills.

Portia Hart, bestselling author and daughter of the late billionaire Remington Hart found dead this morning in the Riverview Hotel.

A young, female reporter stood outside the familiar hotel as Lexi gazed on in horrified silence.

"This morning a woman's body was found on the fourteenth floor of the Riverview Hotel. Although police have declined to officially name the deceased until next of kin has been notified, unofficial sources have confirmed that the body was that of Portia Hart, the popular author of the runaway self-help bestseller, *Simply Portia*, and the daughter of the late billionaire, Remington Hart."

Lexi tried to think. The woman's body had been found on the fourteenth floor. She pictured the angry man who had chased her down the stairs and wondered again what he'd been doing on the stairwell in the middle of the night.

Was he trying to get out of the hotel without being seen...like me?

Could the man have been coming from the fourteenth floor? Lexi's date had been staying on the tenth floor, and she'd left via the stairs as usual, just as she'd been instructed. Thinking back, it seemed to fit. She must have had at least a four-floor head start to outrun him.

Of course, it didn't hurt that she knew the big hotel like the back of her hand. She'd snuck out of it plenty of times trying to avoid the security guards that patrolled the lobby and parking garage, and she'd known from habit to make a sharp right turn as soon as she had flown through the exit door.

A slight gap in the railing had allowed her to slip around to the back of the big concrete parking structure. From there it had only been a five-minute walk to the side street where she always parked her old silver Mustang. Ten minutes later she'd been back in her little apartment, closing the shutters and double-checking the locks.

"Authorities haven't released the cause of death yet as the investigation continues." The reporter gestured toward the chaotic scene behind her. "We'll be bringing you live updates throughout the day. Stay tuned for more details after this commercial break."

Pushing herself up and off the sofa, Lexi made her way to the bathroom on shaky legs. She bent over the sink and splashed cold water on her face, then raised her eyes to her reflection.

Her normally spiky cap of platinum blonde hair had been matted down by the pink wig she'd worn the night before. Smeared eyeliner and mascara formed black rings around her red-rimmed eyes, emphasizing the unhealthy pallor of her skin.

Grimacing at her reflection, Lexi knew she'd have to quickly pull herself together. Molly expected her girls to be picture perfect when they arrived for a date. She squeezed her eyes shut, too tired of her own lies to pretend anymore.

Why bother calling it a fucking date? Why not just call it what it is? The idiot I met last night wasn't a date; he was a paying customer. Or at least, that had been his intention.

Everyone knew what that was called. And it wasn't called dating.

Lexi crossed to the shower and turned on the water; she wanted to wash away all traces of the evening before. She scrubbed her face and body with a soapy washcloth, then let the warm water flow over her, watching with a wistful expression as iridescent bubbles swirled down into the drain.

If only all my problems could be washed away so easily.

Pulling on a well-worn robe, Lexi emerged from the bathroom and stood in front of the television; a commercial for a used car dealership filled the screen. She picked up the remote and began switching through the channels, stopping on Channel Six.

A tall, handsome reporter was conducting a live interview outside the Riverview Hotel. People swarmed in the background as the reporter stuck a microphone toward a man standing next to him.

Lexi froze, sure that her eyes were playing tricks on her. Maybe she'd taken one too many pills. Or perhaps it was the lack of sleep. She rubbed her eyes and looked again at the screen.

No, it wasn't her eyes. The man from the evening before was definitely on the screen. Lexi jabbed at the remote, trying to increase the volume, but the station had cut to a commercial break. Her tired mind spun as she tried to make sense of the last twenty-four hours.

I'll call Molly and tell her what happened. She'll know what to do.

But Lexi didn't reach for her phone. She knew Molly Blair too well. The no-nonsense operator of the town's only escort agency wasn't the type to offer up sympathy or provide a shoulder to cry on.

Especially if she thought Lexi might scare off a client or jeopardize her business in any way.

She'll just tell me to stop whining and keep my mouth shut.

Perhaps that was the answer; she would just lay low and stay out of trouble. It was best not to get involved.

Besides, I don't know if the man on the stairs did anything wrong. And he doesn't know who I am. I'll just have to make sure he never finds out.

Assuring herself that the deadbolt on the front door was still firmly in place, Lexi returned to the bedroom and closed the door behind her. She sank onto the bed and pulled the covers up over her shoulders, starting to shiver even though the temperature outside was inching toward a hundred degrees.

CHAPTER SIX

Rage flooded through Xavier Greyson as he drove east on Waterside Drive, heading toward the interstate. He needed time to figure out his next move, and he had to do it fast. His grand scheme wasn't going to plan and, although he'd made only a few minor mistakes, the missteps could end up costing him a fortune.

Checking the speedometer, he eased up on the gas. No need to attract the attention of some nosy cop. The thought raised another nasty possibility in his mind.

If the cops find out I was there, if they piece it all together, those mistakes will cost me my freedom .... maybe even my life.

The cops were already suspicious of Portia's death, he knew that for a fact. Why else would they call Riley Odell to the scene?

A state prosecutor wouldn't visit a scene unless the cops thought a crime had been committed. A suspected suicide, or even an accidental overdose, wouldn't require a prosecutor's help.

And Riley wasn't just any prosecutor. She happened to be the one person from his past who had seen through his act. Xavier's anger returned at the memory of the steely-eyed prosecutor and her immunity to his charm.

He'd been running his con for almost ten years, and after all that time she was still the only one that had even come close to catching him.

That cold bitch made me realize how important it is to eliminate all witnesses; I really should find a way to thank her for that one.

Sucking in a deep breath, Xavier forced himself to count to ten, before slowly exhaling. He couldn't let Riley Odell get in his way now. Not when he was so close to escaping with all that money.

No matter who was working against him, he had to finish the plan. And he needed to make sure that no one would find out who he really was, or what he'd done. Only then would he be free to disappear into the life of luxury he'd always dreamed of.

He smiled, thinking of the lovely villa on the coast waiting for him. Slowly the smile faded.

But first I need to clean up a few loose ends.

Careening past the exit for the interstate, Xavier continued on for another few miles, then turned the car sharply onto a dirt road. He bumped along the uneven surface until it ended at the muddy shore of a wide lake.

The still water simmered under the afternoon sun, turning the water's surface to glass. Xavier climbed out of the car, strolled to the water's edge, and gazed out over the lake with a grim smile.

It was the perfect spot to bring a certain young woman who'd seen too much. The opaque water would drown any meddlesome stories she might tell.

Putting a hand up to shield his eyes from the sun's harsh glare, Xavier dug a hand into his pocket and pulled out a lightweight phone. He wondered briefly if he should wipe his prints off of it, or maybe crush the cheap device under his heel.

Instead, he turned and threw it as far as he could into the lake beyond. A faint splash confirmed that it had landed a respectable distance from the shore.

Once back in the car, he opened the glove box and fished out a sleek black iPhone. He checked the phone, pleased to see that he'd missed a call. There was one new message waiting for him. Dropping the phone into his shirt pocket, he started the car and bumped back down the path toward the main road.

As much as he wanted to drive in the opposite direction until Willow Bay's unimpressive skyline had disappeared in his rearview mirror, he knew he had to go back into town and finish the job he'd started.

If there were doubts about the cause of Portia's death, his whole scheme would be thrown into jeopardy.

And this wasn't just any con. This was his biggest con yet, and the one he'd been planning to retire on. His days as a handsome, young con man were numbered, and he knew it.

He'd relied on his youth and charm to scam lonely women out of their money for years, but his looks and his luck couldn't hold out forever. One of them was bound to run out eventually.

Running a hand through his thick hair, he leaned forward and checked for any sign of gray in the rearview mirror. Then he sat back, satisfied that he still had a few good years left.

But I've got to get out while I'm still on top...and before I get caught.

As the car raced down the highway, Xavier's mind drifted back over his career. Back to his first big con in Miami almost a decade earlier.

Miriam Feldman had been a rich widow looking for romance, and his good looks and carefree attitude had quickly won her over. He'd managed to pilfer almost twenty thousand dollars before she'd learned the truth and filed a complaint.

After the police had questioned him, Xavier knew it was only a matter of time before they'd have enough evidence to charge him.

The only way to ensure he wouldn't be arrested, the only way to ensure his freedom, was to eliminate the only witness.

It was an easy call. What his father had called *a necessary evil.* If Miriam Feldman were gone, the police would have no case against him, or so he'd told himself.

He hadn't counted on Riley Odell refusing to give up on the case; within days he'd been forced to skip town, arriving in Aruba with a new look and a new backstory. Within weeks he'd found another target. By the end of the summer, he'd moved on again.

Every summer after that there had been a new trip to an exotic location. A new target to work, and more sophisticated techniques to try out.

Some summers he'd managed to slip away with his takings before his target had figured out she was being played. Other times he'd had to protect himself through more deadly means. It was all just part of the game.

The phone in Xavier's pocket vibrated against his chest, and he was tempted to answer it. But he had to be careful. He couldn't afford any more slip-ups. He had to make sure his story was straight, and that he had his act down pat.

The acting was key; it could make or break the success of the con. And this con called for a whole new persona.

It was for the best anyway. He was no longer young enough to pass for a college boy on summer break. He was ready to retire the old act and start anew.

The thought was exciting and a little scary. If he screwed up, he could end up on *America's Most Wanted*.

I've literally killed for this opportunity. I can't fuck up now.

He'd also conned too many people and burned too many bridges as Xavier Greyson to back down. Portia Hart had given him a final chance to avoid living out his life as a fugitive of justice in some third world country. He now had the chance to live a life of luxury and ease.

And isn't that what everyone really wants, despite the crap Portia had written in her ridiculous book?

Driving past the Riverview Hotel, Xavier observed the crowd and began to recalculate his plans. The girl on the stairs was a witness. If he wanted to rest easy in the future, he'd need to find out who she was and make sure she couldn't tell anyone what she'd seen.

After that, he'd have to deal with Riley Odell.

CHAPTER SEVEN

Veronica was powdering a thin sheen of perspiration off her forehead when the Willow Bay CSI van rolled up to the hotel. A four-person crew dressed in protective gear jumped out and hustled toward the hotel's staff-only entrance. Hunter trained the camera on the investigators as Veronica spoke into the microphone.

"I'm here outside the Riverview Hotel as the tragic death of Portia Hart is beginning to sink in. Crime scene investigators have arrived on the scene, hoping to uncover what happened last night in room 1408. There's still no official word from the medical examiner's office or the WBPD as to the cause or manner of death."

After they'd finished the live report, Veronica saw that Willow Bay's new media relations officer, Tenley Frost, had appeared on the scene. Dressed in a pristine white blouse and a pencil skirt, Tenley's glossy auburn hair skimmed her shoulders in a long bob.

The polished woman had been Channel Ten's star reporter before her recent maternity leave, and Veronica had been surprised, and more than a little relieved, when Tenley had accepted the media relations job instead of returning to her previous role at the station.

"Hello, everyone," Tenley called out to the gathered press in a confident voice. "I know you're all anxious for an update on the situation. I've been in your shoes before, so I do understand."

Voices rose in agreement as the reporters, camera crews, and gawkers jostled for position.

"Unfortunately," Tenley continued, sounding a bit smug, "I won't have an official statement prepared until *after* the WBPD have completed their initial investigation. I just wanted to let you all know so that you can go get some lunch or...*whatever.*"

Dismissing the crowd with a vague smile, Tenley spun around and made her way toward Hunter. Her smile widened as she greeted her ex-boss, and Veronica forced herself to look away from the obvious display of affection.

Hunter certainly seems to be taking Tenley's departure gracefully.

She felt an uncomfortable pang of...what? Jealousy? Shaking off the disturbing idea, she turned to see Nick Sargent suddenly standing beside her.

"You missed Tenley giving her statement," Veronica said, noting that his eyes were trained on Hunter and Tenley. "Although come to think of it, you didn't miss much."

"They make an attractive couple, don't you think?" Nick lowered his voice. "I bet Tenley was glad she was able to jump ship before the station goes under."

Veronica frowned up at Nick in confusion.

"You do know that Channel Ten is facing financial difficulties, don't you?" Nick sounded incredulous. "Don't tell me Hadley's kept the situation a secret from you and the rest of his crew?"

"He hasn't said anything to me," Veronica murmured, looking over at Hunter, who was laughing at something Tenley had said. "He doesn't seem to be worried..."

"Well, he *should* be worried. Most of his team are thinking of finding something more...stable. I'd recommend *you* do the same."

"Me?" Veronica was starting to get annoyed by the reporter's patronizing tone. "Thanks for the advice, but I'm perfectly happy where I am."

Nick raised an eyebrow.

"You really don't want to leverage all that attention you got after your special report on the Willow Bay Stalker? It could be a springboard into something much bigger than *local news.*"

The disdain apparent in his voice surprised Veronica. What was wrong with being a local reporter? She'd been thrilled to finally get a chance to stand in front of the camera, and the possibility of breaking a story that impacted her own community filled her with a sense of purpose.

Opening her mouth to protest, Veronica saw Nick staring over her head with the intensity of a lion who had just spotted a gazelle.

She spun around to see that Riley Odell had slipped out of the big hotel and was heading for the parking garage, causing the gathered reporters to rush forward shouting questions.

"Ms. Odell, can you tell us why you've been called to the scene?"

"Is this officially a crime scene, Prosecutor?"

"Was Portia Hart murdered?"

"Do you have a suspect in custody?"

Riley ignored all the questions as Officer Ford stepped forward and herded the reporters back to the designated press area.

A flood of questions filled Veronica's mind as she watched Riley vanish into the garage. They were the same questions the other reporters had asked.

Why was the city's new prosecutor involved with the investigation into Portia Hart's death? Had the ME already determined Portia Hart's death was in fact suspicious? Did they suspect it was a homicide?

Veronica looked back to gauge Nick Sargent's reaction to Riley's unexpected appearance, but the handsome reporter had already disappeared into the crowd. She recalled the scorn in his voice when he'd spoken about reporting local news. She knew Nick had been in the business for a while, and that he often traveled on assignment.

Sounds like Nick is the one fed up with local news, so maybe he's the one who should be thinking about getting a new job.

"You didn't want to ask Riley Odell any questions?"

Hunter had finished his conversation with Tenley and was standing beside her. He held the big camera with one hand and shielded his eyes from the sun with the other.

"I thought I'd go to her office and try to get an exclusive interview instead," Veronica responded before she'd had a chance to think through the idea. "She kind of owes me one."

Flashing his white teeth in an amused smile, Hunter studied Veronica's face expectantly, as if waiting for the punchline.

She crossed her arms over her chest and cocked her head.

"I'm not making this up. After I testified at Boyd Faraday's trial, she told me to call her if I ever needed anything."

The smile widened, then turned into a loud laugh.

"I doubt she meant you should call her to get inside information on a death investigation," he teased. "She probably meant you could reach out to her if you had any concerns about the case. Or if you needed support after your, uh...traumatic experience."

A flush of embarrassment heated Veronica's cheeks, and she suddenly wanted to wipe the smirk off his face.

"You may be the expert on traumatic experiences," she replied in a tight voice, "but I'm not the one that has panic attacks, am I?"

The look of surprise and hurt on Hunter's face made Veronica immediately regret her words. He had only confided in a few people about his PTSD. She still didn't know the whole story behind it, and now, based on her foolish comment, she probably never would.

"You're not really that naïve, are you? You think Riley Odell will give you an exclusive just because you testified in one of her cases?"

His smile was gone, and his words stung, just like he knew they would. Hunter knew better than anyone else how insecure Veronica was about her lack of reporting experience.

Hearing a persistent buzzing inside her bag, Veronica used the incoming call as an excuse to drop her eyes and search for her phone. She didn't want Hunter to see how much his criticism hurt.

"Ronnie? Why didn't you say good-bye to me this morning?" Ling Lee's voice vibrated with worry. "I've been watching the news. It's *terrible*. Nick Sargent says Portia Hart may have died of an *overdose*."

"Ma, why are you watching Channel Six instead of Channel Ten?" Ling Lee ignored the question.

"What if there's another killer on the loose, Ronnie? What if-"

"Ma, I'm at work now." Veronica raised her eyes; Hunter was already walking back to the van. "I need to go, and I won't be home until late, so please be sure to feed Winston."

Hurrying toward the van, Veronica disconnected the call and dropped her phone back in her purse. She managed to jump into the van's passenger seat just before Hunter started up the engine and steered the vehicle down the hotel's big drive.

"Where are we going?" Her voice sounded small. She cleared her throat and tried again. "Are we going back to the station?"

"*I'm* going back to the station," he said, keeping his eyes on the road, "and *you're* going to get that exclusive interview with Riley Odell. We need to find out what really happened last night in Portia Hart's hotel room."

CHAPTER EIGHT

The high-pitched ding of the elevator announced the arrival of Alma Garcia and three other crime scene technicians. As they stepped into the hall, Nessa could see they were all wearing white protective coveralls and booties and carrying a variety of cases and equipment. She lifted a hand in greeting, then motioned for them to join her in front of Room 1408.

"This is crazy, right?" Alma said, watching the crew cordon off the entrance to the room with security tape. "I mean, the one time we get a celebrity to come to Willow Bay, she ends up dead."

Unpacking a bulky black camera from its case, Alma attached a 50mm lens and began snapping photos of the hall and doorway. Nessa knew that by the time Willow Bay's senior crime scene technician left the hotel, she would have a photographic record of every inch of the scene as she'd found it.

"I guess Vanzinger filled you in on the situation when he called?"

Alma nodded and stepped over the threshold into the room.

"He said the body had signs of a possible struggle, and that you guys suspect someone else may have been in the room with Portia Hart prior to her death."

A pale streak on the gray marble floor caught Alma's eye. She aimed the camera toward the ground and snapped several shots, then looked back through the door. Using her camera to zoom in closer, Alma focused on a patch of carpet in the hall.

"What is it?" Nessa followed Alma's gaze. "You see something?"

"We need to cordon off this whole corridor, including the stairwell," Alma called to her team. "We have traces of dried fluid on the floor inside and outside the room."

Nessa stared at the floor, trying to see what Alma was seeing.

"Let's not get too excited," Alma warned. "It could be nothing, but we need to know what it is and where it came from."

Pointing down the hall to the stairwell exit, Alma glanced back at Nessa. Her eyes gleamed behind her protective glasses.

"Whatever it is, there's a trail of it leading toward the stairs."

"A trail of what, exactly?"

The deep, exasperated voice startled Nessa. She spun around to face the hotel manager she'd met earlier in the lobby. Dennis something. He looked as unhappy as he sounded.

"Sir, I need you to step back toward the elevator," Alma commanded, stepping forward to block the man from moving further down the hall. "This is a restricted area. No one will be allowed to enter this corridor until we complete our investigation."

Stealing a glance at the manager's angry face, and then at his name tag, Nessa tried a softer approach.

"Mr. Robinson, I know this must be a huge inconvenience to you and your guests, but we've opened an official investigation into Portia Hart's death. We need to determine how she died, and we haven't ruled out foul play yet."

Dennis Robinson opened his mouth, then snapped it shut again. A variety of emotions played over his face as he absorbed her words.

"You mean Ms. Hart may have been...*murdered*?"

"Well, it certainly is a possibility," Nessa said, wondering how long it would be before Dennis Robinson spouted off this information to the press. "Which means we need to do everything we can to protect your guests and this community until we know exactly what happened in this room last night."

Gazing toward the room with a forlorn expression, Dennis sighed and shook his head.

"Well, I hope it doesn't take very long. That's our finest suite. I'm losing eight hundred a night while this investigation goes on."

The man's callous words caused Nessa's back to stiffen. Her voice rose an octave, and she gave her southern drawl full rein.

"We're gonna be here just as long as it takes to find out what happened, Mr. Robinson. And we'll need to talk to all the employees, of course, to find out what they may have seen. And any guests who stayed on this floor."

Alma moved toward Dennis, ignoring his startled protest, and shooed him back down the corridor. When they reached the elevator, Alma pointed a gloved hand at the camera mounted on the wall over his head.

"I'll stop by the security desk later. We need to review video from the cameras on this level, the lobby, and all entrances or exits."

"And the parking garage," Nessa called out as the manager stepped into the elevator, still shaking his head.

Hurrying back down the hall, Alma knelt to open a hardcover case. She pulled out a handheld device and flicked a switch. A bright beam of light illuminated the floor as Alma stared into a small display on the back of the device.

"It's my new toy," Alma murmured to Nessa. "Portable high-intensity light. Helps find trace evidence and check for bloodstains."

"Blood?" Nessa frowned. "But Portia wasn't bleeding..."

Alma didn't seem to hear her. She bent and searched through her case until she found a small container. Twisting open the lid, she extracted a small plastic strip, then crouched next to the stain.

Nessa held her breath. She'd seen the little strips before. If the strip turned green, then that meant the stain contained hemoglobin.

"Bingo!"

Alma's raised voice caused all three of the other technicians to come to the door. They looked out at Alma through their protective glasses with expectant eyes.

"Looks like someone was bleeding in this room."

Alma held up the plastic strip; it had turned green.

"Although I'd say it's been diluted with water," she added. "And must have been tracked out here sometime after housekeeping came in and cleaned the floor."

Possible scenarios of how the diluted blood had gotten on the floor flooded Nessa's mind. Was it Portia's blood? Or had someone else been in the room? Would there be enough blood to test for DNA?

"I'll collect the specimen to see what we can find out at the lab," Alma said as if reading Nessa's mind. "And we can compare our results to what Iris finds at the autopsy."

Knowing the CSI team was just getting started, and that the investigation would take most of the day, Nessa looked at her watch.

"I'm going to join Vanzinger and Jankowski for the autopsy," she told Alma, already walking toward the elevator. "Iris said she'll do it this afternoon. I bet she's prepping as we speak."

Stepping onto the elevator, she thumbed the button for the ground floor. Her phone vibrated in her pocket just as the elevator started to descend, and she knew who was calling before she looked at the display. Jerry would be wondering where she was.

"I know...I'm late for the viewing," she said, trying not to sound defensive. "But the call this morning ended up being a bigger deal than I thought. I'm sorry but-"

"Nessa, take a breath." Jerry sounded more amused than angry. "I've been watching the news, so I figured you wouldn't be back in time. I was just calling to tell you I've rescheduled the appointment until next weekend."

Relief washed through Nessa at his words. She wasn't sure if she was relieved because he wasn't mad, or because she wouldn't have to go see the new house he wanted to buy.

"Thanks, honey. I feel terrible to have to miss it."

She tried to sound disappointed for Jerry's sake. He wanted a bigger house now that Cole and Cooper were getting older, and now, as chief of police, she was making enough money to afford it.

But Nessa was in no hurry to move. They'd chosen the little house on Cranberry Court when they'd first moved to Willow Bay almost six years before. The boys had been so young back then, and they'd gone through so many good times since, that the modest house seemed like an integral part of their family. The only place in Willow Bay she felt truly safe.

"I understand," Jerry assured her. "The press is going wild with this one. Looks like you're going to be tied up for a while."

Jerry knew better than to ask for details. That was one of the things that Nessa loved about him. He let her keep the unpleasant details of her job out of their house as much as possible. When she was at home with Jerry and the kids, she didn't want to think about the ugliness she faced in her role on the police force.

"Yes, I'm just heading downtown to meet with Vanzinger and Jankowski now. It'll be a long day so don't count me in for dinner."

"Okay, I'll take the boys for pizza or something."

Hearing a whoop of joy in the background, Nessa realized Cole and Cooper had been listening in on the call. She rolled her eyes at the obvious excitement in their voices.

"Well, don't miss me too much, you little pizza monsters."

Nessa disconnected the call just as the elevator doors opened onto the lobby. She could see right away that the crowd outside the hotel had swollen into a mob. Pushing out through the security exit, Nessa avoided the press area and hurried toward her black Dodge Charger, which she'd parked in the loading zone.

Slipping into the driver's seat, she nosed away from the curb and headed down the drive toward the highway. She looked in her rearview mirror, glad to have escaped without being noticed by the growing swarm of reporters. They were all desperate to find out what had happened to Portia Hart.

And they're all looking to me and my team for the answer.

A pang of doubt rippled through her at the thought. Was she ready to lead an investigation that was sure to garner national attention? Or had she gotten herself in over her head?

Suddenly, she found herself missing her old partner, Pete Barker. He'd always been able to make her feel better, even in the most stressful situations, and he'd always had her back, no matter what.

Barker's heart attack a few years back, followed by his early retirement, had put an end to their partnership, but not to their friendship. Picking up her phone, she tapped on his name in her favorites list.

'Hey, Nessa, I was just talking about you."

Just hearing Barker's familiar voice made Nessa feel a little safer.

"I wondered why my ears were burning," Nessa replied. "Good thing I called to find out what you've been saying about me this time."

"I was just watching the news with Taylor, and I was saying that I'm glad I'm not you right now. This thing with Portia Hart looks like it's going to be a major pain in the ass."

Smiling despite herself, she relaxed back against the seat.

"Actually, that's why I was calling you. For moral support. Between you, me, and the fence post, I'm not sure I'm up for this."

The slight tremor in her voice exposed the truth of her words; she heard Barker's heavy sigh and scolded herself as she imagined the worry filling his sad puppy dog eyes.

"Don't be stupid," he said, although his voice had softened. "You're gonna be fine. This is the kind of stuff you're good at. Just don't take any crap from any of those reporters. They're like vultures circling the kill. You just ignore them and focus on being the chief of police."

"Yeah, I guess," she agreed, feeling better. "Besides, what other choice do I have?"

"You could come work with me and Frankie. We're always looking for good detectives at Barker and Dawson Investigations."

"Yeah, and if I was a PI, I'd be spending Saturday going out for pizza with the boys, instead of at the medical examiner's office viewing an autopsy."

Nessa laughed along with Barker, but as she pulled into the WBPD parking garage, and saw a fleet of news vans waiting outside, she wasn't sure the idea was so funny after all.

CHAPTER NINE

Frankie Dawson reached out a skinny hand to search for the phone, wanting to silence the shrill ringing that had woken him from a deep sleep. His fingers settled over the slim device just as the annoying noise stopped. Letting his body sink back into a comfortable position on the sofa, he was half-asleep when the phone erupted again.

"What the fuck..."

Swinging his feet to the floor, Frankie sat up and grabbed the phone. He glanced toward the clock as he swiped to answer. It was half-past noon.

"This is Barker and Dawson's Investigations," Frankie said with an audible yawn. "How can I help you?"

"My name is Maxwell Clay." The man's voice was crisp. "I'm an investigator with Sterlington Trust Insurance Group, and I'm looking to retain a local agency in Willow Bay to help me with a case."

Wiping the sleep from his eyes, Frankie sat up straighter.

"What kind of case are you talking about, Mr. Clay?"

"It's a death investigation...on a life insurance claim. I need to verify the cause of death for an insured who was visiting your town."

Clay cleared his throat and lowered his voice as if someone might be listening in.

"As I'm sure you've heard in the news, Portia Hart was found dead this morning in her room at the Riverview Hotel."

"Oh, yeah," Frankie agreed automatically, even though he'd slept through both the morning and lunchtime broadcasts, "I think I heard something about that."

"Portia Hart had a sizable life insurance policy with Sterling ton Trust, and I'm investigating the circumstances around her death."

Frankie stood, stretched out his back, then stepped over to his desk, which was cluttered with wrappers and napkins from the fast-food dinner he'd eaten the night before.

"I need to determine if we'll want to contest the claim," Clay continued, "and on a high-profile case like this, I find it's usually wise to partner with a local investigator. Someone who knows the community and has the proper connections."

Scratching at the stubble on his unshaven chin, Frankie frowned.

"Why don't you just ask the cops what happened? Or the ME?"

"I wish it were that easy," Clay replied. "But I need the information fast, and the police tend to take their time."

"You're in a hurry to pay out a bunch of money?"

"No, but her brother is the beneficiary, and he'll likely be in a hurry to receive the money as soon as possible. And in a small town like Willow Bay, the local cops will likely shut me out."

Frankie nodded at the words.

"Yeah, I know what you mean. The cops get all bent out of shape if they think a private investigator is trying to do their job. Like I'd want to be a fucking cop."

After a startled pause, Clay agreed.

"Exactly, well, Mr. um...I'm sorry, I didn't catch your name. Am I speaking with Mr. Barker or Mr. Dawson?"

"You're speaking with Frankie...Frankie Dawson, PI."

"Well, Frankie, I saw on your website that your partner, Mr. Peter Barker, used to be a detective on the local police force. Does that mean he still has inside connections?"

The mention of his partner's name caused Frankie to look over his shoulder; he was suddenly sure that Barker had somehow come into the office without being seen.

Confirming that the coast was still clear, Frankie readily agreed.

"Yeah, sure he does. Barker's best buddies with the new chief."

"Wonderful. I hope to arrive in Willow Bay later today. How about I come by your office first thing tomorrow and we'll settle the arrangement?"

Frankie once again thought about Barker. He doubted his partner would be too happy about working on a Sunday.

He'll probably want to spend the day prancing around the fucking park.

Lately, Barker had been spending every weekend playing happy families with his new girlfriend and his daughter. The satisfied grin that had become a regular fixture on Barker's face was beginning to annoy Frankie, but he wasn't about to let it ruin a lucrative new gig.

"Uh, I guess that'll work...where you comin' from?"

Clay was silent. For a minute Frankie thought he'd lost the connection. Then the insurance investigator cleared his throat.

"I'm in Hart Cove, just north of Palm Beach. If I leave now, I can get to Willow Bay before nightfall. I'll be at your office tomorrow morning no later than ten."

Frankie's interest waned at the thought of a Sunday meeting. Especially one that would require him to be up well before noon.

"Um, Mr. Clay, I better talk to my partner and-"

But Clay had already disconnected the call.

"Talk to your partner about what?"

Jumping at the deep voice that sounded behind him, Frankie spun around. Barker stood in the doorway wearing a suspicious frown.

"And what the hell happened in here?" Barker looked around the little office with disgust. "You've been sleeping in the office again?"

"What the hell are you doing sneaking up on me?" Frankie countered, trying to slow his racing pulse. "You trying to make me have a heart attack, too?"

Barker rolled his eyes and crossed to his own desk. He dropped into his chair and surveyed the neatly organized surface.

"This is what a desk is supposed to look like, Frankie," Barker said. "Not like that pile of crap you got."

Swiping the greasy wrappers and wadded-up napkins into the overflowing trashcan under his desk, Frankie decided he'd better break the news about their new case before he lost his nerve.

But as he opened his mouth, Barker flipped on the little television mounted on the wall and leaned back in his chair.

"You hear about Portia Hart?" Barker asked. "It's a real shame."

Shocked to hear the name of the woman Maxwell Clay was investigating coming from Barker, Frankie closed his mouth and looked toward the television.

His eyes widened as he saw Veronica Lee standing in front of the Riverview Hotel and read the words that were scrolling across the bottom of the screen.

Portia Hart, bestselling author and daughter of the late billionaire Remington Hart found dead at Riverview Hotel this morning.

The reporter's long dark hair and green eyes were familiar to Frankie. The Willow Bay Stalker had taken Veronica Lee hostage when Frankie and Barker had been working a related case.

Several months had passed since then, but Frankie still had a slight limp from injuries sustained during the chase that had ended with Boyd Faraday's arrest.

"The WBPD has opened an investigation into the death of the popular self-help author who was in Willow Bay as part of the nationwide book tour for her bestselling book, *Simply Portia*," Veronica said, holding up a book with the picture of a cheerful blonde woman on the cover.

"Reggie had that book." Barker pointed a beefy finger at the screen. "She loaned it to Taylor just the other day."

Running a hand through his wilted brown hair, Frankie turned toward his partner with a hesitant smile.

"I didn't realize Portia Hart was like...well, a *celebrity*. I mean, if I'd known then I might have told Clay that I needed time to-"

"What're you talking about, Frankie?" Barker asked, his eyes still on the television screen. "Clay who?"

"Maxwell Clay." Frankie swallowed hard. "He's the insurance investigator who just hired us to find out how Portia Hart died."

Barker raised both eyebrows and stared at Frankie as if he'd lost his mind. When Frankie just stared back, Barker dropped his head into his hands.

"You gotta be kidding me," he moaned. "You agreed to help some sleazebag insurance guy try to slime his way out of paying an insurance claim for one of the most popular celebs in the country?"

An overwhelming desire to smoke a cigarette took hold of Frankie. He reached into his shirt pocket and pulled out a loose stick of gum. Tearing off the wrapper, he stuck it in his mouth and began to chew.

"Listen, Barker, this could be a good case for us. If we find out what happened to Portia, we could end up as heroes."

When Barker didn't look up, Frankie tried again.

"And with national attention, we're bound to get some publicity. We are not exactly rolling in new cases, you know."

Taking out his phone, Barker acted as if Frankie hadn't spoken. He tapped out a number and waited.

"Hey there again, Nessa." Barker issued an awkward laugh. "I know...it's a real treat for you to get to talk to me twice in one day."

Frankie rolled his eyes as he realized that Barker was calling to ask for permission.

"Anyway, I'm here with Frankie and I got a quick question for you. I'm gonna put you on speaker if that's okay."

Nessa's unmistakable southern drawl filled the room.

"Hi Frankie, how's it going?"

"Swell, Nessa, it's going really-"

Cutting Frankie off with an irritated wave of his hand, Barker raised his voice.

"I know you're busy, Nessa, so I'll make this brief."

"Frankie's made a deal with an insurance investigator working a life insurance claim on Portia Hart. Apparently, he wants us to confirm her cause of death."

Barker pinned Frankie with a stern glare.

"I'm sure the guy's trying to find a reason to contest the claim. Would you have a problem with us looking into this? I wouldn't want to step on your toes or anything."

The silence on the other end of the connection worried Frankie. He chewed hard on his gum and avoided Barker's eyes.

"I don't have a problem with you guys taking on the case," Nessa finally said, "but your client may not like what you're likely to find."

"What do you mean?" Frankie asked. "What won't they like?"

"The insurance company probably has a clause that allows them to reject the claim if Portia committed suicide," Nessa explained. "So, I'd bet they're hoping you come back with a cause of *death by suicide*. That'll save them a million bucks, or whatever ridiculous amount Portia Hart had in her policy."

Leaning over Barker's desk, Frankie spoke toward the phone.

"So, you're saying Portia didn't kill herself? Was it an overdose?"

"I'm not saying any such thing, Frankie," Nessa warned. "I'm just telling you both that this isn't a cut-and-dried suicide, and your insurance investigator's not gonna like the fact that we've opened an official investigation. No telling how long it'll take for us to figure out what happened. It could take weeks...or even months."

Frankie stood up and crossed his arms over his thin chest.

"I bet we can help you find out what happened quicker than that...right, Barker? If we're on the case, we can speed things up."

Barker gave the phone an uncomfortable glance, then shrugged.

"I mean, I guess we might get people to talk to us that won't talk to cops," Barker said. "And we aren't bound by as many rules. So, if it doesn't bother you, then-"

Nessa's voice cut through Barker's muttering.

"Look, Barker, you don't have to treat me with kid gloves."

She was beginning to sound impatient.

"I'm a big girl. My ego can handle a little competition from the private sector. So, have at it. You guys see what you can find out. If you find out anything I can use along the way, I'd be grateful for any info you want to pass on."

Relief flooded Barker's face, and he gave Frankie a thumbs up.

"That's great, Nessa. I'll be sure to keep you in the loop, and sorry to bother you. I'll talk to you later."

"Hold on, now. I have a question for you," Nessa said. "You said the investigator is looking into a claim, but you never told me who the beneficiary is. That's a pretty important piece of information."

Thinking back to his conversation with Maxwell Clay, Frankie tried to remember if the investigator had mentioned the name of the beneficiary. Whoever benefited from Portia's death would be a natural suspect if foul play were suspected.

Barker seemed to read Frankie's mind.

"So, you're treating Portia Hart's death as a suspected homicide?"

"I'm pursuing all possibilities," Nessa corrected. "As should you, if you want to find out the truth for your client."

Frankie nodded in agreement, but the idea that he might once again be searching for a killer unnerved him.

After all, he'd barely survived when he and Barker had tried to track down the Willow Bay Stalker.

"Sorry, Nessa." Frankie was suddenly worried he'd gotten involved in something far more dangerous than he'd anticipated. "I didn't get all the details yet, but the guy said the beneficiary was Portia's brother, I think. He acted like the guy was pretty eager to get his hands on the payout."

"The brother?" Nessa sounded intrigued. "Okay, well, I'd appreciate hearing anything else you find out."

The thought that Willow Bay's chief of police was wanting information from his investigation made Frankie's spirits perk up.

"Sure thing, Nessa. Clay's coming in tomorrow morning, so I'll find out then and we'll let you know."

After Barker had disconnected the call, he turned to Frankie.

"Tomorrow morning? What time?"

"Ten o'clock," Frankie muttered, ignoring Barker's frown, and returning his gaze to the television. "Look at all those people wanting to know what happened. It's crazy..."

Turning on his computer, Barker pulled the keyboard toward him and began typing. He kept his eyes on the monitor as he spoke.

"I'll start the background work on Portia Hart. That way we'll be ready to hit the ground running once Clay comes in and signs the paperwork tomorrow."

Frankie wasn't listening. He was still watching the crowd milling around in front of the Riverview Hotel.

"You know, if Portia Hart is such a big celebrity, with fans always hanging around, then someone must have seen something."

Frankie's words were soft as if he was speaking to himself.

"There's always someone who knows what happened...someone who saw something. We just have to find a witness."

CHAPTER TEN

Lexi Marsh opened red, tired eyes to look at the big numbers on the clock; it was after one. She'd gotten a few hours of fitful sleep, but her nerves were still on edge. Reaching for the pills on the bedside table, she knew immediately from the light weight of the bottle in her hand that it was empty.

"Shit...all gone," she groaned, letting the bottle fall to the floor as she stood up and stumbled into the living room.

Scanning the room for her phone, Lexi was relieved to see she'd stuck it on the charger by the television. She stared at the dead screen with mounting dread, suddenly remembering what had happened the night before.

A woman was killed at the hotel, and that man...that horrible man...

Her hand shook as she picked up the remote and turned on the television. The station was still tuned to Channel Six, but the news was over. A woman in faded jeans and waterproof boots was watering a bed of flowers as she spoke in a loud, cheerful voice about the importance of keeping soil moist during a drought.

Thumbing the *MUTE* button, Lexi picked up her phone. She swiped past the notifications about missed calls and unread messages and tapped on Molly Blair's number.

She needed more pills to help her calm down. Everything would seem better once she had taken her medicine.

Six rings later an automated voice informed Lexi that the person she was calling was not available.

"Molly, I need to talk to you."

Lexi tried to think of something to say that would make Molly call her back.

"It's about my...my date last night. There may be a problem, so please, call me back."

She dropped the phone on the table and turned to see that the gardening show had been interrupted for a special news bulletin. Lexi wrapped her arms around herself as she stared at the screen.

The same handsome reporter stood in front of the Riverview Hotel. Snatching the remote, Lexi turned up the volume. Nick Sargent's deep voice filled the room.

"Questions surround the death of self-help author Portia Hart. Sources claim that the popular author was found by the hotel cleaner."

The reporter stared into the camera with dark, solemn eyes as he spoke.

"The daughter of the late billionaire Remington Hart was reported to be unresponsive in the bathtub with an empty pill bottle beside her."

His words sent a chill through Lexi, and she held a hand to her throat as if the pills she'd swallowed earlier might be stuck within.

"The police aren't saying if the death is a possible suicide, an accidental overdose, or something more sinister," Nick continued with a grim shake of his head, "but they have opened an official investigation, and a source inside the department labeled the death as *suspicious.*"

Lexi numbly absorbed the information. The police thought the poor woman's death had been suspicious and they'd opened an investigation.

Did that mean that Portia Hart had been killed? Questions flooded through Lexi's muddled brain as she tried to think.

The police will question the hotel guests. Will they find out I was there?

She thought of the man she'd visited on the hotel's tenth floor the night before. Her *date* as Molly would call him. Would the awful man tell the police she'd been there? Would he put the cops on to Molly?

Panic fluttered in Lexi's stomach at the imagined what would happen if the police found out the truth about Molly's sordid little business enterprise.

Will the cops track me down, too? Will I get in trouble for what I've done?

An even more disturbing possibility caused her heart to thump heavily in her chest. What if Portia Hart *had* been killed by the man in the stairwell? What if he was able to find out who she was?

And what if he comes looking for me?

Motivated by the urgent need to warn Molly about the pending situation at the hotel, and desperate to get more pills to calm her shattered nerves, Lexi hurried back into her bedroom and threw open her closet door.

Pulling on a fresh pair of jeans and a thin tank top, Lexi grabbed her purse and charged toward the front door.

Remembering that she'd set her phone on the bedside table, Lexi spun around and darted back to retrieve it. The phone began to buzz and vibrate in her hand as soon as she picked it up.

She looked at the display and sighed. She hadn't thought the day could get any worse.

"Hi, Mom, what's up?"

"What's up is that I've been trying to call you and you won't answer, that's *what's up*."

Loretta Marsh emitted a high-pitched laugh that was anything but amused. It reminded Lexi of the Wicked Witch of the West.

"Sorry, Mom. I've been busy. I'm taking a summer class, and-"

"Spare me the lies," Loretta Marsh snapped. "It's just embarrassing for the both of us. I know what's been going on."

Lexi kept her face expressionless as if her mother would be watching her reaction. But even the eagle-eyed Loretta Marsh couldn't see through a cellular connection.

"What are you talking about, Mom? There's nothing going on."

"I'm talking about you lying. About you pretending that you're still taking classes at that community college. I know it's not true."

Relieved that her mother didn't know about the work she'd been doing for Molly, Lexi tried to think up something to say.

Her shoulders slumped as she realized it was no use. Her mother was right; she had been lying, and there wasn't much use in saying otherwise.

"I didn't tell you because I knew you would act like this." Lexi forced the words out of her dry sticky mouth. "Now I've gotta go. I'm late for work already."

"So, those *strangers* you take care of matter more to you than your own mother? Is that what you're saying?"

For one dreadful moment, Lexi thought her mother actually did know about her dates. Then she realized Loretta Marsh must be talking about the job she'd made up to get her mother off her back.

Lexi had claimed to have found work as a home healthcare aide. The imaginary job helped Lexi explain how she'd been able to afford an apartment without a roommate, and where she went on the many nights she spent out of the apartment.

"No, of course not."

Lexi's words sounded unconvincing to her own ears, and she wondered for the millionth time why she bothered lying to her mother.

"But I do have to go now. Bye, Mom."

As she crossed the room and put her hand on the doorknob, Lexi saw that the television was still on. A photo of Portia Hart's face filled the screen. Lexi stopped to study the carefree, smiling face, wondering why bad things seemed to always happen to good people.

She looks so happy there. And now, just like that, she's dead.

As Lexi opened the door and stepped into the unbearable heat of the summer day, a disturbing conviction settled in her mind.

If I'm not careful, I may wind up dead, too. Only no one will even know who I was, and you can bet my photo won't be posted on the evening news.

CHAPTER ELEVEN

The Channel Ten news station was unusually quiet when Hunter Hadley arrived. The crew scurried around like frightened mice, darting sideways looks at him as he crossed to his glass-walled office, but not calling out the usual greetings and updates. Hunter sank into the chair behind his desk with a puzzled frown.

"Got a minute?"

Veronica Lee appeared in the doorway. Her green eyes were unusually bright, and her face was illuminated by the sunlight streaming in through the big picture window. Hunter dropped his eyes to stop himself from staring.

"Sure, come on in. Sit down."

"I'll stand if that's okay with you." Veronica's voice was neutral, but her back was stiff. "I just thought you might like to know that there's been some gossip about the station, and..."

"And you're volunteering to be the one to break the news to me?"

Veronica nodded, then swallowed hard.

Giving her a reassuring smile, Hunter cocked his head, raised his eyebrows, and leaned back in his chair to listen.

"Well, it's just that Gustavo told everyone that he quit because the station is in financial trouble. That we're going *bankrupt*." Her voice faltered on the word. "I also heard pretty much the same thing from Nick Sargent earlier today."

Hunter winced. Unprepared for the question, he sat up straight in his chair and met Veronica's worried gaze.

"We aren't going bankrupt," he said, running a big hand through his dark brown curls, unsure how much he should say. "Sure, we've lost some of the local advertisers lately, so things are a little tight, but that doesn't mean we're in trouble."

He hesitated, tempted to leave it at that. He didn't want Veronica or the rest of the crew to worry needlessly. But then, he couldn't risk them hearing the whole truth from anyone else either. If the wrong message was sent out, he could end up losing more of his crew.

"I'm glad to hear it," Veronica said, letting out a deep breath. "I knew Gustavo must be mistaken, and Nick Sargent...well, he seemed to enjoy the idea that Channel Ten was in trouble."

"Listen, Veronica, I'm sorry that-"

"No, I'm sorry, Hunter. We're in the middle of breaking news and I'm wasting time listening to gossip. Forget I said anything."

Brandishing her notebook in her hand, Veronica's voice filled with enthusiasm.

"I'm going to track down Portia Hart's next of kin for an interview. I figure someone will have to come to Willow Bay to view the body. If I'm waiting outside the ME's office, maybe I'll get a chance to ask a few questions."

Hunter raised a hand to stop her from leaving. He needed to tell her the truth. But a loud rap on the doorframe made them both jump.

A young man in khakis and a polo shirt stood just outside the doorway of his office. The man nodded as he met Hunter's eyes.

"How can I help you?"

Hunter noticed the heavy bag hanging over the man's muscular shoulder. It looked worn out and oddly familiar.

He glanced again at the man's square jaw and dark complexion.

"I'm Finn," the young man said, his voice deep and solemn. "Finn Jordan."

Hunter's eyes widened in surprise, and for a minute his throat was too thick to speak.

"You're Jordie's son?"

Nodding, Finn dropped his eyes and cleared his throat.

"Yes, Sir. Saul Jordan was my dad."

"Was your dad? You mean..."

Pain knifed through Hunter. Could Jordie really be gone? Finn raised his eyes, and the sadness within confirmed Hunter's fear.

"When did he...pass?"

It hurt to say the words, and Hunter looked away, fighting to keep his composure. He watched Veronica hurry out of the room, heard her close the door behind her as he turned back to Finn.

"What happened?"

"Cancer," Finn said, his face tight. "He thought he had longer. The docs told him six months, but it was more like *six weeks*. He was planning on calling all his friends after he'd decided not to do any more chemo. Set up time to say his good-byes. Said he wanted to get his energy back first. Only he never did."

Hunter thought of his old mentor's wide smile and all-knowing eyes. Saul Jordan had taken Hunter under his wing when he'd started out as a young reporter. He'd been the kind of role model Hunter's own father never had been. Hunter tried to remember the last time he'd taken the trip out to Memphis to visit Jordie. Had it really been more than two years?

"My dad asked me to give you this," Finn said, dropping his eyes to the envelope he held in his hand. "Made me promise him I'd bring it to you in person."

Hunter could see a flash in Finn's eyes. Anger? Resentment? Hunter wasn't sure. The only thing he knew, was that the boy must be hurting. Losing a dad like Saul Jordan must hurt pretty bad.

His hands trembled as he took the envelope and opened it, wondering if Jordie's hands had been trembling when he'd sealed it.

Hunter,

My time's about up so I'm gonna need to call in that favor you owe me. You know what I'm talking about, so don't try to play dumb now.

Finn's a good boy, and I taught him everything I know. But he's gonna need someone to look after him once I'm gone. Watch out for him. Tell him what you've learned. Give him a base to come to when he needs it.

Don't let me down, and don't let Finn know I asked you to babysit him. A man has got his pride after all.

And remember what I always told you. Make it count today, cause you might not get tomorrow.

Your old pal,

Jordie

Hunter's eyes fell on the worn travel bag over Finn's shoulder. "Is that your dad's old rucksack?"

Finn nodded, his eyes resting on the letter.

Folding it carefully, Hunter put it in his pocket. He tried to keep his voice casual as he walked back to his desk.

"Just so happens I need a cameraman around here. If you're anything like your dad, I'd be a fool not to add you to my crew."

Finn's back stiffened, and his eyes flashed again.

"You'd be doing me a favor," Hunter continued. "I had a cameraman quit yesterday and I'm short-staffed. I'd need you to start right away."

After an awkward pause, Finn nodded.

"For some reason my dad really liked you, so I'll help you out until you find a replacement. Then I'm gone."

"Where to?"

"Wherever I can find a place that feels like home I guess."

Hunter nodded, relieved that Finn had given in so quickly.

"Well, you'll stay at my place in the meantime."

Hesitating, Finn looked over his shoulder.

"Only if Gracie can stay as well."

Hunter hurried to the door, a wide smile spreading across his mouth. He rushed across the room to kneel by a white Labrador retriever, who sat at attention by Veronica's desk.

"Gracie? How you doing, girl?"

Hunter ruffled the dog's fur, and she looked up at him with wide, solemn eyes. Time seemed to stand still as he met her gaze. He felt like he was back in Kabul. Like ten years hadn't really just passed in the blink of an eye.

"She's not been the same since Dad died."

Finn's voice sounded behind Hunter, and he heard the pain underneath the words.

"You're missing old Jordie, aren't you, girl?" Hunter sighed and looked up at Finn.

"You and Gracie have a home with me as long as you want it. Now, store your bag over there, and let's meet the crew."

CHAPTER TWELVE

Veronica slung her bag over her shoulder and headed toward the door. She wanted to get to the medical examiner's office in time to talk to Portia Hart's younger brother. According to her research, Julian Hart was Portia's only living relative, and the heir to the enormous fortune Remington Hart had left behind after his fatal plane crash almost a decade earlier.

"Veronica, wait up," Hunter called out from the door to his office.

She turned to see that the young black man who had interrupted their earlier conversation stood next to him.

"This is Finn Jordan," Hunter said as Veronica approached. "He's going to help out on the camera crew for the time being. He's worked with some world-class reporters, so we're lucky to have him."

Gesturing toward the white Labrador beside him, Hunter added in a proud voice, "And that's Gracie, an old friend of mine."

Veronica smiled down at the big dog, wondering once again about Hunter Hadley's background. They'd worked together for more than a year now, and she still knew very little about the station manager.

"And Finn, this is Veronica Lee, our roaming reporter and something of a local celebrity."

Rolling her eyes at the phrase, Veronica looked at Finn with curious eyes. He smiled and nodded but didn't say anything. He didn't look old enough to be a seasoned pro, but who was she to question Hunter? Her boss knew the industry and the craft better than anyone she knew. If he thought Finn was the right guy for the job, she wouldn't argue.

"I'll show Finn around and introduce him to the crew," Hunter said. "And once he's set up with his gear I'll let you know. Maybe by then, you'll be ready with that breaking interview."

Veronica turned away before Hunter could see how nervous she was. He was putting a lot of trust in her to pull together a story that would keep viewers tuned to Channel Ten. He seemed so confident that she would come through, but she wasn't so sure.

Will I really have the nerve to ask a man who just identified his sister's dead body for an interview?

The thought disturbed her. She'd often wondered what she would be willing to do in pursuit of a big story. Suddenly, she wasn't so sure she wanted to find out.

* * *

Several people were standing outside the Willow Bay medical examiner's office when Veronica drove by in her Jeep. She recognized Nessa Ainsley's red curls, as well as Iris Nguyen's sleek bob.

Steering the Jeep into the parking garage, Veronica found an empty space on the second floor and rushed down the dim stairwell, hoping to catch the chief of police and the medical examiner before they disappeared inside the big concrete building.

Momentarily blinded by the dazzling sunshine as she stepped out onto the sidewalk, Veronica raised a hand to shield her eyes and headed toward the front of the building. She was relieved to see Nessa and Iris still talking outside.

"Hi, Nessa, how are you?" Veronica called out, trying not to think about the last time they'd been together. "Can I ask you a few questions about Portia Hart's death?"

Appraising Veronica with narrowed eyes, Nessa put both hands on her hips and shook her head.

"Well, I'm not feeling very generous with the press right now," she said. "Not after your competition over at Channel Six made sure we didn't have a chance to notify Portia's kin before *everyone in the known world* heard about it."

Veronica's heart dropped at Nessa's rebuke, and she wondered again if she was doing the right thing. Perhaps she should just leave Julian Hart alone. She could always go back to the hotel and try to find witnesses there.

Along with every other reporter in the state.

Wearing a solemn expression, Iris stepped closer and put a small hand on Veronica's arm, as if to stress the importance of her words.

"We reached Portia Hart's brother on the phone and asked him to come identify his sister's body; he's on his way to Willow Bay as we speak. Hopefully, you and the other reporters around here will show him some sympathy and let him mourn in peace."

The clatter of high heels on the pavement sounded behind her before Veronica could respond. She turned to see a petite woman in a neon pink shift dress. Her snow-white hair had been cut into a pageboy, and she wore huge black sunglasses.

"You're the police chief I saw on the news," the woman gasped, pointing at Nessa. "I'm Portia Hart's agent, Jane Bishop, and I need to talk to you. I don't care what they're all saying. Portia was *not* on drugs and she would never kill herself."

Veronica pulled out her notebook and scribbled down the woman's name and noted the statements she'd made.

"She'd been seeing someone," the woman said, her voice rising. "She was trying to hide it, but I..."

Nessa raised a hand to stop Jane Bishop from saying anything else, regarding Veronica's notepad with disapproving eyes.

"Ms. Bishop was it?" Nessa turned back to the distressed woman and guided her toward the door. "You come inside with me and we'll talk in private."

Veronica watched in frustration as Nessa led Portia's agent into the cool interior of the building. She stared through the window, considered going inside, then spun on her heel and walked back to her Jeep. She needed to get to her laptop.

Sitting in the driver's seat with the windows up and the air conditioning on, Veronica typed Julian Hart's name into the search engine.

If Portia Hart's little brother was on his way to Willow Bay, she might get the opportunity to approach him in person. If so, she would need to know a lot more about him. Convincing a total stranger to trust her enough to grant an interview wouldn't be easy.

A list of almost fifty million search results appeared, but within a few clicks Veronica determined that Julian was Portia Hart's only sibling; he was also an artist who avoided the spotlight almost as much as Portia had chased it.

Clicking on an image, Veronica studied an abstract painting of waves crashing against a rocky coastline. The painting was titled "Hart Cove at Dawn" and Julian Hart had signed the bottom with a dramatic flourish.

Intrigued by the mix of contrasting colors and textures in the landscape, Veronica wanted to know more about the man who had painted it. She suspected that Julian Hart had used the pain of losing his parents to inspire his art.

I wonder if he'll cope with the loss of his sister in the same way.

She felt a stab of pity for the man who seemed to have everything in the world, other than a family. She read through the search results with growing interest.

Portia and Julian had inherited a fortune after their wealthy parents died in a dramatic plane crash a decade earlier. Then, after an initial flurry of coverage, they'd all but vanished from the public scene.

Only after Portia Hart's book, *Simply Portia*, had hit the bestseller list last year, had she become a household name, and a social media darling. Portia's name and face had appeared in hundreds of reviews, articles, and photos, and the Hart name was once again synonymous with money and fame.

But from what Veronica could see, Julian Hart had shunned the spotlight, preferring to stay at his family home in Hart Cove to work on his art. She could find only a few mentions of him online, and all the references were focused on his famous parents, his famous sibling, or his artwork.

Portia Hart's brother didn't seem to use social media and didn't appear to have much of a social life.

Closing her laptop, Veronica pondered her next move. If she waited outside the medical examiner's office, she might get lucky and catch Julian Hart coming or going. In a perfect world, he would agree to an interview, maybe even tell her what he thought had happened to his big sister.

Or maybe I'll stand out there sweating for no reason while Nick Sargent hunts Julian Hart down and gets my scoop.

She gritted her teeth at the idea of Nick Sargent getting to Julian Hart first. The Channel Six reporter was ruthless.

He won't care about Julian Hart's grief or respect his privacy.

Her indignation drained away as she recognized the hypocrisy of her own thoughts. Was she any better than Nick Sargent after all?

The buzz of her cell phone saved Veronica from having to answer that question. Hunter Hadley had sent a text.

Our new camera guy is ready to roll. He'll meet you at the scene.

Veronica didn't need to ask which scene. Portia Hart's sudden death was the only story in town. Easing the big Jeep out of the narrow space, she pulled out of the parking garage and took a last, regretful look at the entrance to the ME's office. She wondered what information Jane Bishop had provided as she headed back toward the Riverview Hotel.

CHAPTER THIRTEEN

Jane Bishop's hand trembled as she picked up a glass of water off the tray Wesley Knox had set on the desk. Nessa waited for the older woman to take a drink, noticing the dark smudges under her eyes. She wasn't sure if Jane had been crying, or if the stifling heat had caused the woman's mascara to melt.

"Thank you, Wesley," Iris said, sitting down at her desk across from Nessa and Jane. "I'll let you know once we're ready to start."

Glancing at her watch, Nessa forced herself to remain quiet while Jane regained her composure. If the woman really did know something about Portia's death, Nessa couldn't afford to rush her. So far Jane Bishop was the only person who claimed to know why the popular author had ended up dead in a hotel bathroom.

"Portia never took any drugs...not even pain killers," Jane finally said. "She was dedicated to a natural, unmedicated, unstimulated lifestyle. It's all in her book...you've read her book, haven't you?"

When neither Iris nor Nessa responded, Jane looked shocked.

"Haven't you read *Simply Portia*?"

"No...although I did buy it," Nessa admitted. "It's on my bedside table, but I've got two little boys and I don't get much time to read."

Jane tutted and pointed a stern finger in Nessa's direction.

"Then you definitely need to read it. It'll help you simplify your schedule and make more room in your life. Most people have a schedule that's just as cluttered as their house."

Smiling in polite agreement, Nessa looked at her watch, then over at Iris, who was supposed to be performing the autopsy on Portia Hart. Iris raised her finely arched brows and nodded, silently reassuring Nessa that she was doing the right thing by waiting to hear what Jane Bishop had to say.

"Ms. Bishop, I'm Iris Nguyen, the chief medical examiner, and I'm very sorry for your loss."

The medical examiner's words sounded sincere, even though Iris must have uttered the same phrase hundreds of times before.

"If you can help us determine the circumstances around Portia Hart's death, we'd be grateful," Iris continued. "We were just preparing for the autopsy, and–"

"Can I see her?" Jane interrupted in a hoarse whisper. "If I see her, I'll know it's true. That this isn't just a bad dream."

Sitting back in her chair, Iris looked over at Nessa, who shrugged. After a slight pause, Iris picked up the phone on her desk.

"Wesley, can you prepare Portia Hart for a viewing?"

Ten minutes later Jane Bishop stood outside a glass partition, staring down at Portia's swollen, discolored face. With a soft cry, Jane turned away from the horror beyond the window and shoved her dark sunglasses over her eyes.

"That *bastard*," she managed to spit out. "This is all *his* fault. "

"Which bastard?" Nessa asked. "Whose fault?"

Taking Jane by one trembling arm, Nessa led her to a row of chairs against the wall. Jane's knees buckled, and she abruptly sat down.

"The bastard Portia met in the Bahamas a few months ago," Jane said. "She was only supposed to be going for a long weekend but ended up staying almost a month. I knew a guy had to be involved. She wouldn't tell me anything specific, but I had a bad feeling...then I saw him that time in New York."

"Did you get the man's name?"

Jane shook her head, then stood and pushed past Nessa.

"I need to use the restroom," she muttered as she flung the door open. "I think I'm going to be sick."

* * *

Iris sliced a y-shaped incision into Portia Hart's chest, then pulled the skin up to reveal the rib cage. Nessa closed her eyes as the diminutive medical examiner lifted a small electric saw and began to cut away the cartilage holding the ribs in place.

Jane Bishop's words echoed through her mind.

That bastard...this is all his fault.

Feeling Wesley beside her, Nessa opened her eyes to see the brawny forensic technician leaning in to help Iris lift out the rib cage. She closed them again as they took photos, then began to remove and weigh the internal organs.

After what seemed like hours, Iris stepped back, pulled off her gloves, and pushed up the plastic face shield.

"She has liquid in her lungs and stomach," Iris said, her voice grim. "I'm confident that the cause of death is drowning, or more precisely, hypoxia and acidosis leading to cardiac arrest."

"But what about the pills?" Nessa asked. "Did she take too many? Could they have caused her to drown?"

Iris shrugged as she watched Wesley collecting and packaging specimens to send to the lab.

"It's possible that the pills could be a contributing factor. We'll have to wait for the test results to know what she took, if anything."

Gesturing toward Portia's limp hand, Iris sounded hopeful.

"We did find traces of something under her fingernails, so we took clippings to see if we can get viable DNA."

"Good." Nessa tried to sound optimistic. "And while you're checking for drugs in her system and skin under her fingernails,

Alma will be testing the residue we found on the hotel floor. She thinks it might be water from the bath mixed with traces of blood."

"Well, I doubt it would be Portia's blood," Iris said. "The only external injury I saw during the autopsy were her broken fingernails, and they didn't seem to have bled much."

Nessa suddenly wondered if they were misreading the evidence. Perhaps Portia had simply fallen and broken her fingernails after taking too many pills, then lost consciousness and drowned in the tub. Maybe it had just been a horrible, senseless accident. But her intuition chaffed at the idea. All the little inconsistencies at the scene seemed to add up to homicide

And if it really was homicide, the killer is still out there, somewhere.

A jarring ring startled Nessa out of her brooding. She turned to see Wesley Knox cross to a phone mounted on the wall. After a short exchange with the caller, Wesley hung up and called over to Nessa and Iris.

"That was Detective Vanzinger. He said to tell you that Julian Hart showed up at the police station. He's bringing him over here to identify his sister's body."

Noting the look of distress on Nessa's face, Iris frowned.

"What's wrong, Nessa? I thought you'd be happy. It's your chance to talk to someone who may be able to shed light on Portia's death."

"I am...I guess," Nessa replied with a sigh. "It's just that Julian Hart will ask how and why his sister died, and we still don't know."

CHAPTER FOURTEEN

Tucker Vanzinger tried to think of something to say to the quiet man walking beside him, but his mind drew a blank. He wasn't sure what the proper etiquette was; should he try to make small talk, or leave the young man alone with his grief?

What can I say to a brother who is on his way to identify his sister's body?

Glancing over at Julian Hart, Vanzinger wondered if he should try to prepare the poor man for what he was about to see.

It's messed up to have to see any dead body, but seeing the body of your sister? That must really screw with your head.

Julian hid behind dark sunglasses as they walked toward the bulky concrete medical examiner's office, and he kept his head down as if trying to make himself less visible, which wasn't an easy task.

Standing as tall as Vanzinger, at least six foot two or more, Julian was lean compared to Vanzinger's muscular frame, with long limbs clad in pressed khakis and a long-sleeved linen shirt.

The younger man didn't seem to be sweating despite the scorching heat of the mid-July sun, and Vanzinger felt momentarily embarrassed as he swiped a big hand across his own damp forehead.

"Mighty hot one today, huh?"

The words croaked out of Vanzinger's dry mouth, and Julian raised his head with a start as if he'd forgotten Vanzinger was next to him.

"Yes, it's hot," Julian agreed without much enthusiasm.

After another minute of silence, he added in a low voice, "I imagine if hell were real, it would feel just like this."

Before Vanzinger could reply, they reached the glass door of the building, and Vanzinger pulled it open for Julian to walk through. Spotting Maddie Simpson behind the counter, Vanzinger raised a big hand in greeting.

"Hey, Maddie, how're you doing?"

He detected an underlying smell of decay in the still, cool air as he turned to gesture at Julian.

"This is Mr. Hart. We're here to see Iris and Nessa."

Smoothing back a short strand of jet-black hair, Maddie flashed Vanzinger a rare smile. He normally got only a muttered complaint from the woman who had worked for the city ever since she'd graduated from Willow Bay community college as a sullen twenty-two-year-old. Her attitude hadn't improved in the thirty years since.

"Iris is expecting you, Mr. Hart," Maddie responded, resting curious eyes on Julian. "I'll let her know you're here."

"Thank you," Julian murmured, pushing his sunglasses up on his head, revealing pale blue eyes framed by spiky black lashes.

Once Maddie had disappeared into the back, Vanzinger turned to face Julian, who looked slightly shell-shocked.

"Iris Nguyen is the medical examiner, and Nessa Ainsley is the chief of police," Vanzinger explained. "They'll review what they found during the autopsy and ask you to view your sister's body in order to make a positive identification."

"Chief of police?"

A frown creased the smooth skin of Julian's forehead.

"Why are the police involved? What happened to Portia?"

Looking toward the door in hope of rescue, Vanzinger sighed.

"It's best to wait until we're in the back to discuss the details of your sister's death. That way we'll be assured of privacy."

Julian stared at the door leading to the back with wide, almost glassy eyes; finally, it opened to reveal a muscular man in blue scrubs.

"Mr. Hart?" the man called out, looking toward Julian and Vanzinger. "I'm Wesley Knox, the forensic technician handling your sister's case. The chief will see you now."

As Vanzinger followed Julian into the back, he wondered who Wesley had been referring to. Both Iris and Nessa were now the official chiefs of their respective departments. Both women had overcome the city's good-old-boy culture to earn their positions; it was the kind of progress Vanzinger had doubted would ever happen.

Things in Willow Bay sure have changed since the first time I joined the department.

Then all thoughts fled as Wesley led them into the narrow viewing room. Vanzinger stared at the long window that separated the room from the autopsy suite, relieved to see the blinds were firmly closed, blocking the view. He put a comforting hand on Julian's shoulder just as Iris entered the room, and Nessa followed close behind her.

"Good to meet you, Mr. Hart. This is Nessa Ainsley, the chief of police, and I'm Willow Bay's medical examiner, Iris Nguyen."

Iris wore a clean, white lab coat over black pants. Her elfin face and kind brown eyes were framed by dark, glossy hair styled in a neat bob. She extended a hand toward Julian, but he didn't seem to notice. His eyes were on the window.

"Is she in there?" he asked. "Is Portia in there?"

Iris nodded, and Vanzinger could feel Julian's shoulders begin to shake under his hand.

"When you're ready, we'll open the blinds. Your sister will be fully covered in a white sheet. Once you feel prepared, Wesley will move the sheet to show you only her face and shoulders. After you've made the identification, we'll go to my office so I can ask you a few questions and answer any questions you may have."

"Okay, I'm ready," Julian said, shrugging off Vanzinger's hand and straightening his shoulders. "I want to see my sister now."

* * *

Twenty minutes later they were all sitting around a small table in Iris' office. A cup of herbal tea was sitting untouched on the table in front of Julian. His stoic expression and dry, stunned eyes were beginning to worry Vanzinger.

Is the guy in shock? Does he realize what has happened?

Julian had worn the same blank expression since he'd seen Portia's ruined face on the gurney. It was as if he refused to acknowledge the horror of what he was seeing.

"I know your parents died in a plane crash back in 2010," Iris said, her voice soft. "Do you have any other family?"

Shaking his head, Julian kept his eyes on the table.

"No, it was just me and Portia after the crash," he said, pushing a lock of dark hair off his forehead. "We liked it that way. At least we used to before Portia's book came out."

Nessa leaned forward in her seat.

"So, you and your sister lived together?" she asked.

"We used to. My parents built a house in Hart Cove that we jointly inherited," Julian agreed. "It's on the east coast, north of Palm Beach, but I'm not sure what that has to do with my sister's death."

"We're trying to determine why your sister died, Mr. Hart."

Vanzinger was glad to hear the emotion in Julian's voice, even if it was frustration.

"We don't understand what happened, and we need to find out everything we can about Portia so we can figure it out."

Julian met Vanzinger's eyes and held his gaze.

"Do you think my sister...did this to herself? Did she want to die?"

The question surprised him, but Vanzinger kept his face neutral.

"We don't know, Mr. Hart, what do you think? Would your sister what to harm herself? Had she tried to hurt herself before?"

"No, I don't think she would," Julian replied, looking away. "But she's been...away a lot lately, so I...I don't know for sure what she might have done."

"Was your sister taking any medication?" Nessa asked. "Do you know if she was under a doctor's care?"

The glassy look had come back into Julian's eyes, and he slumped back against his chair without responding.

"We found an empty bottle of pills in her room. Do you know what they were for?" Nessa continued. "Did your sister have an addiction to alcohol or drugs?"

Folding his arms over his chest, Julian shook his head, and Vanzinger saw a flush of emotion fill his cheeks. Nessa's question had hit home.

"Do you know where your sister got the pills from?" Vanzinger asked, watching for Julian's reaction.

"No, I don't have a fucking clue," Julian suddenly yelled. "My sister did whatever she wanted, no matter what I said."

He jumped to his feet and moved toward the door.

"She didn't tell me what she was doing half the time, and she certainly didn't ask for my permission."

He reached for the doorknob as Nessa stood and followed him across the room. She put a hand on the door to stop him from leaving.

"Do you know who your sister was dating, Mr. Hart?" Nessa asked. "We've been told she may have recently met someone in the Bahamas. Do you know anything about that?"

"I already told you. I don't know anything about her love life, or who she might have been sleeping with," Julian said between gritted teeth. "Now move your hand so I can go."

Vanzinger stood to face Julian's angry glare.

"Mr. Hart, we'll need to work together if we want to find out what happened to your sister. I know you're hurting, but we just want-"

"Fame can do things to you, Detective," Julian interrupted. "It can make you think the wrong things are important. I tried to warn her, but...well, Portia made her own choices. There's nothing I can do about that now. She's gone, and now I just want to be left in peace."

CHAPTER FIFTEEN

The silver Mustang turned onto Kingston Road, then slowly rolled by Molly Blair's tidy house. Lexi had the air conditioner blowing at full blast, but her palm was sweaty as she held the phone to her ear. Molly still wasn't picking up. When the call rolled to voicemail yet again, Lexi steered the car around the corner and into the back alley. Molly didn't like attracting attention from the neighbors, so Lexi had made a habit of coming through the back gate.

Opening the car door, she set one foot on the hot pavement and looked up and down the street, checking for passing cars or nosy neighbors. Seeing neither, she hurried along the fence until she reached the gate. The latch opened easily, and she slipped inside.

Lexi crossed the brown, dried out lawn, climbed the short flight of stairs to the back deck, then navigated around the hot tub to the sliding glass doors.

"Molly?" Lexi knocked on the glass and tried to peer through, but the blinds were drawn. "Molly, are you in there?"

Lexi listened but could hear nothing from inside. Sweat began to trickle down the small of her back as she wondered where Molly could have gone. She needed to talk to her boss and tell her what had happened the night before. And she needed more pills.

Banging her fist on the glass in frustration, she called out again.

"Molly, please! I need to talk to you!"

She had just turned to walk away, when the lock on the big glass door clicked up, and the door slid open several inches. Angry eyes glared out at Lexi, barely visible through a narrow opening in the blinds.

"What the fuck do you want?" Molly snapped.

She opened the blinds a little wider and poked her head out, looking past Lexi to see if anyone was with her. When she saw that the patio and backyard were empty, she turned her eyes back to Lexi.

"I need to talk to you," Lexi pleaded. "I need to tell you about the man at the hotel. It's been on the news and–"

"Shut your mouth," Molly ordered, throwing a furtive look over her shoulder. "I'm busy right now...we'll have to talk later."

Scared that Molly would close the door in her face, Lexi reached out a hand and grabbed the frame.

"This can't wait," Lexi insisted. "A woman's been–"

"I said I'm busy," Molly repeated, lowering her voice to a furious whisper. "And I'm not alone. Now get out of here. I'll call you when I'm free to talk."

Panic set in as Lexi realized there would be no pills until later. She made one last attempt.

"I don't feel good, and I...I don't think I should work tonight," she moaned, blinking back tears. "Unless I can get some more pills..."

Uttering a string of muffled curses, Molly stuck her head out again to study Lexi's sweaty face. She frowned as she took in the wide, blood-shot eyes and unwashed, matted hair.

"You look like shit," Molly said in disgust. "Wait here."

She disappeared behind the blinds for several minutes, then reappeared holding a handful of pills in a small plastic bag.

"Go home and take a shower." Molly pushed the bag through the gap in the door. "Get cleaned up and ready for tonight."

Grabbing the bag with eager hands, Lexi turned and hurried back down the path and out the gate. She opened the door to the Mustang, oblivious to the oven-like conditions, and slid into the driver's seat. Only after swallowing two of the pills dry did she start the engine, open the car windows, and head home.

* * *

Lexi didn't make it back to her apartment. Once the pills had kicked in, she felt too jittery to go home. She wanted to find out what was going on at the hotel. She needed to see for herself if the man was still there, although she knew she was unlikely to see him wandering around outside.

If he is a killer, he's probably halfway across the country by now.

Driving past the hotel's front entrance and the parking garage, Lexi parked the Mustang on the usual side street and then sat motionless in the car, clutching the steering wheel. Finally, she reached down and opened the glove box. A deflated pack of cigarettes lay on top of a messy pile of napkins, receipts, maps, and a never-used 2010 Ford Mustang owner's manual.

She knew without looking that there were only four cigarettes left in the pack. Taking one out, she stuck the filtered tip in her mouth and closed her eyes, enjoying the familiar smell of the tobacco.

I should put this back in the pack. Or better yet, I should just throw the whole pack in the garbage. Get rid of them once and for all.

But instead, she reached into her purse and extracted a thin Bic lighter. Climbing out of the car, she lit the cigarette and began walking toward the hotel. She'd just gotten to the front of the hotel's self-parking garage when she heard a voice beside her.

"That shit'll kill you. You know that, right?"

A tall, lanky man in baggy jeans and a green football jersey stood on the sidewalk, staring at the cigarette in her hand.

"Yeah, I know. I've been trying to stop, but...it's hard."

Reaching into his pocket, the man pulled something out and extended his hand toward her. She saw a flash of silver and recoiled, before seeing that it was just a stick of gum wrapped in foil.

"Somebody's jumpy," he said, still holding out the gum. "I used this to quit a two-pack a day habit. No joke. If I can do it, you can."

Lexi transferred her cigarette to her left hand and took the stick of gum with her right. She decided she liked the smooth feel of the foil on her fingers.

"Thanks," she said, but the man's phone had started to chirp, and he turned away and held it to his ear.

Looking toward the hotel's entrance, Lexi watched the television crews, police, and hotel guests milling in front of the lobby, while a steady stream of cars and taxis drove up the drive to drop off and pick up passengers.

As if in a bad dream, she saw a man emerge from the crowd and look her way. Even at a distance, she thought she recognized the man she'd seen in the stairwell the night before. The man seemed to feel her watching him, and he lifted his eyes to meet hers just as a yellow taxi pulled up in the drop off lane, blocking her view.

Breathless, Lexi slipped behind a row of trees along the drive. She dropped her cigarette on the ground at her feet, using her heel to grind it into the parched earth. Staying hidden behind the trees, she slipped up closer to the entrance and peeked out.

A stout woman with white hair and black glasses was climbing out of the taxi. Lexi could see that the woman was talking on a phone as she turned to pay the driver. When the taxi pulled away, the man had disappeared.

Scanning the crowd with nervous eyes, Lexi couldn't see him anywhere. Had he gotten into the taxi? Had he gone inside the hotel?

Perhaps it hadn't been the man in the stairwell after all. She'd seen only his face, and the lighting had been bad. It was best to just follow Molly's advice and go home. She could take a shower and pull herself together.

She spun around and hurried back toward her car, not seeing the man on the sidewalk until he was only inches away. She screamed as he grabbed her arms and held her in place.

"What the fuck?"

It was the skinny man in the green jersey. He released her arms and stepped back.

"I already got hit by a car this year," he said, sounding more amused than angry. "I don't need another broken leg."

Heart pounding, Lexi stared at the man with frightened eyes.

"Hey, it's okay. I'm not gonna hurt you."

Lexi ignored his words and tried to move past him.

"Whoa, there. Are you sure you're gonna be all right? You look a little...dazed."

"I'm fine," she murmured, looking over her shoulder. "I just need to get out of here."

The man followed her gaze back toward the hotel.

"You stayin' at the Riverview?" he asked

Shaking her head, Lexi once again pushed past him. She stepped off the sidewalk and felt her ankle twist underneath her. She tottered and almost fell, but the man reached out and steadied her.

"Maybe I should help you get home." A frown of concern creased his forehead. "My name's Frankie. I'm not a psycho or anything, I promise."

Taking a tentative step, Lexi felt a sharp pain in her ankle.

"My car's just around the corner," she gasped, holding on to Frankie's scrawny arm. "If you can help me get there..."

Frankie walked slowly, letting Lexi hold on to him as she hobbled along. She felt his eyes taking in her disheveled appearance and felt a wave of shame wash over her. When they got to the Mustang, Frankie opened the door and Lexi fell into the driver's seat.

"Come on, you can't drive like that," Frankie said, shaking his head. "You'll get into an accident."

"I only live a few blocks away. I'll be fine," Lexi insisted, worried that he might see the bag of pills she'd left on the passenger seat.

"A few blocks away?" Frankie looked doubtful. "Which street?"

Her mind refused to come up with a plausible lie. Then the name of the street she'd just come from spilled from her lips.

"Kingston Road," she blurted out. "Now please, I just want to go home and take care of my ankle."

"Listen to me, uh...what's your name?"

"Molly," she said, pulling the door closed and starting the engine.

"Listen, Molly. Let me call you a cab or an Uber or something," Frankie called through the glass. "You shouldn't be driving

But the car was already in motion, and neither Lexi nor Frankie noticed the man watching from the hotel lobby as the Mustang pulled onto the highway.

CHAPTER SIXTEEN

Xavier Greyson slipped into the hotel lobby, taking advantage of the crowd and chaos to blend unnoticed into the busy scene. Once he was safely through the doors, he stepped behind a marble column, reassuring himself he couldn't be seen by anyone outside.

Pulse racing, he forced himself to take several deep breaths. He couldn't fall apart now. At first, he'd been alarmed to see the girl from the stairwell standing outside the parking garage, instantly recognizing her even without her pink hair, but now he thought maybe it was all for the best. If she was hanging around the hotel, it would be easier for him to find her and shut her up.

Deciding the safest thing to do was to act normal and not call attention to himself, Xavier pulled out his phone and held it to his ear, pretending to be deep in conversation. He crossed the lobby, stopping next to the big window that looked out onto the taxi drop-off lane and the pedestrian path to the parking garage.

The girl from the stairwell was nowhere to be seen. She'd definitely recognized him, too, but she hadn't cried out or alerted the police. Why not? Had she not connected his soggy, unexpected presence in the stairwell with Portia Hart's highly publicized drowning death the same evening? Could she really be that naïve?

He thought of the shock and fear he'd seen on her face, obvious even at a distance, and dismissed the idea.

She recognized me and she was afraid, so she must suspect something.

Maybe that was why she'd disappeared. She was scared and knew he would be coming after her. Or, perhaps she was the opposite of naïve. Perhaps she was smart enough to sense the danger.

I need to find out who she is and why she was in the stairwell in the middle of the night. And why she's still skulking around here the day after.

A disturbingly familiar voice interrupted his thoughts. Still holding the phone to his ear, he glanced back to see two women in the midst of an emotional conversation. The woman wearing a bright pink dress looked familiar. He took another look.

For the second time that day, Xavier's heart jumped in alarm. Portia's agent, Jane Bishop, stood only a few feet away. Her bright cap of white hair and her loud, penetrating voice were unmistakable.

Turning back to the big window, he listened to the women's conversation with growing dread.

"...it doesn't make sense. Portia would never do this to herself. Someone is responsible and I have a feeling I know who it is."

"She seemed so happy last night," the other woman said. "Her reading was flawless, and she was incredibly engaged during the signing. It took ages, but she spoke to everyone in line without any sign of impatience or fatigue."

Xavier assumed Jane must be talking to the hotel's event planner, but he didn't dare look back. She might recognize him from their one brief encounter a month before when she had stopped by Portia's hotel room in New York City during the book tour's first stop.

Xavier had answered the door thinking it would be room service with his breakfast tray. The old woman had been surprised to see him, and she'd been hard to get rid of.

At the time he hadn't been worried that Jane had seen his face. That had been before he'd discovered the truth about Portia. Back when he'd thought they might really be able to start a life together.

Before he'd had to adjust his plans to better meet his long-term financial goals.

But the sight of Jane Bishop at the Riverview Hotel was an unwelcome complication. And the conversation he'd overheard indicated she was, once again, going to be difficult to get rid of. The police would be asking questions of everyone Portia had known. It would only be a matter of time before they talked to Jane.

Calculating his options, Xavier snuck a quick look back at the women. The event planner was handing Jane a box of books.

"These were left after last night's reception." The woman sounded almost apologetic. "Portia signed them all yesterday. They're the last ones she'll ever sign, so I thought you'd want them."

"Thank you...for everything." Jane's voice cracked as she took the box. "I've got to get to the airport now, but I plan to come back soon. This isn't over."

Jane hurried past Xavier's motionless figure; only his eyes moved to follow her as she exited the hotel.

You're absolutely right, you old busybody, this is definitely far from over.

Xavier waited until Jane had joined the long queue of people waiting at the taxi stand, then hurried out the hotel's side entrance.

* * *

The yellow car idled next to the curb as Xavier gripped its steering wheel and watched the queue outside the hotel with growing impatience. Willow Bay's taxi operations obviously weren't up to the task of handling the rush caused by Portia Hart's sudden death.

Waiting until just the right moment, he steered the taxi into the flow of slow-moving cars. He pulled into the loading zone and waited for the doorman to open the passenger door for the next person in the queue.

"Where to?" he asked, not looking around.

"The airport, please."

Jane Bishop slid a cardboard box full of books onto the seat next to her and buckled her seat belt, then took out her cell phone and began tapping in a message. Xavier surveyed her in the rearview mirror, instinctively adjusting his dark sunglasses and pulling his black baseball cap lower as he accelerated onto the highway.

Taking the exit for the airport, he stayed in the right lane, observing the speed limit. He couldn't afford to attract the attention of a cop who might be driving by. He'd heard too many stories about criminals getting snagged because they'd gotten stopped for a minor traffic violation. He was determined not to make any more mistakes.

"Wasn't that the airport exit?"

Jane looked back at the sign they'd just passed in confusion.

"The new entrance for taxis and public transport is just up here," Xavier said, noting with satisfaction that all the other cars on the highway had turned off toward the airport as the road narrowed to two lanes.

Xavier could see Jane in the rearview mirror staring up at him with a puzzled frown. Perhaps she'd recognized his voice. Or maybe she realized they were now the only car on the highway.

Seeing the turnoff to Mosquito Lake, he slowed and twisted the wheel, ignoring Jane's cry of surprise and protest. Before she knew what was happening, he had reached over the seat and grabbed the phone from her hand, dropping it onto the floor at his feet.

He floored the gas, barreling and bucking down the rutted dirt road until he'd reached the shore, then slammed on the brakes. Jane had already opened the rear door and was scrabbling through it as Xavier jumped out and grabbed a handful of short white hair.

Wrenching her all the way out, he pulled her toward the back of the car. She resisted, slipping in the mud, and falling hard at his feet.

Her black-framed glasses askew, she squinted up at him, but the sun was too bright, and she had to squeeze her eyes shut.

"Here, let me make it easier for you." Xavier bent forward, blocking the sun as he removed his cap and glasses. "That better?"

Jane gasped as she recognized his handsome features.

"I knew it!" she gasped. "I knew you were *bad news.*"

"And I knew you couldn't mind your own fucking business," he responded through gritted teeth. "I guess we were both right."

Spinning on his heel, he stomped back to stand in front of the trunk. Hesitating, he squared his shoulders, took a deep breath, and popped it open. The taxi driver's wide, unseeing eyes stared up at him through the clear plastic bag Xavier had used to suffocate him.

Jane got to her feet and tried to stumble away, but Xavier's long arm shot out, and he grabbed the back of her mud-splattered dress, yanking Jane's compact body against him.

"Oh no, you're not going anywhere."

Dragging her toward the trunk, Xavier felt the phone in his pocket buzz. He'd need to finish up with Jane soon. He had other things that had to be taken care of right away. If he didn't act quickly, his whole plan would fall apart.

Xavier wrapped one strong arm around Jane's throat and squeezed while using his other arm to keep her hands trapped by her side. Within minutes her body sagged limply in his arms.

"It's time...for you to...disappear," he gasped, maneuvering her closer to the open trunk. "Now don't make...this...difficult."

Forcing her head inside the trunk, he could tell by her renewed resistance that she was still conscious and that she'd seen the taxi driver's body stuffed inside.

Summoning all his strength, Xavier shoved Jane into the trunk and slammed the lid shut. He stood in stunned silence, surprised to have gotten her inside so quickly.

Maybe things are looking up. Maybe my run of bad luck is over.

Walking around to the driver's side of the car, Xavier opened the door and bent down to feel around the floor well. His fingers settled on Jane's phone, and he scooped it up. A sudden banging in the trunk caused him to jump and drop the phone on the ground.

He strode to the back of the car and pounded his fist on the lid several times, then leaned close and yelled out.

"Go ahead, bang all you want, old lady. It doesn't matter...nobody's gonna hear you where you're going anyway.'

The phone in his hand trilled, and once again he dropped it. Bending to retrieve it, he bumped his head against the bumper. Grabbing the phone, he hurled it toward the water without thinking.

The splash made him feel a little better, and he exhaled as he watched the ripple in the lake fade away, determined not to let the stress get to him.

I'm almost there...just a few more loose ends to take care of and I'll be done. The hard part will be over.

Turning back to the car, Xavier started the engine and lowered all the windows. Then he put the taxi into drive. The yellow car began to roll slowly down the steep bank toward the lake. He managed to step away and shut the door just as the taxi reached the soggy shore.

When the car stopped halfway into the water, and he could still hear Jane pounding against the lid, Xavier's fear that the whole plan had been a terrible mistake returned.

Forcing himself to stay calm, he got behind the car and pushed. The wheels began to move again, and within minutes the yellow roof of the taxi had disappeared into the lake's murky depths.

The hot air around the lake was quiet and still for a few blissful seconds. Then an airplane roared overhead, prompting Xavier to turn away and head back toward the highway. Taking the phone out of his pocket, he tapped on the *Willow Bay Quick Rides* app and typed in the address of the little mom and pop gas station he'd located on the map earlier. It was only half a mile further up the highway.

Fifteen minutes later he was sitting in the back seat of a blue Toyota sedan chatting to the driver, who had introduced herself as Connie. She explained that she'd retired to Florida to escape the chilly Chicago winters.

"I don't miss all that snow in the winter," she said, turning up the air, "but these Florida summers are pretty intense. Especially with this latest dry spell."

Xavier nodded, making sure to keep his sunglasses and hat on, and his tone neutral.

"Yeah, it's a good day to spend in the water." He allowed himself a small smile. "I'm sure there are plenty of nice lakes around here."

Sitting back in his seat, Xavier looked at his watch, exhausted and anxious to get back to the hotel. Someone might wonder where he'd gotten to. And, of course, the other woman who could screw up his plan was still out there.

He pictured the fear written on the girl's face in the stairwell, and then again outside the hotel that afternoon. That kind of fear made people do stupid things. Eventually, she'd panic and end up telling someone what she'd seen.

That meant, no matter how tired he was, he couldn't let himself rest until he made sure she would never have the chance to tell anyone where he'd been the night Portia died. If he asked around discreetly, he would likely be able to find out who she was and why she was skulking around the hotel.

Taking out his phone again, Xavier navigated to his new app and swiped through the latest updates. He wanted to keep track of all developments. He had to make sure he was prepared to do whatever was necessary to avoid becoming the main subject of the next big story.

CHAPTER SEVENTEEN

Finn Jordan steered the Channel Ten news van up to the front entrance of the Riverview Hotel. He came close to side-swiping the police cruiser that was blocking cars and pedestrians from crossing the secured perimeter around the employee entrance and the door leading to the stairs.

"I'll go park over there next to the Channel Six van." Finn ignored the uniformed officer who was waving for him to move out of the unloading zone. "You go get us a spot in the press pen. I'm sure as a *local celebrity* you won't have a problem getting a place at the front."

Annoyed by Finn's bossy tone and sarcastic comment, Veronica didn't bother responding. She opened the door and jumped out into the crowd.

Winding her way through the throng of people, she looked toward the spot where Nick Sargent and Gustavo had been stationed earlier in the day. Neither man was anywhere to be seen. In fact, it looked as if half the reporters had decamped.

Looking at her watch, she saw that it was already six o'clock. Perhaps they'd gone to get dinner. The thought made her stomach growl. She hadn't had lunch and was suddenly ravenous.

With a defiant sigh, she marched into the lobby and headed toward the restaurant, which appeared to be packed.

A teenage hostess explained there would be at least a thirty-minute wait for a table, but that the bar had just opened for dinner, and that single seats were available. Veronica turned toward the dimly lit bar with a resigned sigh.

I guess I better get used to the single seats.

Finding an empty stool near the end of the long wooden bar, Veronica caught sight of herself in the mirror. She smoothed back a stray lock of hair and wiped at a smudge of mascara under her left eye, cursing the relentless heat and humidity.

"Don't worry, you look fine," an amused voice said from across the bar. "But I bet you could use a cold drink. What'll it be?"

Veronica's cheeks flushed pink as she turned to see the bartender standing in front of her. When she didn't speak, he raised dark eyebrows and tried again.

"What can I get you?"

"Sorry," she said, clearing her throat. "Perrier with lime, please."

The bartender smiled and nodded.

"You're a serious drinker, I see."

Veronica ignored the teasing comment as she picked up a food menu off the bar and began studying the options.

"I'm just going to look at the menu. I'm famished."

Setting a glass in front of her, the bartender filled it with cold sparkling water and added a twist of lime.

"My name's Benji. Just let me know when you're ready to order."

Once Benji turned to walk away, Veronica lifted her eyes to take a closer look. She had a habit of people watching. She liked to study people and try to figure out their story. It was one of the reasons she'd become a reporter. There was something interesting about most people if you looked deep enough.

Tall and lean, Benji had a five o'clock shadow and dark hair that curled over his white collared shirt. Veronica noted his strong, tan forearms as he wiped the counters with a rag.

As he turned to a man at the end of the bar, she examined his profile, admiring his strong jawline, high cheekbones, and classic Roman nose.

Catching her appraising gaze, Benji smiled, revealing deep dimples. Mortified, Veronica dropped her eyes and stared fixedly at the menu as if it might hold the secret of immortality. She didn't raise her eyes again until she heard a man's voice at her elbow.

"Mr. Hart, your room will be ready shortly," the man said, bumping Veronica's arm as he ushered a man onto the stool next to her. "Benji, get Mr. Hart a drink of whatever he wants on the house."

"Of course, Mr. Robinson," Benji said in a polite voice, although his dimples had faded. "What will it be, Mr. Hart?"

Unsure if she had heard the name correctly, Veronica turned to see a young man with dark, floppy hair and thick-framed glasses.

"I'll just take a glass of water, please," he said, settling onto the stool with a deep sigh.

Veronica stared in stunned surprise. Could the man really be Portia Hart's younger brother, Julian? Was it possible that the man she'd been looking for had just walked up and sat down next to her?

"Mr. Hart?" Veronica asked, unable to control herself. "Are you by any chance Julian Hart, Portia Hart's brother?"

Regarding her through smudged lenses, the man seemed unsure how to answer. He finally nodded and turned back to Benji, who had returned with his drink. Downing the water in several long gulps, Julian set the empty glass on the table.

"Same again, please," he said to Benji, sliding the glass forward.

The bartender picked up the glass and spun around to refill it. When he returned, Veronica was surprised to see a flash of irritation on his handsome face.

Benji set the water down without a word, then stepped out from behind the bar to clear one of the bar tables.

"I'm sorry for your loss."

An awkward silence fell as Veronica searched for the right words. "You must be devastated."

Taking off his glasses, Julian rubbed his eyes with his fists and twisted his head to look at Veronica.

"Thanks. I guess I'm still in shock. It just doesn't seem real."

His eyes were a deep blue, and without his over-sized glasses, Veronica thought he was really quite attractive. She'd seen online that he was thirty years old, only a few years old than she was, but in person, he appeared to be younger.

"Do you have anyone here with you? To support you?"

Shaking his head, Julian offered a wan smile.

"Portia was my only family. Without her I...well, I'm on my own."

"I'm sorry to hear that," Veronica said. "My mother is the only family I have, other than Winston...he's my cat...so I can imagine how lonely I'd feel if something happened to her."

As Julian raised his glass to take another drink, Veronica noticed a small heart-shaped birthmark on his right wrist, just under the cuff of his long-sleeved shirt. She'd never seen a birthmark with such a clearly defined shape before.

It's the type of mark that would be easy to identify in a morgue.

The macabre thought flitted unbidden through her mind, and she winced. Perhaps her thwarted visit to the medical examiner's office had left a bigger impression than she'd realized.

"Did you get the chance to identify your sister?" she asked, hoping she didn't sound callous.

"Yes, the police called me in, but they seemed more interested in trying to smear my sister's name than in doing their job and finding out what really happened."

Veronica heard bitterness in his voice, and she couldn't blame him. Who wouldn't be bitter? When Julian had woken up this morning, his world had been the same as usual, and then he turned on the television or radio, and suddenly nothing would ever be the same again.

"I heard that you found out about her death from news reports," Veronica said, feeling guilty. "I'm sorry about that."

Frowning over at her, Julian shrugged.

"Why should you be sorry? The media is always trying to use someone's tragedy to increase their ratings. It's not your fault."

Veronica turned to face him with an apologetic grimace.

"Maybe I should have introduced myself earlier. I'm Veronica Lee, Channel Ten's local roaming reporter. I'm here covering the story."

The color drained from Julian's face as he absorbed her words. Jumping up from the stool, he shook his head in disgust.

"I should have known you had an ulterior motive for being so nice to me. Most beautiful women do. But I guess that's what I get for letting my guard down. Shame on *me*."

Striding toward the exit, Julian bumped into a man in a baggy jacket and hotel name badge that identified him as the hotel manager. The manager straightened his glasses and turned angry eyes on Julian.

When he saw who had bumped into him, his expression melted in an obsequious smile.

"Oh, Mr. Hart, I was just coming to tell you your room is ready."

Julian froze in place, looking past the hotel manager with blazing eyes. Finn Jordan stood in the lobby, camera in hand. At the sound of Julian's name, he turned and raised the camera.

"You there," the manager called out, pointing at Finn. "Get that camera out of this hotel right now! This is *private property*."

Finn seemed unfazed by the hotel manager's outburst. He continued pointing the camera in Julian's direction as Veronica stepped forward and blocked his shot.

"What the hell?"

Finn glared at Veronica over the camera.

"Why'd you do that? You ruined a good shot, and now Julian Hart is gone."

"He wouldn't talk to the police because he doesn't trust them," Veronica said. "I was hoping he'd talk to me. But I screwed it up, and now we may never find out what he knows about his sister's death."

CHAPTER EIGHTEEN

Nessa swallowed the last bite of her sandwich and threw the paper wrapper into the trashcan under her desk. She wiped a smear of mustard off her hands with a napkin and took a swig from her water bottle. So much for dinner. Now she needed to decide which item on her to-do list to tackle next.

Flipping through the pages in her notebook, Nessa decided she would call Jane Bishop first. Portia Hart's agent had been adamant that her client would never have taken drugs, much less kill herself with an intentional overdose, and she'd likely been right.

From what Iris Nguyen had uncovered in the post-mortem, Portia hadn't died of an overdose. Of course, it was too soon to tell what role the drugs may have played in her drowning, but Nessa's intuition was siding with Jane.

Someone out there is responsible for Portia's death. But who... and why?

When Jane's voicemail picked up after the fifth ring, Nessa realized the woman was probably still on her flight back to New York.

"Ms. Bishop, this is Chief Ainsley with the Willow Bay Police Department. I'd like to ask you a few more questions. If you can give me a call back, I'd appreciate it."

Looking through the pages of notes and reminders, Nessa decided it was time to call the team together for an update and strategy session. Iris had estimated Portia's time of death to be between midnight and two a.m. That meant she'd been dead for more than eighteen hours; the window of opportunity to solve the mystery of what had happened in Room 1408 was starting to close.

She picked up her cell and tapped on Vanzinger's number.

"I was just gonna call you, Chief. We're gathering in the briefing room now for an update. That is if you're available."

Caught off guard, Nessa stared at the phone, then laughed.

"I guess great minds really do think alike, Vanzinger. I was just calling you to suggest the same darn thing. I'll be right there."

Vanzinger sat at a long table across from Detective Jankowski, Riley Odell, and Alma Garcia. He jumped up when Nessa came through the briefing room door and pulled out the chair next to him.

"Have a seat, Chief. We were waiting for you to get started."

Nessa cast a sharp glance in his direction, suspecting sarcasm, but his face was the picture of innocence. Perhaps he didn't think she was trying to micromanage after all. Allowing her shoulders to relax, Nessa took out her notebook and turned to the last page of notes.

"Well I'm here," she murmured. "You get started, Detective."

Giving an easy nod, Vanzinger stood and crossed to the whiteboard at the front of the room. He taped a headshot of a glamorous blonde woman to the top, then used a black dry erase marker to write Portia Hart's name.

"Okay, let's document what we know so far," Vanzinger suggested. "Then we can move to what we need to find out."

"Well, we know Portia drowned, and that her time of death was somewhere between twelve and two a.m." Nessa offered. "And we know that she had two broken fingernails and bruises on her shoulders that indicate a possible struggle."

Alma raised her hand, but Nessa wasn't finished.

"I also spoke to Portia Hart's literary agent, a woman from New York named Jane Bishop. She claims that Portia never took drugs and that she would never take her own life. She also was adamant that Portia had a secret boyfriend that may be involved with her death."

"When did you talk to her agent?" Vanzinger looked surprised. "And what else did she say about this guy?"

Feeling guilty that she hadn't yet shared the important detail with the lead detective on the case, Nessa pretended to check her notes as she answered.

"Jane Bishop arrived at the ME's office out of the blue when Iris and I were preparing to start the autopsy. She was pretty torn up and wanted to see Portia."

Nessa looked up with a grimace.

"Unfortunately, the sight of Portia's dead body made Jane sick to her stomach. She ended up leaving for the airport before I could get any useful information, other than she thought Portia had met some guy in the Bahamas this summer. She said the guy was *bad news*."

"Did you get a name?" Vanzinger asked. "Or a description?"

Nessa shook her head.

"She said she didn't know his name, but that she did see him one time. I have a call into her now to try to get a description."

Writing Jane Bishop's name on the board, Vanzinger turned back to the group.

"Okay, what else?"

"We know that Portia Hart was worth a lot of money," Riley offered, "and that her only surviving family member is her younger brother, Julian Hart."

Riley's comment prompted Nessa to turn back a few pages in her notebook to find her notes on Barker's earlier call.

"An insurance investigator named Maxwell Clay from Sterlington Insurance contacted Pete Barker. He asked him to investigate Portia Hart's cause of death. Barker thinks this guy wants to prove she committed suicide."

"Why would he want to do that?" Vanzinger asked.

"So that his company doesn't have to pay the claim," Riley suggested in a dry voice. "Suicide invalidates most policies."

Nessa's mouth tightened into a disapproving line.

"Hoping that someone was miserable enough to kill themselves, so your company saves money? That seems pretty cold-hearted," Nessa said with a huff. "It's as bad as being an ambulance chaser."

"Well, it doesn't look like Mr. Clay will get his wish in this case." Jankowski spoke with grim satisfaction. "Even though someone tried to make it look like a suicide, or maybe an accident."

Riley crossed her arms over her crisp cotton blouse and frowned. "So, who's the beneficiary of Portia's life insurance policy?"

"Barker said it's her younger brother, Julian Hart. Although why he'd need more money I can't imagine. The guy's a billionaire."

"He's also the person who was prescribed the pills Portia had in her room the night she died," Alma added, putting her hand down.

All eyes turned to the crime scene technician.

"Early tests on the residue in the prescription bottle indicate it contained Oxycodone, more commonly known as oxytocin," she said, checking her notes. "The tracking number matches a prescription called into a Florida-based pharmacy for a patient named Julian Hart."

Using the marker to draw another column on the whiteboard, Vanzinger added Julian Hart's name, then wrote *Insurance Beneficiary* and *Prescription at Scene* underneath.

"I think we'd better have another chat with Mr. Hart." Vanzinger drew a line under Julian's name. "We need to ask him how his pills got in Portia's room."

"And I'd also like to ask him about the life insurance policy," Riley said, opening her laptop. "What was the name of the insurance guy?"

"Maxwell Clay," Nessa answered, "with the Sterlington Group."

Vanzinger added Maxwell Clay's name to the whiteboard while Riley typed on her keyboard. After several minutes of frantic tapping, she looked up with a puzzled frown.

"Maxwell Clay isn't on the state's list of registered private investigators and he isn't listed on the Sterlington Group website as an employee," Riley murmured. "But there is a Maxwell Clay listed as an independent insurance broker in Hart Cove."

"Hart Cove?" Jankowski pushed a stray lock of blonde hair off his forehead. "Where's that?"

Riley shrugged, still tapping on her keyboard.

"Hart Cove is a little town on the east coast, just north of Palm Beach. Looks like Remington Hart's grandfather founded the town."

"I guess if you're that rich owning a whole town is no big deal." Jankowski sounded as if he disapproved. "And you probably feel like you can do whatever you want."

Ignoring Jankowski's bitter comment, Nessa turned to face Riley.

"So, if Maxwell Clay's not an insurance investigator, and his company isn't the one on the hook to pay out the claim, then why did he ask Barker to look into Portia Hart's cause of death?"

"There's only one way to find out," Riley responded.

"Right," Nessa agreed, "and Barker told me Clay would be at his office tomorrow morning. I think we better send a welcoming party. In the meantime, I'll wait for Jane Bishop's call."

Vanzinger nodded, reviewing the whiteboard.

"How about I call Julian Hart and arrange another interview for tomorrow afternoon?" Riley sounded almost enthusiastic. "That'll give us a chance to get a statement from Maxwell Clay."

Vanzinger jotted a few notes on the board.

"I guess that leaves me and Jank to review the security footage from the hotel," he said, shooting Jankowski a grin. "Sound like fun, bro?"

Jankowski grunted but didn't respond, so Nessa stood and crossed the room. She pulled open the door, then looked back over her shoulder.

"I'm gonna go home and tuck my boys into bed. Call me if you have any updates that can't wait for tomorrow."

As she walked out to her Dodge, Nessa felt as if she was leaving something undone. Could she have missed some vital clue? Doubt again settled in her chest.

Maybe I should stay and look through the security footage with Vanzinger and Jankowski. Or do a background check on Maxwell Clay.

But she knew she needed to let her team do their job, and so her legs kept moving. She was soon driving into the setting sun toward home.

CHAPTER NINETEEN

Riley stared at the closed door, wondering why she hadn't walked with Nessa to her car. There was nothing she could do at the police station that she couldn't do in her own office, or in her own apartment. But it was Saturday night and the thought of going back to City Hall's empty corridors or eating a lonely dinner in her quiet apartment depressed her.

"I'm going back to the hotel." Jankowski stood and slid his laptop into his backpack. "I want to talk to the security guard and the rest of the staff working last night."

Vanzinger nodded his agreement.

"Yeah, better get them to make a statement while it's still fresh."

Waving a distracted hand at Jankowski's retreating back, Riley stared down at her computer and began clicking through the search results on Julian Hart. Most links led to stories about the death of his billionaire father ten years earlier. A few mentioned his artwork or referred to his famous sister.

"Remington Hart left both of his children a huge fortune," she said, trying to think through the possibilities. "Would Julian kill his own sister over an insurance claim when he's already loaded?"

She looked up and caught Vanzinger's blue eyes, then looked back down at her screen with a flustered scowl.

"Maybe I should get a subpoena to review Portia Hart's bank accounts and see what's going on."

"You still using that old *follow the money* trick?" Vanzinger scoffed. "I thought you'd be after some DNA. Isn't that what a jury wants nowadays?"

Riley's cheeks burned, and she berated herself for letting his words get to her. She was surprised at how much his sarcastic remark stung. Why did she even care what he thought anyway? A hard edge crept into her reply.

"Of course, but they also want a motive, and that usually leads back to only a few things...and money is always a good bet."

"Well, you can chase the motive if that's what you want, but I think you'll need more than that to prove to a jury that Portia didn't take her own life...or accidentally take one too many pills, for that matter. We need some physical evidence."

"We need to follow the money," Riley insisted.

Vanzinger's eyes lit up. He pulled his cell phone out of his pocket and tapped out a number.

"You just gave me a great idea."

He held the phone to his ear.

"Hey Alma, I know you just left, and I'm sorry to be a pest, but I've got a question for you." Vanzinger winked at Riley. "Let me put you on speakerphone."

"You're not a pest," Alma replied. "Call me anytime you like."

Riley darted a sideways glance at Vanzinger and rolled her eyes, irritated by the flush of color that had risen in his cheeks at Alma's suggestive tone.

"Okay, so we wanted to ask you a question."

"We?" Alma sounded wary.

Riley sighed and sat forward.

"Hi Alma, it's Riley. I'm still here going through the case with Vanzinger. Apparently, he thinks he has a brilliant idea, but I'm still not sure what it is."

Alma laughed, but Riley thought the crime scene technician's cheerfulness sounded forced. She wondered why Alma seemed different with her lately. It was almost as if Alma was mad at her.

Does Alma think there's something going on between me and Vanzinger? And is she as interested in him as she seems to be?

"Well, go ahead, Vanzinger," Alma said. "What's the question?"

"You dusted for fingerprints at the scene, right? You dusted her purse, her wallet, the hotel room safe?" Vanzinger asked. "Anywhere and everywhere she may have had some money?"

"Well, my team is pretty thorough, but I'll have to check to see what prints we collected." Alma sounded as confused as Riley felt. "Are you thinking this was a robbery gone wrong?"

Vanzinger caught Riley's eyes on him again as she listened to Alma's response. This time she didn't look away, and he offered her the teasing smile that always used to make her melt.

"Just following the money, Alma. You know what they say..."

"Well, I'll check and let you know what I find out. As far as I know, Portia Hart's personal effects haven't been turned over to her family, so we could always go through them again if you think it could help."

"That'd be highly appreciated, Alma." Vanzinger gave Riley a thumbs up. "I'll wait to hear back."

Disconnecting the call, he dropped his phone into his pocket and turned to leave. Riley couldn't stop herself from calling after him.

"Where are you going now?"

"I'm going to watch the security footage the hotel turned over. See if I can spot anything fishy."

He raised his eyebrows and cocked his head.

"I'll let you watch them with me if you bring the popcorn."

* * *

Vanzinger's office was small but neatly organized. Riley sat stiffly on the chair next to him as he stuck the memory stick into his computer's USB drive and waited for the device to be recognized.

"Iris estimated Portia Hart's time of death to be between midnight and two, and we know Portia left the reception sometime after eleven."

Two files appeared on Vanzinger's screen. He clicked on the top file and waited as the video player loaded.

"I asked to get the video feed from the camera by the fourteenth-floor elevator landing, and the exterior camera by the stairwell exit."

Riley felt a rush of anticipation as the hotel corridor appeared on the screen, but she let out a disappointed puff of air as she saw the poor quality of the video. The picture was fuzzy, and the dim lighting made it hard to make out any details. From what she could see, the corridor was empty.

Straining to see any sign of movement in the dark hall, Riley tried to ignore the musky scent of Vanzinger's cologne as he sat only a foot away. She'd been alone so long she'd almost forgotten how intoxicating it could be to feel the heat of a man's body next to hers.

"Look, someone's coming out of the elevator." Vanzinger pointed to a figure on the screen. "It's Portia going back to her room."

A curtain of pale blonde hair topped the willowy figure of a woman teetering down the hall. She soon blended into the dark shadows outside Room 1408.

"Now we wait to see if anyone else goes in," Riley said in a low voice as if someone in the corridor might hear her.

"Or if anyone comes out," Vanzinger added, checking his watch.

Riley caught herself staring at his muscled arm, wondering what he'd done with the watch she'd given him all those years ago.

It's probably in some pawnshop over in Tampa by now.

Shooting Vanzinger an exasperated sideways glance, Riley almost missed the flash of movement at the end of the hall. She looked up just in time to see a figure in dark pants and a hoodie slip through the shadows toward the door to the stairs.

Vanzinger's gasp confirmed he'd seen the figure as well.

"Gotcha!"

His voice vibrated with anger as the figure disappeared through the big metal door. Tapping on an icon to skip backward in the video, Jankowski watched the clip again.

"There was definitely someone in her room around that time," Vanzinger said. "And it looks like he was waiting for her when she came in."

Clicking on the second file, both Riley and Vanzinger watched the screen with anxious eyes. They weren't expecting to see the girl with pink hair slam out of the exterior door and disappear through an opening along the walkway.

"Who the hell is she, and–"

Before Vanzinger could finish his sentence, the door opened again, and a dark figure in a hoodie raced through with his head down. The man headed toward the parking garage without noticing the gap in the wall the young woman had slipped through.

"There was a man in Portia's room." Riley sounded stunned to have found solid proof that Portia hadn't died alone. "And that girl may be the only witness out there who can identify him."

CHAPTER TWENTY

The sun rose early, lighting the water of the Willow River with a dazzling brightness that made Lexi's eyes water. Sunday mornings on the Riverwalk were free from the loud, bustling crowds that frequented the restaurants, bars, and retail boutiques each evening. She sat alone on a wide wrought iron bench facing the water's edge.

Lifting her head, Lexi heard the bells pealing at the Methodist church a few blocks away on Waterside Drive. She felt a sudden pang of nostalgia for the days when she'd go to Sunday service with her parents. That was before her father had walked out. Before her mother had run away to Jacksonville to start a new life.

The first line of a song she used to sing at Sunday school played again and again in her head as the sun sparkled off the calm water.

This little light of mine, I'm gonna let it shine...this little light of mine...

A mosquito buzzed next to Lexi's ear, and she swatted at it with a lazy hand. She'd been up most of the night, pacing her tiny apartment and jumping at any noise. Too suffocated and trapped to sit still, she'd eventually crept out into the predawn darkness, hoping to find a sense of peace by the lake.

Something rustling in the bushes caused her to jump, and she turned to see two squirrels dart out and scramble up a nearby tree. She smiled as their bushy tails disappeared into the branches.

Her smile faded as she heard her phone trilling. She didn't need to look at the display to know who was calling. She'd purposely chosen the gentle, pleasing ringtone for Molly Blair, hoping to make the unpleasant woman's calls more bearable.

After waiting all night for Molly to call her back, Lexi was tempted to ignore the call. She took her phone out and looked at it with resentful eyes.

Maybe I should just run away. I could get some help...I could get better.

The phone stopped ringing, and for one, blissful moment, Lexi felt a surge of relief. She'd done it. That was the first step. Ignore the calls. Leave town. Pretend nothing that had happened during the last twelve months was real. It was all just a terrible dream.

Shoving the phone back in her pocket, Lexi felt the edge of the plastic bag that Molly had given her. It held only two more pills. Panic rose in her chest at the thought of what she would do after the two remaining pills were gone.

I'll go to the rehab that guy Frankie told me about. I'll go to Hope House.

But doubt and fear joined the swirl of panic as she wondered how she would cope with the withdrawal. She'd tried it on her own already several times. Each time had seemed harder than the last, with the nausea, sweating, and anxiety reaching unbearable levels.

Grabbing her phone, Lexi jabbed the screen and held it to her ear.

"Molly? Is that you, Molly?"

"Lexi, I need you to come over here."

The request surprised Lexi.

"Come to your house? Like...now?"

"Yes, I need to...to talk to you. And I have more pills."

Lexi raised her eyebrows and held the phone out to stare at it. Molly was usually paranoid about mentioning anything to do with pills, drugs, or illicit activities over the phone. Perhaps Molly was mellowing. Or maybe she'd been up all night and was just too tired to care.

Picturing the bottle of pills that awaited, Lexi closed her eyes and sighed. Who was she kidding anyway? There was no way she would be able to leave Willow Bay without a supply of pills to hold her over. She had tried going cold turkey before, and it was a painful, dangerous method.

I'll go to Molly's and get a supply. I'll use them to wean myself slowly.

"I'm not at home now," she told Molly, "so it'll take a while."

"Just get over here...*now*."

Before Lexi could reply, Molly disconnected the call.

* * *

Lexi's silver Mustang sped away from the Riverwalk, almost sideswiping a neon blue Prius as she made a wide turn onto Bay Street. Molly's back gate was ajar when Lexi steered the Mustang into the alley behind Kingston Road only a few minutes later.

She parked along the curb, then looked over her shoulder, reassuring herself that her suitcase and backpack were in the backseat. All she had to do was get the pills, and she could be on her way to Jacksonville. She'd call her mother and break the news once she'd gotten on the highway.

Stepping into the stifling heat, Lexi felt her temples begin to throb. She shaded her eyes from the harsh morning sunshine with one hand and stuck her other hand in her pocket to pat the deflated plastic bag, comforted by the two hard tablets within.

Pausing at the gate, she wondered if Molly had gone out. Why else would she leave it open? She looked toward the detached garage and saw with relief that Molly's sleek black Jaguar was parked inside.

The sound of water bubbling stopped Lexi halfway to the backdoor. Could Molly really be using the hot tub in the excruciating heat? She walked forward and peered over the side and into the swirling water. Leaning closer, Lexi saw something floating just under the foamy, frothing water.

Molly Blair's pale, slack face bobbed under the surface, and her unseeing brown eyes stared up through the undulating water. Lexi watched in horror as the water churned around Molly's lifeless body.

"Molly?"

Her voice croaked out the name, and she reached down to pull the woman out of the water, even though she knew without a shadow of a doubt that Molly was already gone.

The sound of soft footsteps behind her made Lexi spin around. She froze in shock as she recognized the man from the stairwell. Before she could open her mouth to scream, the man grabbed her around the waist and clapped a hand over her mouth.

"You took your time," he muttered in her ear. "I was just going to come looking for you. I really have to-"

Bringing her heel down hard on his foot, Lexi threw her head back and cracked her skull against the man's forehead. He bellowed and released his grip as Lexi ran toward the gate, her heart thumping and her legs shaking. She'd almost made it to the gate when a big hand closed around her arm and jerked her backward.

Her scream pierced the air, then abruptly stopped as the man once again held a strong hand over her mouth. Dragging her toward the hot tub, he pushed her head down into the gurgling water.

Lexi clawed up at him, scratching at the leather gloves he wore in growing desperation. Grasping at anything she could hold on to, she wrenched her hand back and pulled off one of his gloves. He pushed her head under the water with angry hands, and she gulped in a burning mouthful before managing to get her face above the surface.

"Stop fighting, you stupid-"

The sound of the gate banging against the wooden fence caused the man to stop and look up. Lexi used the distraction to bring her knee up between his legs, and the man screamed in pain. His hands dropped away, and she lost her balance, tumbling into the water on top of Molly's lolling body.

Flailing against the water, Lexi grabbed onto the side of the tub and tried to pull herself out, but a wave of dizziness caused her legs to give way. She sank back in despair, sure that the man would be on her again any minute and certain her body would never be able to withstand another assault. She fought to keep her head up as she wavered in and out of consciousness.

It can't end like this...can it? No, I can't give up. I can't let him win.

"Molly?"

She heard the voice above her and looked up to see worried eyes in a thin, unshaven face. Skinny arms reached down, straining to pull her up and out of the water, and gentle hands deposited her on the wooden deck.

"Are you okay, Molly?"

Squinting up, Lexi recognized the man who'd given her the stick of gum the night before. What was his name?

"Frankie?"

Her voice was a raw whisper.

"Yeah, it's me." His voice was strained. "You almost crashed into me and my partner back on Bay Street. I thought we'd better make sure you were okay. You didn't look very good last night."

Eyes widening, Lexi tried to sit up, but the spinning in her head caused her to sink back down.

"That man...he...he killed Molly."

"Who is that guy? He ran into the house. Barker went after him."

Frankie pointed toward the sliding glass doors, then frowned.

"And what do you mean he killed Molly? Aren't you Molly?"

Shaking her head, Lexi tried to explain.

"No, I'm Lexi Marsh. Molly's...in...in there." Choking out the words, Lexi struggled to remain conscious. "That man killed her."

Frankie pushed himself to his feet and leaned over the edge of the hot tub. After a long pause, he sat down next to Lexi, his face stricken. Pulling out his cell phone, he tapped three times on the display and then held the phone to his ear.

Lexi could hear the faint voice of the 911 operator on the other end of the call. When Frankie spoke, his voice was shaky.

"I need to report a homicide and an assault. The house is on Kingston Road...hold on."

Frankie looked at the house, then down at Lexi.

"You know the house number?"

She nodded, starting to feel a little less dizzy.

"It's 5025 Kingston."

The fact that she was asking the police to come out to Molly's house seemed surreal. She'd been keeping her work for Molly a closely guarded secret for so long it still seemed wrong to reveal the address.

"Okay, they're gonna send a car over," Frankie told her, looking down at her with a curious expression. "Now, are you gonna tell me what's going on?"

Sitting up, Lexi ran a hand through her wet hair. Tiny drops of water dripped onto her shoulders as she considered her options. If she told the police the truth, she may get in trouble.

She'd taken drugs without a prescription, and she'd taken part in an illegal escort operation. Both offenses could result in jail time and a permanent record. And the man who had tried to kill her was still out there. If she told the police what she'd seen, he'd be back.

"I was at the Riverview Hotel Friday night," she heard herself say. "And I saw that man...the one who attacked me. He was coming down the stairs and he looked angry that I'd seen him."

"Friday night at the Riverview?" Frankie cocked his head and frowned. "You mean when Portia Hart was killed?"

Lexi nodded and took a deep breath.

"I think he was trying to get to me through Molly," Lexi said, her voice cracking. "He wanted to shut me up. He killed her and...and he was gonna kill me next."

Lifting a thin hand, Frankie gave her shoulder an awkward pat as sirens began to wail in the distance. A big man stepped out of the back door and waved at Frankie.

"I couldn't catch up to him. He must have had a car nearby."

Frankie nodded and looked down at Lexi.

"You gotta tell the cops what happened," he said, sensing her reluctance. "You're the only one that saw the guy who killed your friend. The same guy that was in the hotel the night Portia Hart died. You're gonna be a star witness."

Lexi recoiled at the idea, wishing she were strong enough to get up and run away before it was too late.

"Cheer up," Frankie said, trying to smile. "You'll probably end up on the news and everything. You'll be famous when the press hears your story."

Fear settled in Lexi's chest as she imagined just what the police and the press would uncover if they dug into her past. She shivered as the first police car roared up outside the gate.

CHAPTER TWENTY-ONE

Hunter Hadley dropped the phone on his desk with growing unease. He'd gone into the station early, even though Sunday was usually the one day of the week he allowed himself to take the full day off. He'd been working on the developing Portia Hart story for several hours when he'd received a call from his contact at the Willow Bay Police Department. A woman had been attacked and killed in her home on Kingston Road.

All that Hunter knew so far was that the police had responded to a 911 call and found a woman's body floating in the backyard hot tub. According to his contact, there was at least one witness at the scene.

Typing the address into his computer's search engine, Hunter saw that the house on Kingston was owned by a woman named Molly Blair. He didn't recognize the name, but he figured the homeowner was likely to be the victim.

According to his search, Molly Blair was thirty-eight years old and had purchased the house on Kingston three years earlier. He could find no arrest or criminal record. She seemed like an ordinary Willow Bay citizen.

Hunter wondered who would want to kill her, and why?

Viewing the house on *Google Earth*, he noticed it was located in a downtown neighborhood only blocks away from the Riverwalk.

Which meant it was only blocks away from the hotel where Portia Hart had drowned on Friday night.

Can it be a coincidence that two women drowned to death under mysterious circumstances less than ten blocks and forty-eight hours apart?

He looked out through the glass wall of his office, anxious to get Veronica and Finn out to the scene, but Veronica's desk was empty. Picking up his phone, he tapped on her number and waited. After the sixth ring, her voicemail picked up. He waited for the beep.

"A woman's body was found this morning at a house on Kingston Road. Looks like a homicide."

He didn't try to hide his impatience.

"That's only blocks from the Riverview Hotel. We need to jump on this; meet me at the station when you get this message."

Disconnecting the call, he thought again about Veronica's question yesterday. She had a right to know the station was up for sale, and she was bound to find out sooner or later. The whole crew would know eventually, so he might as well come clean.

"Hunter, come see this!"

Finn Jordan stood by the door looking at him with the same wiseass grin Jordie used to wear. Hunter hadn't realized how much he'd missed that grin. A sharp pang of grief pierced him at the realization he'd never see Saul Jordan's grin again.

Refusing to give in to the melancholy, he followed Finn's broad back out to the newsroom. Gracie sat at attention next to a desk that held dual monitors and Finn's old rucksack.

The white Lab's tail thumped back and forth as Hunter approached. He scratched the dog's head and looked at the monitors; both were lit up with footage of Veronica outside the Riverview Hotel the previous evening.

"This is the segment on Portia Hart's death that I was putting together when you left last night. I finished it this morning."

The pride in Finn's voice was unmistakable, and as Hunter watched the screen he began to smile. The young man was a chip off the old block. He had talent, just as his father had.

Hunter nodded his approval when the segment had finished.

"Okay, I'm impressed. You really do take after your dad, and that's saying something. He was one of the best in the business."

Finn's grin faltered as the words sunk in, and for a minute Hunter feared he had made a blunder by mentioning Jordie. Maybe the wounds were still too fresh. Perhaps he should avoid bringing up Jordie for the time being. Even good memories could be painful.

"Thanks, man...that means a lot coming from you." Finn's voice thickened, but his eyes were dry and bright as they met Hunter's. "My dad respected your opinion. He always said you had a good eye."

Hunter's throat tightened, and he spun around to hide the emotion in his face, looking toward the door.

"Have you talked to Veronica this morning? I just got a call on a big story. I want you guys on the scene right away."

"Yeah, she said she was on her way." Finn sounded excited. "We were gonna go back to the hotel this morning. Maybe get an interview with the hotel manager, or maybe a couple of the guests."

"Good, well as soon as she gets here you guys come into my office and I'll give you the details. In the meantime, I'll tell the team to work your segment into the noon broadcast."

Striding back into his office, he saw that Gracie had followed him in. She crossed to the window and stared out into the parking lot. Hunter followed her gaze.

A big red Jeep had just pulled into an empty space. They both watched as Veronica jumped out, smoothed back her long dark hair, and slung her bag over her shoulder.

Before she could walk toward the building, a white Mercedes rolled up and park beside her. Hunter frowned as he watched the driver open the door and step out.

There was something familiar about the man's dark, tousled hair and glasses, and he recognized the neatly pressed khakis and long-sleeved linen shirt.

Thinking back to the segment Finn had just shown him, Hunter remembered seeing a glimpse of Julian Hart standing in the hotel lobby. Portia Hart's devastated younger brother had quickly turned away, but the resemblance was unmistakable.

Why is Julian Hart out there talking to Veronica, and what does he want?

Hunter's sense of unease returned as he watched Veronica. He was too far away to see the expression on her face, but her body language suggested she was tense, and that the conversation was strained.

Resisting the urge to rush outside and intervene, Hunter forced himself to remain calm. His sudden instinct to protect Veronica disturbed him.

He couldn't let himself get too emotionally involved with his staff, although he knew it was common for people working together in stressful environments to associate their heightened emotions with their co-workers.

And he couldn't think of any situation more stressful than the last time Veronica had gotten too involved in a story. She'd cornered a serial killer and had ended up as his hostage.

Hunter's pulse raced as he remembered the night he'd had to face Boyd Faraday. Luckily, he'd managed to outsmart the killer, and Veronica's life had been spared.

But it had been a close call, and Hunter couldn't help worrying that the next time she chased down a killer to get a story, she might not be so lucky.

Of course, Julian Hart wasn't a deranged stalker. He was a grieving brother. A rich, handsome artist with a sensitive side. Perhaps that's just what Veronica needed. She certainly deserved to be happy.

As he watched Veronica reach out a gentle hand and rest it on Julian's arm, Hunter told himself she was only trying to console the guy. That was the kind of person she was.

Her compassion was one of the main reasons he admired her. And it wasn't any of his business in any case. It shouldn't matter to him who she spoke to.

Then why does the sight of her touching Julian Hart make me want to put my fist through this window?

Forcing his eyes away from the scene outside, Hunter knelt next to Gracie's warm, solid body and rubbed her soft fur. He breathed in deeply, then let out a slow exhale. He couldn't let himself slide backward.

Not after all the progress he'd made in the last few months. His therapy sessions with Reggie Horn had been going well, and he'd managed to wean himself off his medication.

A sudden fear washed over him. What if his lack of medication was making him relapse? Perhaps he didn't have as much control over his PTSD as he'd imagined.

"I can't go back there, Gracie," he murmured, staring into the Labrador's deep brown eyes. "I can't lose myself again."

* * *

Veronica dropped her bag on her desk, seemingly lost in thought.

"Hey, you got my message, right?" Hunter asked as he walked toward her. "About the homicide over on Kingston?"

She stopped short and stared up at him blankly.

"I guess that means you didn't."

Finn appeared beside them carrying a camera case. His rucksack was already over his shoulder. He looked ready to roll.

126

"You ready to go, Veronica? I just saw that Channel Six is already on the scene. Your buddy Nick Sargent must live in his van."

Smiling at her confused expression, Finn headed toward the door.

"I'll fill you in on the way to the scene. Now let's get moving."

He turned back to Hunter and laughed.

"I think Gracie wants to stay here with you."

Hunter glanced down to see that Gracie had settled in by his feet. She looked up at him with contented eyes and yawned. When he raised his head Finn and Veronica were halfway to the door.

"Wait!"

Everyone on the news crew turned to look at Hunter as Veronica and Finn jerked to a stop. The word had come out louder than he'd intended. Seeing the startled and expectant faces all around him, Hunter couldn't bring himself to say what needed to be said.

He wanted to tell Veronica and the rest of the crew about the station's impending sale, but he had to pick the right time.

Blurting out the situation in the midst of two breaking stories would make it seem more dire than it actually was. He'd have to wait until things had calmed down.

"What did Julian Hart want?" He hadn't known he was going to ask the question until it came out of his mouth. "I saw him outside."

"He agreed to an interview," Veronica replied, not sounding very happy. "And he apologized for overreacting last night."

Raising his eyebrows, Hunter tried to mask his surprise.

"That's good. You've managed to get a real scoop then."

"Yeah, I guess so," Veronica agreed. "We're supposed to meet up later this afternoon. Hopefully, he won't change his mind."

Finn walked to the door and pulled it open.

"Let's go, Ronnie."

Veronica stopped in mid-stride and put her hands on her hips.

"Who told you to call me that? Only my mother calls me Ronnie."

"I'm a reporter," Finn said, holding open the door. "I can find out just about anything if I'm motivated."

Rolling her eyes, she hurried out the door. Hunter watched it swing shut behind her, then looked down at Gracie and sighed.

"You know what, girl? I kind of wish I were going with them."

He headed back to his office picturing the chaotic scene he'd worked the day before.

It had been good to be back in action. It'd felt right, somehow. He thought of Veronica and Finn racing toward another dramatic scene and felt the old thrill. That jolt of adrenaline he used to experience when he'd first started out as a reporter.

Maybe I can find what I lost in Kabul. Maybe it isn't over for me after all.

CHAPTER TWENTY-TWO

Knowing the temperature inside the locked van would be unbearable, Finn started the engine and let the air conditioner run while he loaded up the camera and grip gear. Veronica leaned against the door and pulled her notebook out of her bag. She wanted to make a few notes about her conversation with Julian Hart before she was pulled into another story.

The unexpected arrival of Portia Hart's brother had rattled her, and she'd been concerned by his disheveled appearance.

He was obviously having a hard time dealing with his sister's death, and Veronica suspected he was pretty much alone in the world, now that Portia was gone.

Veronica had tried to apologize for not telling him she was a reporter as soon as they'd started talking the day before, but Julian had stopped her. He'd seemed embarrassed that he'd stormed out in a huff. And he'd thank her for not using the footage on Channel Ten's late night or early morning broadcast.

As she waited for the van to cool off, Veronica replayed his words.

When my face wasn't on the news, I kind of hoped I'd been wrong. That you hadn't talked to me just to get a story. That I might be able to trust you.

His words had been spoken with such earnest sincerity that she'd reached out and put a hand on his shirtsleeve. She now wondered about the impulsive gesture. At the time it had felt like the right thing to do. He was alone and hurting, and she had offered comfort.

But now Veronica wondered if she was allowing herself to get too emotionally invested in Julian Hart's story. Shouldn't she keep an objective distance so that she could report the facts without her own feelings skewing them?

"You coming or what?"

Looking up from her notebook, Veronica saw that Finn was already sitting in the driver's seat. He'd rolled down the passenger window and was staring at her with wide, impatient eyes.

"Oh, yeah, sorry."

She opened the door and climbed in.

"I was just making some notes to reference later."

Finn navigated the big van out of the station's parking lot and onto Townsend Road, then turned to look at her.

"What did Julian Hart want? You guys seemed to be having a pretty intense conversation."

"I'm surprised you have to ask," she snapped. "I thought you already knew everything about everything."

Her tone was defensive, although she wasn't sure why she felt as if she had something to hide.

Oh, you know why, Veronica. You're hoping to hear the rest of Julian's story. You think he's going to share all his family secrets with you.

But she couldn't tell that to Finn. Or to anyone. Julian had confessed that Portia's life wasn't as perfect as her book had portrayed to the rest of the world. But he'd done so off the record.

Veronica thought back to his tortured admission.

There are things no one knows, and I...I need to find out the truth. I need closure. Will you help me find it? Off the record?

While she hadn't committed to anything, Veronica had agreed to meet Julian later. Now she was wondering if that had been a mistake. Perhaps she should have told him bluntly that her job was to report on the story, not to get involved in the story.

She forced herself to close her notebook. She had another breaking story that needed her attention; further thoughts about Julian Hart and his sad blue eyes would have to wait.

"Okay, so where are we going and what's the big story?"

She looked out the window as Finn turned toward downtown.

"A woman's body was found this morning at a house on Kingston Road. She was attacked and killed in her own backyard. They found her floating in the jacuzzi."

Jerking her head around, Veronica gaped at Finn.

"Another woman is *dead*? It's only been twenty-four hours since Portia Hart's body was discovered."

Finn nodded just as the automated voice from the GPS told him to turn right onto Bay Street. He swung the van around a corner and narrowly missed hitting two teenagers who were crossing the intersection on bicycles.

"Yeah, and this time there's a witness."

He sounded excited.

"We'll probably get a description or even a sketch of the killer."

The street was blocked off to through traffic, and a line of cars dutifully waited in the sweltering sun as a uniformed officer waved them onward toward a detour sign. Veronica recognized Officer Andy Ford's freckled face.

"Let me out here," Veronica ordered, her hand already on the door handle. "I'll ask Andy to let us through."

Jumping down from the van, Veronica approached the policeman with a friendly smile.

"Hey, Andy, how's it going?"

The young policeman's anxious face softened into a smile when he saw Veronica. He waved several cars toward the detour sign as he called out a greeting.

"How's your mother doing?'

Trickles of sweat dripped down Andy's face as Veronica stopped in front of him.

"She still keeping the kids in line over at Willow Bay High?"

Veronica nodded, suddenly glad that her mother was the principal of the town's main high school. Most people who'd graduated from Willow Bay High in the last two decades knew Ling Lee. It could open certain doors for Veronica when she was pursuing a story.

"Yeah, she's still got them all running scared," Veronica teased.

"Oh, no. She doesn't need to scare anybody," Andy protested as if he felt obligated to defend his old principal. "The school's part of my patrol area. It's easy to see that everybody still loves your mom, Veronica. Just like when I was there."

"Thanks, Andy. I'll be sure to tell her you said hello."

Veronica pointed back at the van.

"But, in the meantime, you wouldn't mind letting us through the barrier, would you, Andy? I think there are other crews already on the scene."

Andy nodded and glanced back over his shoulder. The satellite dish on top of a white van was visible past the stop sign.

"Channel Six got here first," he said. "Nick Sargent arrived a few minutes after we pulled up. It took the rest of his team a bit longer."

Pushing the barricade to the side, Andy waved the Channel Ten van through. He caught sight of Finn's face through the windshield.

"You got a new guy on your crew?"

"Yep, that's Finn Jordan. He started as our new cameraman yesterday, but he already acts like he's in charge."

Veronica climbed back into the van. As Finn drove past Andy onto Kingston Road, she extended a grateful thumbs up.

But her cheerful expression melted when she saw that Nick Sargent was in the middle of a live feed and that Gustavo was working the camera.

"Park next to them." Veronica looked at her watch. "We'll have to set up the feed right away to be ready by noon."

As she stepped out of the van, her attention was captured by Nick Sargent's solemn voice. He spoke directly into the camera.

"A local woman was killed today by an assailant who is still on the run. No official word yet on the name of the victim, but neighbors tell us that the house behind me, located at 5025 Kingston Road, is owned by local resident Molly Blair."

Astonished that Nick had once again revealed the name of a victim before official identification and next-of-kin notifications had been performed, Veronica cast a withering glare at the newsman.

Looks like some reporters will do anything for a story.

Pushing back a pang of guilt at the thought, Veronica tried to focus on her notes, but she was unable to block out Nick's deep voice.

"Sources in the WBPD tell us that the woman's body was found floating in the hot tub and that another woman was at the scene and may have witnessed the crime."

Nick paused to look down at a slip of paper in his hand as if he'd just been handed a last-minute update. It was a tactic Veronica had seen the Channel Six reporter often use to add drama to his reports.

"And now, just in, we are hearing speculation that this morning's homicide may have a connection to the death of Portia Hart yesterday at the Riverview Hotel. The celebrity author was found dead in her luxury suite only blocks away."

The words sent a cold shiver down Veronica's spine despite the soaring temperature. The idea that some maniac was going around Willow Bay drowning women was ludicrous. Wasn't it?

"You think Portia Hart's death could really be related to this homicide?" she asked Finn as he appeared beside her. "I mean...what would an ordinary woman living in this quiet neighborhood have in common with a super-rich celebrity like Portia Hart?"

Finn shrugged and raised the camera.

"That's what we've gotta find out," he snipped. "That's why it's called *investigative* reporting. Now get ready to go on air. We're running out of time."

A high-pitched chime filled the air, causing Veronica to start and reach frantically into her pocket to silence the phone.

"Sorry, I thought it was on silent," she muttered to Finn. "It's my mother calling. She probably just saw the Channel Six report."

"Well, answer it!" Finn demanded, sounding indignant. "It's *your mom*. You don't just ignore your mom."

Frowning at Finn's outburst, Veronica tapped on the display and held the phone to her ear.

"Hi, Ma. I'm at a scene and about to go on air."

"I know where you are," Ling responded matter-of-factly. "I can see your location on the *Find My Phone* app you installed."

Her calm demeanor slipped as she continued.

"Why else do you think I'm calling? I see my daughter is at the scene of a murder, and the assailant is still on the loose. What should I do? Wait for the police to call and tell me you've been hurt again?"

"I'm not going to get hurt, Ma. The police are all over. In fact, I can see Andy Ford right now. He said to tell you hello."

Ling sniffed and Veronica could picture her mother's expression.

"Andy Ford is a nice boy, but he can't protect you if you're running around trying to interview a deranged killer. You'll get yourself-"

"Ma, I'm not interviewing killers. I'm reporting on the situation so the public knows what's going on and people can protect themselves. It's a big responsibility."

Sighing, Ling's voice lost its fight.

"But who's going to protect you, Ronnie, when you're fulfilling this responsibility? And who's going to take care of Winston if something happens to you?"

The thought of the old, orange Tabby brought a smile to Veronica's face. She knew her mother was trying to use Winston to guilt her, but she'd only managed to make her more determined.

"Winston would agree with me," she said, softening her tone. "He knows what it's like to lose someone you love to murder."

She glanced up to see Finn's raised eyebrows. Someday she'd have to fill him in on Winston's history. The fact that the cat had witnessed his previous owner's murder was something few people knew. Veronica still didn't like talking about it.

"I just want you to be safe and happy," Ling insisted. "That's what I've always wanted."

Tucking a strand of hair behind her ear, Veronica sighed. It was always the same old refrain. But if her mother was really concerned about her daughter's happiness, she should have more faith in her. Veronica felt the urge to say what she'd been thinking for so long.

Why don't you trust me enough to tell me the truth about my father? How can I ever be happy if I don't even know who I am?"

Turning her back on Finn, Veronica lowered her voice and spoke into the phone, not trying to hide the hurt.

"Try to have some faith in me for once, Ma," she said, knowing it wasn't the time or place to raise the subject of her father again.

The silence on the other end of the line brought a stab of remorse. Better just to apologize. She needed to get back to work, and it was easier to pretend she was fine. After all, she'd been doing it for years.

"I'm sorry, Ma, just forget about it. It doesn't matter."

Veronica tried to make the lie sound convincing.

"And I promise I'll be careful. You'll see, nothing's going to happen to me."

When she turned around Finn was staring at her with a curious expression. Veronica was relieved when he didn't say anything about the call. He just picked up the camera, raised his hand, and began the countdown to go live.

Five, four, three, two, one...

"Good morning, Willow Bay. This is Veronica Lee reporting live from Kingston Road where a woman was attacked and killed earlier today. The Willow Bay Police Department is now searching for the suspected assailant who is still at large..."

CHAPTER TWENTY-THREE

The girl in the hospital bed pulled the thin blanket over her shoulders. She appeared to be shivering, although her skin looked pale and sweaty under a spattering of bruises. Nessa imagined the chill of the air-conditioned room must be a shock to the girl's system after the furnace-like conditions outside. Summoning a reassuring smile, Nessa stepped into the room.

"Hi, Alexandra, I'm Nessa Ainsley, Willow Bay's chief of police."

The girl's puffy blue eyes widened in fear.

"Am I in trouble?" she asked, swallowing hard.

"No, of course you're not in trouble."

Nessa crossed to stand beside the bed, masking her surprise.

"I'm just here to make sure you're okay, and I want to talk to you about what happened this morning."

Dropping her eyes, the girl sunk deeper into the covers.

"Well, *I* don't want to talk about it." She turned her face away. "Besides, I already told the detectives everything I know."

Nessa pointed to a chair by the bed.

"Do you mind if I sit down, Alexandra?"

"I guess not, but only if you stop calling me Alexandra."

The petulant retort reminded Nessa of Cole's tendency to pout whenever he wasn't getting his own way. She hid a smile as she slid onto the chair and opened up her notebook.

"Okay, what should I call you, then?"

"Most of my friends call me Lexi, although my mom calls me Alex." After a slight pause, she added, "I prefer Lexi."

Nessa cleared her throat.

"Well, Lexi, I know from your earlier statement that you drove your car over to Kingston Road to see Molly Blair. Why'd you go over there this morning?"

"Molly called me." Lexi's voice was flat. "She asked me to come by right away. She didn't say why."

"What was the nature of your relationship?"

Lexi's eyes darted around the room as if seeking an escape.

"We were...friends," her voice quavered on the last word. "She started helping me out after my mother moved to Jacksonville."

"Okay, I see."

Nessa jotted a note in her book, but she wasn't buying Lexi's story. The emotion Lexi exuded when she spoke of Molly Blair was one of anger or resentment, not grief.

"So, Molly was kind of like a surrogate mother to you, then?"

Lexi's mouth tightened into a thin line as she shrugged.

"Something like that," she conceded.

"Then you must be pretty torn up that she's gone."

Reaching for a glass of water by the bed, Lexi ignored the question.

"I really just want to get out of here," she said, sipping at the water. "I'm fine. I don't know why they even brought me here."

"The doctors want you to stay overnight for observation. They say you ingested a lot of water and might have blacked out during the...the incident. Best to keep an eye on you."

Nessa had also overheard the nurses saying Lexi's vital signs were unstable, but that wasn't something she had been supposed to hear.

"I'd like to show you something, Lexi."

Pulling out a thin laptop, Nessa opened it on her lap and clicked on an icon. Within seconds a video began to play. It showed an exterior door of the Riverview Hotel. Suddenly a young woman with pink hair charged through the door and disappeared into a gap in the wall. Almost immediately a man barreled out, running with his hooded head down. He flew past the gap in the wall without slowing, and the clip ended.

"That was footage from a security camera outside the Riverview Hotel," Nessa said, watching Lexi's face drain of all color. "And I think that young woman running out the door might be you."

Shaking her head in denial, Lexi crossed her arms over her chest. "I don't know who that is, but she looks nothing like *me*."

Nessa bit her lip, wondering what Lexi hoped to gain by lying.

She looks petrified. What or who could be scarier than the man who came storming out of the hotel after her? What is she hiding, and why?

Leaning back in the chair, Nessa studied Lexi's face. Behind the fear and the bruises, she was a lovely young woman, with high cheekbones, big blue eyes, and a long, slender neck. But there was a vulnerable tilt to her chin, and her hands trembled as they clutched the blanket to her chest.

"I can see that you're really scared, Lexi. And I don't know why, or what might have happened to you before today. But if you tell me what's wrong, I can try to help you."

Nessa's heart dropped as a guarded expression hardened Lexi's face and she looked away with pursed lips.

"That man is still out there." Nessa stood and crossed to the window. "He might be out there hurting someone else right now, and I may not be able to catch him if I don't have your help."

A frown appeared between Lexi's eyes, and her hand trembled as she lifted the cup of water to her dry lips. She was just about to speak when a nurse came bustling in to review her chart, ignoring Nessa as she turned to her patient.

"How are you feeling, dear?"

"I'm okay," Lexi replied in a shaky voice, "but I...I just need a little pain medicine and then I'll be good to go."

Peering at Lexi over her glasses, the nurse raised her eyebrows.

"What kind of pain are you experiencing?"

"My head, my back..." Lexi's voice trailed off. "Just like...general pain. If you can give me something to help, I can get out of here."

A sudden understanding clicked in Nessa's brain. How had she missed the signs? The pale skin, trembling hands, and paranoid behavior were all signs she'd seen before in the addicts who were occasionally picked up for illegal or erratic behavior.

"A doctor would have to prescribe any medication." The nurse put the chart back on the end of the bed. "I'll ask Dr. Ivanhoe to come see you. You can talk about a possible discharge then."

Waiting for the nurse to disappear through the door, Nessa moved back to the side of the bed and stared down at Lexi.

"You don't have to be scared of me, Lexi," Nessa assured her in a low voice. "I'm not going to arrest you for anything you tell me in relation to the man in that video. I'm not worried about your drug use...other than to help you get help if you want it. But I am interested in finding the man who killed Molly Blair."

Lexi glared up at Nessa with bitter eyes.

"You want to help me? That's a *laugh*."

Tears stood in Lexi's eyes as she spit out the words.

"That's exactly what Molly said before she hired me and got me hooked on pills. But she didn't help me...she just used me. Just like you want to use me to catch that psycho."

"I don't want to use you, Lexi," Nessa insisted, feeling her own anger rising. "I want to *help you*. But I also have a responsibility to protect the people in this town. If you know something that could save someone else's life, you have to tell me."

Dropping her tear-streaked face into her hands, Lexi let out a tortured moan. Her thin shoulders shook with emotion, and Nessa found herself leaning over to pull the girl into a consoling hug.

"It's okay, honey," Nessa soothed, running a soft hand over Lexi's short blonde hair. "You're going to be all right."

Lexi let her head sag onto Nessa's shoulder, and she sobbed like a little girl as Nessa waited for the storm to pass. Finally, Lexi raised her head and wiped at her eyes with the edge of the blanket.

"Molly ran an escort service and I was...one of her girls." Her words were soft but edged with pain. "I went to the Riverview on Friday to meet a date. That's what Molly called our clients."

Nessa squeezed Molly's hand but remained silent.

"When I was leaving down the stairs...I always used the stairs so security wouldn't notice me...well, I heard these footsteps, and I looked up..."

Lexi's voice faltered, and Nessa could see the fear on the girl's face as she replayed the events in her head.

"He looked so angry. He started charging down toward me, so I just ran. I didn't have time to think about it, but I knew he would hurt me if he caught me."

"And you were able to slip away?"

"Yeah, I usually park on the side street. That way I don't have to see anyone in the garage. I knew a shortcut and...I left. The next day I heard about that writer dying in the hotel, but I wasn't sure..."

Nessa nodded her understanding.

"You couldn't have known who he was or what he'd done."

Sniffing back tears, Lexi shook her head.

"I didn't know...I swear I didn't. But then I saw him the next day outside the hotel, and I couldn't help but think it could be related."

Adrenaline shot through Nessa's veins at the words.

"The man was still at the hotel the next day?"

Lexi nodded and the fear returned to her eyes.

"He was outside with the reporters and he saw me. I'm sure of it. But a car blocked my view and then he was gone."

Lexi drew in a long, trembling breath.

"Next time I saw him I was at Molly's house. He popped up behind me and said he had been waiting for me."

Reaching for the water, Lexi took a sip, then started coughing. By the time she'd regained her ability to talk, she was sweating again, and her trembling had worsened. Nessa was tempted to call the nurse, but she still had questions.

"How do think the man found you?"

Lexi considered the question, then shrugged.

"Maybe he figured out why I was there and asked around. Molly made an arrangement with someone at the hotel, so, the man...the *psycho*...must have tracked her down to get to me."

"Do you know who Molly's contact was at the hotel?"

Shaking her head, Lexi grimaced and clutched at her stomach.

"I'm not feeling so good. I think I'm gonna be sick."

Nessa reached for the nurse call button, feeling bad for pushing Lexi too hard. The girl needed help, and she needed protection. The rest of the questions would have to wait.

* * *

Frankie Dawson was just coming through the hospital doors as Nessa was leaving. He took her arm and pulled her toward the lobby.

"How's Lexi?" He sounded worried. "Is she staying overnight?"

Nessa shrugged, uncertain what Lexi would do.

"I know they want her to stay for observation, but I'm not sure Lexi will agree."

Nessa hesitated, knowing she couldn't tell Frankie about the girl's addiction, but wanting him to understand how vulnerable she was.

"Maybe you can talk some sense into her," Nessa said, looking at her watch. "I need to get back to the station. I wanted to have a sketch artist come by and work with Lexi. See if we can get a composite to put on the news."

Frankie scratched his unshaven chin and frowned.

"You think the same guy that killed Molly Blair was involved with Portia Hart's death?" Frankie asked. "You think it's related?"

Not sure what she could say without compromising the investigation, Nessa decided to evade the question for the time being.

"Why are you so interested, Frankie?" she asked. "And why were you and Barker at Molly's house anyway?"

"I'm trying to help the poor girl. She's a fucking mess." Frankie's voice was indignant. "I saw her at the hotel on Saturday, and then Sunday morning she almost crashes into me and Barker when we were heading over to the office."

Nessa snorted.

"You and Barker work Sundays now?"

"We do when insurance companies agree to pay us a big retainer."

A lightbulb went on in Nessa's head.

"Oh, right, Barker told me you guys were going to work for some guy looking into Portia Hart's cause of death."

"Yeah, Maxwell Clay from Sterlington Group or some shit like that. He was supposed to come to the office to sign the paperwork by ten this morning," Frankie explained. "But I was worried when I saw Lexi's Mustang weaving all over the fucking road, so I told Barker to follow her. We saw her Mustang parked in the alley and heard a scream. The rest is all in my statement."

Deciding it was best to break the news to Frankie sooner rather than later, Nessa looked at her watch again and grimaced.

"Sorry to break the news to you like this, but that guy, Maxwell Clay? Well, we looked into him and it turns out he's not an insurance investigator with Sterlington Trust."

"He's not an insurance guy?"

"Well, he is in insurance. He owns an independent agency, but he's not with Sterlington and he's not an investigator. Riley Odell did a quick background check on him and...well, he doesn't check out."

A flush turned Frankie's face red. Nessa wasn't sure if he was angry or embarrassed. Possibly both.

"I was actually planning on asking one of the detectives to look into his background and interview him today," Nessa said, "but now that we've got this other homicide, resources will be stretched pretty thin. Maybe you and Barker can save me some time and get Maxwell Clay to tell you his real story."

"Yeah, we'll get that phony jerk to come clean," Frankie agreed. "And then we'll drop his ass for misrepresenting himself."

Putting a hand on Frankie's shoulder, Nessa spoke in a low voice.

"Would you do me another favor?" she asked. "Would you try to convince Lexi to stay here...at least overnight? If she insists on leaving, I've asked Officer Ford to drive her home and assign a patrol car to keep watch over her house throughout the day."

"You got it, Nessa," Frankie agreed. "But the best way to protect Lexi is for you guys to find the fucker that attacked her."

"We're doing our best," Nessa said, giving him a parting wave.

But as Nessa got in her Charger and headed back toward the station, she wasn't sure that would be enough.

CHAPTER TWENTY-FOUR

Frankie stepped off the elevator and approached the nurse's station, which stood guard between him and the patient rooms in the corridor beyond. He waited as a man in blue scrubs behind the counter scribbled onto a clipboard. Eventually, the man paused and looked up at Frankie with raised eyebrows.

"Sorry to disturb you, Doc, but I'm here to see Lexi Marsh." Frankie looked around as if she might be wandering the halls. "She's a patient up here. Came in this morning."

"Ms. Marsh hasn't been cleared to see visitors," the man said, returning his attention to his paperwork.

Unfazed by the curt dismissal, Frankie used his trump card.

"Actually, Doc, the chief of police has asked me to look in on Lexi. I'm a private investigator and she's asked for my help."

"I'm not a doctor," the man said in a dry voice, not looking up. "I'm the head nurse on duty today, and if the police chief wants you to see a patient on this floor, then she'll have to arrange for that in advance with the patient's doctor."

Frankie was about to open his mouth and try again when he saw Andy Ford coming down the hall toward him. The uniformed officer frowned when he saw Frankie.

"Officer Ford, it's good to see you," Frankie said, throwing the nurse a sideways glance. "Nessa asked me to check in on Lexi, but the staff here won't allow me through."

"Chief Ainsley wants you to talk to Alexandra Marsh?" Andy looked doubtful. "She didn't say anything about that to me."

Frankie guided Andy to the side and lowered his voice, not wanting the hard-nosed nurse to intervene.

"I'm the one who found her, you know," Frankie said, trying to look modest. "And she trusts me."

"I don't trust anyone, actually."

Lexi's voice directly behind him caused Frankie to jump. She was dressed in jeans and a tank top, and her pale face was marred by ugly bruises. She'd washed the sweat and grime off her face since he'd seen her outside Molly's house, and her hair looked freshly washed.

"Ms. Marsh, you aren't supposed to be out of bed."

The nurse was on his feet; his smug indifference had disappeared. Circling the counter, he crossed to Lexi and put a concerned hand on her arm, but she shook him off.

"I'm leaving," she insisted, heading toward the elevator. "There's nothing wrong with me that a little rest won't fix."

Scrambling to join her in the elevator, Frankie pushed past Andy, who was staring after her with a panicked expression.

"The chief told me to give you a ride home," Andy called out as he, too, scurried through the doors. "She'll have my ass if I let you go out there on your own."

Lexi folded her arms over her chest and leaned against the wall as the elevator descended. Frankie noted the sweaty sheen on her skin and watched as she fidgeted with the thin strap of her tank top. He could see she was in even worse shape than she'd been in the first time he'd seen her at the hotel.

Even from their brief encounter, he'd seen that she was on something or coming off of something. And now, after a few days had passed, he could tell she was hurting.

The poor girl is dope sick and doing a shitty job of hiding it.

As the elevator door opened, Frankie put a hand on Lexi's arm and guided her toward the double doors leading outside.

"My cruiser's over there." Andy pointed to a black and white by the curb. "I'll give you a ride back to your apartment, Ms. Marsh. And we'll have a patrol car keep watch over you tonight."

Opening the back of the cruiser, Andy waited for the girl to climb inside. Before he could close the door, Frank had slipped in, too.

Lexi stared at Frankie in surprise, then shrugged and slumped against the back door. She rested her head on the thick glass of the windowpane and closed her eyes. Frankie looked over her bright thatch of blonde hair and watched the hospital recede as Andy pulled away from the curb.

By the time they arrived at Lexi's apartment, she was snoring softly. An occasional moan or whimper escaped her lips as she slept.

"Home sweet home," Frankie called out, nudging her arm with a long, skinny finger. "Time to wake up."

Lexi opened an eye and stared at Frankie in confusion. She raised her head to look out the window and caught sight of her apartment just as Andy opened the door. Climbing out of the car, Lexi walked toward her apartment without looking back.

"We'll have a patrol car outside," Andy called in an exasperated voice. "Let us know if you need anything."

Frankie followed Lexi to her door and waited as she dug into her pocket for the keys. He looked back as Andy Ford got into his cruiser and figured it might be his last chance to convince Lexi to get help. He had to give it a try.

"I can see you're suffering, Lexi. What are you coming off of?"

Lexi froze with the key halfway in the lock.

"What the hell are you talking about?" she said, not looking up. "What did Chief Ainsley tell you?"

"Nobody had to tell me nothin'," Frankie said. "It's written all over your face. You can't fool *me*, little girl."

"I'm not a little girl," Lexi muttered, but she sounded resigned.

Pushing the key into the lock for her, Frankie turned the deadbolt and pushed the door open. He waited for her to go inside, then followed behind her, but left the door slightly open so she wouldn't feel trapped.

"I'm not here to get in your face," Frankie said, "And I know you need to get some rest. But you don't have to go through this alone."

"Oh yeah?" Lexi smirked, dropping onto her sofa. "You want to help me? Maybe get a little piece while you're at it?"

Shaking his head, Frankie tried to keep the anger out of his voice.

"That's messed up." He scratched at his chin and took a deep breath. "I'm not a damn perv. I'm offering to help cause you need a friend. I know firsthand how shitty it is to feel like you're all alone."

Lexi stared up at him with red-rimmed eyes. She suddenly seemed very young and painfully fragile.

"Molly ran an escort business." Her voice was almost a whisper; Frankie had to lean in to hear. "She arranged dates with men who would pay. And she gave me pills to make it all...easier. Oxy mainly. But now she's...gone, and-"

"And you don't have any Oxy."

Nodding, Lexi raised desperate eyes to his.

"Can you help me? Can you get me some pills?" She held his gaze. "Just enough to...to let me wean myself off that shit. I can't go cold turkey...I've tried."

"I can't do that," Frankie said, knowing he had no choice. "The only thing that's gonna help you is rehab."

He pulled his phone out of his pocket.

"I know the lady who runs Hope House. She's a real nice person. If I ask her, I know she'll help you."

Dropping her head into her hands, Lexi shook her head.

"Just leave," she muttered. "Just leave me alone."

"Listen, Lexi, I know it can be tough, but-"

"I said *get the fuck out*," she yelled, jumping up and stumbling over to open the door. "Just get out of my fucking house."

Frankie flinched as the door slammed shut behind him. He thought of the lost look in her eyes and promised himself he'd be back. Lexi Marsh was about to hit rock bottom, and when she did, she'd need someone there to help her pick up the pieces.

* * *

Frankie arrived at the Riverview Hotel in a bad mood. He was worried about Lexi and had been unable to get in touch with Maxwell Clay to reschedule their meeting.

That slimy phony must know I'm on to him.

Tapping on Clay's number yet again, Frankie settled himself on a sofa in the hotel's lobby and prepared to leave another message. He kept the phone to his ear as he surveyed the area, absently listening to the phone ring again and again.

A shrill echo across the room grabbed Frankie's attention. A tall man in a well-tailored suit stood by the reception desk. His phone was ringing in unison with the phone Frankie held to his ear. Tapping the screen to disconnect, Frankie dropped the phone in his pocket and moved closer to the man in the suit.

"You're all set, Mr. Clay," the receptionist said. "Enjoy your day."

As the man turned around, Frankie stepped in front of him, blocking his path to the door.

"Why, if it isn't Maxwell Clay." Frankie crossed his thin arms over his chest. "Just the man I've been looking for."

Recoiling from Frankie's aggressive stance, Clay tried to step around him but found his way barred by Frankie's lanky figure.

"I thought you needed the services of a local PI," Frankie protested. "But you don't seem to wanna take my call anymore."

Clay stopped and stared at Frankie.

"You're Barker and Dawson Investigations?"

"No, I'm Frankie, and I'd appreciate you telling me why the hell you're pretending to be an investigator for some big-time insurance company when you aren't."

A flush of anger filled Clay's thin face.

"Who do you think you are?" the man sputtered. "I waited over an hour for you this morning and you never showed up. And now *you're* attacking *me* with some ridiculous accusation."

"So, you're telling me you really are an investigator with Sterlington Insurance Group?" Frankie asked, beginning to wonder if Nessa had gotten her information mixed up.

"I'm telling you to move out of my way, Mr. Dawson. I have an appointment to get to, and I'm already late."

Sidestepping Frankie's size fourteen shoe, Clay once again headed for the door. He paused when he heard Frankie call out.

"The police are looking into you, Mr. Clay. And if I were you, I'd hope they don't find out you've been going around telling stories."

Clay's shoulders stiffened, but he didn't look back as he pushed through the big glass door. Frankie stared after him in frustration, not sure what he was going to tell Nessa. She'd asked him to find out what the man's intent was, and all he'd managed to do was piss him off and warn him away.

Wondering what he should do next, Frankie stared around the lobby. Portia Hart had mysteriously drowned in this same hotel on Friday night and Molly Blair's body had been found floating in her hot tub only blocks away on Sunday morning. What was the connection between the two women?

Lexi's anguished voice replayed in his mind.

"I was at the Riverview Hotel Friday night, and I saw the man who attacked me.... he was trying to get to me through Molly. He wanted to shut me up. He killed her and he was gonna kill me next."

The Riverview Hotel had to be the link. That's where the killer had seen Lexi sneaking down the back stairs. It wouldn't have been rocket science to figure out Lexi was a pro.

And somehow the killer found out that Molly Blair ran the operation. Once he knew who she was, it would have been easy to track her down and force her to call Lexi.

So, who the hell knew about Molly and her girls?

He looked around the lobby, trying to imagine who could have been Molly Blair's contact at the Riverview. His eyes settled on the reception counter, then strayed to the concierge's station, which was currently unmanned.

Stepping to the polished mahogany desk, Frankie banged his fist on the bell and waited. Within seconds a harried man in wired-framed glasses and an ill-fitting jacket scurried over. His nametag identified him as *Dennis Robinson, Hotel Manager.*

"Good afternoon. How can I help you, sir?"

The manager's eyes didn't match his welcoming words. They took in Frankie's crumpled, unshaven appearance with silent disdain.

"You can start by telling me if you know a woman named Molly Blair," Frankie replied, leaning on the counter.

Raising his eyebrows, Dennis regarded Frankie with suspicion.

"Is she a guest at the hotel?"

"No, she's a guest at the morgue," Frankie replied. "And the man who killed her was seen at this hotel yesterday."

The manager gaped at Frankie, his eyes wide behind his glasses, apparently at a loss for words.

"In fact, the guy who offed her was also seen in here on Friday night. The same night one of Molly's girls came here to meet up with some loser staying at your hotel."

Finally regaining his ability to speak, Dennis inhaled a deep breath and adjusted his jacket.

"I have no idea what you're talking about. We run a legitimate, high-end operation here, and if you're implying otherwise the-"

"I'm not implying anything." Frankie leaned further over the counter. "I'm stating a fact. I know that an escort racket has been sending girls to this hotel. I just have to figure out who specifically was involved on your end."

Red with outrage, the manager pointed toward the door.

"I think you'd better leave before I have to call the police."

"Go ahead, *Denny*." Frankie produced a nasty smile. "Some of my best buddies are cops. They'd love to hear all about your little arrangement with Molly Blair. How much was she giving you to send johns her way and keep your mouth shut?"

Looking around the lobby with furtive eyes, Dennis came around the counter and lowered his voice.

"I can't have you causing a scene in here. Follow me."

The manager scurried across the slick marble floor toward the bar. He didn't look back as Frankie followed him. As they stepped into the dimly lit room, a man behind the bar looked up and frowned.

"Sorry, Benji," Dennis said. "I need you to take a break."

"But I'm still cleaning up after the lunch shift," the bartender protested, throwing Frankie an irritated glare.

"Give us some space, Benji. This shouldn't take long."

Benji shrugged and threw down his dishcloth, then sauntered into the back. Frankie watched his broad shoulders disappear behind the door before turning to Dennis.

"Who all knows about your seedy little set-up?" Frankie asked. "Is that guy Benji involved, too? How about the lady at the front desk? You got everybody working for you? Maybe I should ask-"

"All right, fine," Dennis said, sinking onto a barstool. "I passed on Molly's details to select guests when they made certain inquiries."

Frankie slapped his hand on the bar top, making Dennis jump.

"*Select guests?* Are you fucking kidding me?" Frankie issued an angry laugh. "The men who used Molly's service are anything but *select*. They're screwed up if you ask me."

"That may be, but I received no money from Molly or anyone else. I was just providing an added service to my guests," Dennis insisted. "And I'm the only one at the hotel who knew. I didn't tell anyone else what was going on."

Stepping closer to Dennis, Frankie raised an accusing finger.

"You told plenty of people. Every man you gave Molly's name to is a potential suspect in her death."

Dennis recoiled at the words.

"I want a list," Frankie said.

"Absolutely not," Dennis replied, jumping off the stool. "Even if I had a list, which I don't, I would never be that indiscreet."

Frankie shook his head in disgust.

"Yeah, you're the model of virtue. But the police are gonna want to know who you talked to."

"Then they can speak to me themselves. I'm done here."

Before Frankie could react, Dennis stomped to the door and banged through it.

"You guys done in here?"

Frankie looked up to see the bartender standing in the doorway.

"Yeah, I guess so."

"Looks like Mr. Robinson is pretty pissed," Benji said, picking up a glass and wiping it with a white dishtowel.

Shrugging, Frankie moved toward the door. Then he paused and turned back to Benji.

"Were you working Friday night?"

"Yeah, why?"

"Just wondered if you noticed anything. Anyone hanging around, or did anything unusual happen?"

Benji shook his head.

"No, it was busy because we had an event in the hotel but nothing interesting happened. Most people got their drinks at the free bar in the event hall. Only a few bothered stopping here on the way out."

Frankie nodded, reaching up to scratch at the stubble on his chin.

"You ever see any working girls around here?"

A guarded look descended over Benji's face.

"You mean like...pros? No man, we attract a pretty boring crowd."

"Any of these boring old guys ever ask you how to score a date?"

Benji held up a hand and backed away.

"I don't want any trouble, man." He ran a hand through his dark hair. "I'm new here and I mind my own business."

Before Frankie decided if he believed the words, he felt a buzzing in his pocket. It was Barker, and he wanted an update. Making his way out of the bar and through the lobby, Frankie scanned the faces in the crowd with suspicious eyes. A killer had been in the same building only a day before; he might still be there, waiting and watching.

CHAPTER TWENTY-FIVE

The nausea was getting worse, as was the shaking. Lexi stood in front of the bathroom sink and splashed cold water on her face. She surveyed herself in the mirror, shocked by the red, swollen eyes and pasty, bruised complexion she saw looking back.

How did it all go so wrong, so fast?

Closing her eyes, she leaned her head against the cool glass and tried to think. But the trembling in her hands and the pounding in her head wouldn't go away.

I've got to get some pills. They'll help me feel better so that I can think. Then I'll be able to figure out what to do.

If only Molly were still there. As much as Lexi had hated the coldhearted woman, she had needed her. Molly had been the keeper of the pills, and only she could make all Lexi's problems fade away.

Now that Molly was gone, Lexi was on her own and the possibility of finding a way out of the mess she was in seemed hopeless.

No pills. No money. No hope for the future.

Crossing to the front window, Lexi peered out at the patrol car parked along the curb. She wasn't a hundred percent sure the police officer within was parked there to protect her.

Maybe he'd been sent to keep an eye on her. To trick her into making a mistake.

She let the curtain fall back into place and slid to the floor. It had been almost eight hours since she'd taken the last two pills, and she would start to feel the real withdrawal symptoms soon. The nausea, headache, and shaking were just the preview to the main event.

The last few times she'd tried to kick her habit had ended in racking pain and debilitating anxiety. She'd felt like she was dying, and a part of her had almost wanted to. In the end, she had always succumbed to the relief of the pills.

Now there were no pills.

Well, they are there. I just can't get them.

The thought made Lexi sit up straight. What if the secret stash Molly kept was still safely hidden away?

She'd seen the concealed panel in Molly's study only once, but she'd never forgotten the army of pill bottles and stacks of bags within.

At the time it had seemed like the promised land to Lexi, and she had figured that Molly must be dealing the drugs in addition to supplying them to the girls that worked for her. But that didn't matter now.

Molly wouldn't be selling drugs or setting up dates ever again. And all those pills would just go to waste.

Unless I go in there and take them. Why not? No one would ever know.

Once again, she looked out the window; the police cruiser was still there. This was one of the times Lexi wished she had an apartment with a patio or back porch.

But her simple unit had only one way in and one way out, and that was through the front door leading straight out to the cop car.

Running a frustrated hand through her hair, Lexi looked toward her little bedroom, noting the sunshine streaming through the doorway.

She slipped her bare feet into the dusty running shoes on her living room floor and shoved her phone in her pocket.

Her eyes fell on the cigarette pack on top of the television. There were two cigarettes left. She hesitated, then crumpled the pack and tossed it into the trashcan before racing into the bedroom.

She crossed to the window and looked out over the back parking lot. A few cars sat baking in the heat but otherwise, the lot appeared to be empty. Unlocking the latch, she pushed up the window and let in a surge of hot air.

Grasping the edge of the screen, Lexi dislodged the frame and pushed. The screen clattered to the ground outside.

A horn blared in the distance as Lexi climbed out of the window and dropped to the ground. Glancing around with nervous eyes, she propped the screen back in place.

She backed away, pleased to see that her apartment looked like every other nondescript unit in the long, brick building.

Nothing's out of place and nobody will know I'm gone.

The sun was still high in the afternoon sky as Lexi made her way through the back lot and into the thin strip of forest that edged Channel Drive on its way to the highway. The trees would offer cover from the sun, as well as from the curious eyes of any cops driving by.

Refusing to think of anything but getting to Molly's house, Lexi trudged through the trees, grateful for the shade they provided. She would have to walk almost two miles to get to Kingston Road, and she'd need to take the backroads to make sure she wasn't seen.

Legs trembling, she forced herself to keep moving.

Twenty minutes later she reached the intersection of Channel Drive and Surrey Way. From here on out she'd have to navigate streets without much cover.

Wishing she'd thought to put on a hat, Lexi quickened her pace. She wouldn't last much longer in the sweltering heat.

When she finally reached the turnoff to Kingston Road, she was dripping with sweat and gasping for breath. The police cars and crime scene van in front of Molly's house brought her up short. Standing in the shade of a massive oak tree, Lexi studied the scene.

I've just got to wait until they leave. Once they're gone, I can sneak in.

As she watched from a distance, a Channel Six news van sped past her. A shiver ran down Lexi's spine when she saw Nick Sargent's handsome face on the side of the van. He seemed to always show up whenever bad things happened.

Deciding it wasn't safe to get any closer with the press and the police presence still there, Lexi sank down behind an overgrown thicket of rose hips that bordered the street.

She wrapped her arms around herself and rocked back and forth in a soothing rhythm. Closing her eyes, she began to sing under her breath.

This little light of mine, I'm gonna let it shine...this little light of mine...

Safe in the shady hiding place, Lexi sank into a restless sleep.

*   *   *

The sound of a police siren startled Lexi. She lifted her head and looked around, trying to remember where she was and how she'd gotten there. Fighting back a wave of dizziness, she stood and peeked around the scruffy bushes toward Molly's house.

She watched as a young, female reporter with long, dark hair spoke into a camera, gesturing to the house behind her. Several other camera crews were busy along the street, and police were still blocking through traffic.

Lexi ducked down when she saw a tall man with a red crewcut looking in her direction. His clean-cut appearance screamed cop, and the last thing she needed was to have the police pick her up again after she'd managed to sneak away.

That would end any chance she'd have to score the pills hidden in Molly's house.

While Lexi knew the pills weren't a solution to her problems, and that they were only a temporary fix, she'd been hooked since the very first time Molly had innocently offered her "a little something to take off the edge."

That first day Lexi had been euphoric at the sudden absence of worry or fear or pain. The weight of everything she'd been through had melted away into blissful nothingness. But it was a feeling she had never quite attained again.

Now, after months of constant use, the pills only dulled reality for a few hours at a time, before wearing away and leaving her to face the sickness and the despair that always came in their wake.

Sitting down with her back against the big tree trunk, Lexi suddenly wished she hadn't been too ashamed to tell someone what was going on.

With her mother hundreds of miles away, and Molly dead and gone, she was now truly alone. The thought made her think of Frankie, and what he'd said in her apartment.

"I'm offering to help cause you need a friend. I know firsthand how shitty it is to feel like you're all alone."

He'd seemed sincere, and he hadn't tried anything creepy. He'd even said that he knew someone who ran a rehab center. Someone that helped women like her.

Maybe I should have listened to him. Maybe he could have really helped me get clean.

But it was too late now; she'd sent Frankie away and she was on her own. Her only hope now was to get the pills and then lay low at her mother's new house while she weaned herself off.

Somehow, she'd have to get her Mustang out of the parking lot without the cops seeing, and then it would be a six-hour drive to Jacksonville.

I just need to wait until the cops and the press clear out. It can't take that long, can it?

But waiting would be hard, especially when her hands were shaking, and her nerves were working overtime. The craving for a cigarette returned without warning; Lexi impulsively stood and began an unsteady walk back along Surrey Way. She'd walk to the store and buy a pack of gum. Maybe that would take the edge off.

CHAPTER TWENTY-SIX

Xavier Greyson was pleased to see that the crowd in the Riverview Hotel had thinned out in the last few hours. The police had responded in full force to the latest crime scene, and the press had chased behind them like hyenas attracted to a fresh kill. He had no doubt they were all over on Kingston Road scavenging for the goriest details.

Positioning himself under a widescreen television mounted on the wall, he watched Veronica Lee reporting live outside Molly Blair's house. He kept one eye on the screen and one eye on the crowd, curious to see if the cops would put two and two together.

Will they figure out the connection between Portia Hart and Molly Blair?

He smiled when he thought of the bodies they'd eventually find in Mosquito Lake. The bodies in the trunk of the taxi would surely be a mystery to the clueless cops. They would probably never be able to solve the murders or understand why they'd had to happen.

The smile turned into a grimace as Xavier recognized the woman standing next to Veronica Lee. It was Riley Odell, the assistant prosecutor that had worked on his case down in Miami. She'd been the only one that had ever gotten close to catching on to his con, and she'd almost put a stop to his promising career before it had really gotten started.

But if he thought about it, Riley Odell had been the reason he'd finally resorted to murder. It had been the smug prosecutor's fault that he'd been forced to kill Miriam Feldman in order to avoid going to jail. If only she'd kept her nose out of his love life everything might have been different. Releasing a wistful sigh, he let his mind wander back to that fateful night in Miami a decade earlier.

The small yacht had been anchored for days, bobbing up and down in the warm waters off Miami Beach, waiting for its owner to wrap up her business in the city and sail away to a less crowded port. Xavier, still damp from his swim through the dark waters, waited patiently in the cabin, ignoring the shouts and laughter from the other vessels nearby. He didn't want to be seen, and he couldn't afford to be distracted.

It was going to be his first time, and he wanted it to go flawlessly. He had a tradition to uphold after all. Walking to the oval mirror mounted on the wood-paneled wall, Xavier ran a manicured hand through his wavy blonde hair and smiled. He liked being a blonde. The sun-kissed beach boy look suited him, and the blue contact lenses made him appear wide-eyed and innocent. Admiring the smooth fit of his diving suit over his leanly muscled chest, Xavier stepped closer to the mirror then paused.

Someone was walking down the dock toward the yacht. He recognized the click, click, click of Miriam Feldman's high heels against the wood. Striding across the small cabin, he closed himself in the tiny bathroom. Moments later he heard the cabin door open and close. The rattle of keys falling onto the table, and the thump of first one shoe and then the other hitting the floor, let him know she was settling in for the evening.

As the door to the bathroom swung open, Xavier lunged forward and grabbed Miriam by the throat, giving her no chance to scream for help. Her eyes widened in fear as she saw the terrifying truth in his eyes. He wasn't the playful, seductive man she'd come to know. Instead, she saw the real Xavier: cold, calculating, and utterly ruthless.

Pushing Miriam into the middle of the cabin, Xavier forced her back against the table where they'd spent so many previous evenings enjoying dinner and wine by candlelight. His arms began to shake with the effort, and a trickle of sweat dripped down his face as he squeezed harder. In a last, instinctive attempt to save herself, Miriam lifted her hands to his, trying to claw his fingers away, but her fingernails cracked against the thick diving gloves he wore. When her hands fell away, he released her, allowing her body to slump to the floor.

He nodded in approval as she moaned and stirred. Everything was going just as he'd planned. It wouldn't do for her to be found without water in her lungs. Not if he wanted her death to be labeled an accidental drowning. No, he needed her to be alive when she went into the water.

Dragging Miriam to the door, he opened it and hefted her up the short flight of stairs to the deck. The breeze lifted a strand of her hair and blew it around her face, causing her eyes to flutter open, but Xavier ignored her as he checked his diving gear and strapped on his air tank, before pulling on his fins and diving mask.

He was all set to go. Bending at the knees, he scooped up Miriam's thin body and dropped her over the side of the boat. The splash was louder than he'd intended, but he didn't hesitate; holding the regulator in his mouth, he held his head up and took a giant step off the boat.

Miriam had already begun to flail in the water, and her hands reached out and clutched at his head, gripping onto his mask. Xavier pried her fingers off and then shoved her down, forcing her deeper into the dark water. He switched on his dive light, illuminating her pale, ghostly face as she gaped up at him in panicked terror.

Gazing through the diving mask with cold detachment, Xavier watched as her desperate struggles weakened and then stopped altogether. Within minutes she was floating peacefully, her eyes open in an endless stare. Xavier stared back, fascinated and repelled at the same time.

So that was what it was like to kill someone. His father had often spoken about the thrill of the kill, but Xavier wasn't so sure he agreed. He didn't see what the big deal was. He hadn't enjoyed it, but he had to admit there was a certain satisfaction in knowing he'd found a permanent solution to his problem. All in all, it had been a success.

A close-up image of Riley Odell's probing eyes on the television brought him back to the present and rekindled his lingering resentment. The ambitious assistant prosecutor had been new to the job, and eager to make a name for herself. She'd been quick to believe that Miriam Feldman's handsome summer fling had been siphoning money from her safe as they sailed around the Caribbean.

Xavier had first been questioned by two paunch-bellied detectives who had believed his claims that Miriam had fabricated the story. They'd nodded with empathy when Xavier said she'd been bitter after he'd moved on to greener pastures.

"She's a lonely woman and I feel sorry for her," he'd told the detectives. "You know what they say about a woman scorned..."

But Riley Odell, the state's newest junior prosecutor, hadn't been taken in by his charm, and she'd seen through his lies. She'd been unusually hard and bitter for someone so young, and it was clear she would stop at nothing to bring him down.

When his public defender told Xavier that the police had managed to lift his fingerprints from Miriam Feldman's safe and that a warrant for his arrest had been issued, he knew if Riley got Miriam to testify against him, he was doomed.

So, because of Riley Odell, there had been only one solution. Only one way to make sure a case could never be brought against him, even he if was caught someday. And once Miriam was gone, he'd skipped town. The only thing he'd brought with him was the cash in Miriam's safe and the firm resolution to eliminate any threats to his freedom in the future. It had all gone to plan, until now.

Smoothing back a dark strand of hair, Xavier wondered how, after all these years, he'd once again ended up in Riley Odell's crosshairs.

He'd thought killing Miriam Feldman had solved all his problems and taught him how to keep himself out of prison. But he was beginning to think he'd gotten it all wrong.

Maybe instead of getting rid of Miriam, I should have just eliminated the troublesome prosecutor. Perhaps it's not too late to correct a mistake.

CHAPTER TWENTY-SEVEN

Veronica Lee stood with Riley Odell on the steps of city hall as Finn Jordan worked the camera. A crowd of concerned citizens gathered around them, watching Veronica quiz Riley about the women who had drowned to death in Willow Bay only days apart.

"Do you think the two deaths are related?" Veronica asked with genuine curiosity. "And if so, do you have a theory as to who could have committed the crimes?"

Riley looked toward the camera with an impassive expression, revealing nothing about her opinion one way or the other.

"The investigation into Portia Hart's death is ongoing," Riley stated in a formal voice as if she were reading from a cue card. "All options and possibilities are still being considered."

Frustrated by the cautious answer, Veronica tried again.

"And the recent homicide on Kingston Road? Does the fact that a woman was killed within forty-eight hours of Portia Hart's death impact the investigation?"

"Again, all possibilities must be considered," Riley replied with a small shrug of her narrow shoulders. "We'd be foolish to discount the possibility that the two deaths could be related before we conclude a thorough investigation."

Before Veronica could react, the crowd parted to reveal Tenley Frost's stiff figure. The media relations officer marched up the stairs with ill-concealed fury, stepping in front of Riley Odell and turning to face Finn's camera. Veronica hastened to hold out the microphone.

"Thank you, Ms. Odell, for sharing your comments with the press. I'm sure they appreciate hearing from the state prosecutor's office."

Tenley's words belied the angry gleam in her eyes. She tucked a glossy strand of auburn hair behind her ear and exhaled as if summoning her patience.

"I'm sure everyone here is anxious to find out what happened to Portia Hart, and concerned about the homicide earlier today. However, the mayor's office and the WBPD are not ready to release a formal statement at this time."

Throwing a furious glare in Riley's direction, Tenley continued.

"Rest assured that as soon as we have a statement prepared, we will notify the press. Until then all city employees will refrain from commenting on the ongoing investigations. I can't speak for the state prosecutor's office."

Tenley stepped away from the camera, leaving Veronica to wrap up the shot with a hasty sign-off. Once the camera had stopped rolling, she turned to see Tenley and Riley standing face to face. They looked like boxers meeting before a title fight; neither one wanted to be the first to look away.

"Since when does the prosecutor's office speak to the press before consulting with local officials?" Tenley asked in a tight voice.

"It's my fault," Veronica interjected. "I approached her on the steps in front of the crowd and she was just trying to-"

Tenley turned her fury on Veronica without warning.

"I don't need *you* to explain the way the press operates," she hissed between clenched teeth. "I was reporting the real news back when you were just the *weather girl* in case you've forgotten."

Spinning on her heel, Tenley stomped down the stairs, pushing past Nick Sargent, who had just arrived at the scene. The Channel Six reporter climbed the steps toward Veronica.

"Looks like you have an enemy there," Nick said, watching Tenley disappear into the crowd. "She's probably still mad that you took her job at Channel Ten...and you also usurped her special place with Hunter Hadley."

Veronica couldn't hide her shock.

"Oh yes, they had quite the thing going from what I've heard...at least before she went and got herself *knocked up*."

Veronica felt sick to her stomach. She knew she shouldn't care about Hunter's love life, but she did. There was no use denying it. At least not to herself.

"Sounds like it's none of my business," Veronica responded, waving over to Finn. "And none of yours either."

Following Finn back to the van, Veronica heard Nick call after her. She had swung around to face him before she could stop herself.

"Your boss has left a trail of broken hearts in his wake," Nick said, and Veronica thought she detected a note of anger in his voice. "And if I didn't know better, I'd say that you're about to be his next ex-girlfriend."

The buzz of her phone stopped her from formulating an angry reply. Digging in her pocket, she saw that her mother was calling. Veronica steeled herself for the inevitable complaints and warnings. She knew she was lucky to have a mother who cared so deeply, but the incessant nagging was beginning to wear her down.

"Hi, Ma, what's up?"

"I saw your interview with that new prosecutor," Ling Lee said. "She never did answer the question, but I'm not surprised. It seems like no one will admit what's going on."

"And just what is going on, Ma?"

"There's another serial killer in Willow Bay," Ling insisted. "And he's going around drowning women to death. I want you to be careful. Don't trust anyone you-"

Exhaling in frustration, Veronica interrupted.

"Yes, I know. Don't talk to strangers and don't go out after dark. I've got it, Ma. Now I've got to go."

After an uncomfortable pause, her mother spoke in a stiff voice.

"I fed Winston, and I left food in the refrigerator for you to heat up when you get home. I'm going to the bowling alley."

Veronica thought of her tiny mother in her two-toned bowling shoes lugging around her lucky nine-pound ball. She suddenly wished she was heading to the weekly Sunday night game with her mother. It seemed like ages since she'd allowed herself a night to just relax and have fun.

"I hope you bowl a three hundred, Ma."

But Veronica was talking to dead air. Her mother had already disconnected the call.

* * *

Veronica sat stiffly in the news van wishing she hadn't told Finn she was meeting Julian Hart at the Riverview Hotel. He'd insisted on driving her there, and he'd made no attempt to hide his doubts about Portia Hart's brother.

"I don't trust anyone who hides from my camera," Finn explained, as he steered the news van toward the unloading zone. "So, I'll park this bad boy and wait for you in the lobby. No rush."

Deciding it would be pointless to argue, Veronica climbed out of the van and hurried into the lobby. She hadn't been sure Julian would actually follow up on his unexpected request for help that morning, but she'd given him her number just in case.

His text to meet her at the hotel's bar had come in just after the altercation with Tenley Frost, providing a welcome excuse to leave the tense scene and escape Nick Sargent's snide comments.

The hotel bar was busy, and it took Veronica's eyes a minute to adjust to the dim lighting. She stepped further into the room and saw Julian sitting at a table in the back corner. He was gazing down at the table with a forlorn expression.

"Hi, Julian."

He raised red-rimmed eyes, and Veronica instinctively reached out to put a comforting hand on his sleeve. Her need to protect him was becoming a habit.

"How are you holding up? Have you seen the news?"

He nodded, his face contorting into a grimace of disgust.

"I've seen enough to know that every station in the country's trying to boost their ratings by exploiting Portia's death."

Sliding onto the stool across from him, Veronica pointed to the television behind the bar, which was tuned to Channel Six.

"No, I meant the news about the other woman being found a few blocks from here." She watched as Nick Sargent's face filled the screen. "I was worried it might have upset you."

Julian frowned.

"Why should it upset me?"

He let his eyes flick to the screen.

"I haven't really been following the story, but the woman's death was a homicide, wasn't it? Probably a domestic dispute. I mean, it's sad, of course, but it doesn't have anything to do with me."

When she didn't respond, Julian stood and walked toward the bar. He lifted his head to stare up at the screen.

"Hey, can you turn up the sound?" he called to the bartender. "I want to hear what they're saying."

Veronica saw that Benji was working behind the bar. He picked up a little remote and aimed it at the television. Nick Sargent's smooth voice soon filled the room.

"Earlier today state prosecutor Riley Odell refused to rule out the possibility that the same man may have been involved in the death of Portia Hart on Friday night and the woman brutally killed today on Kingston Road."

Nick spoke directly to the camera, and Julian stared into the reporter's eyes as if transfixed.

"While the name of the victim has not officially been released, neighbors say the slain woman is local resident Molly Blair."

Gesturing for Benji to turn off the television, Veronica took Julian's arm and guided him back to the table.

"I'm sorry. I thought you would have seen the news."

He didn't seem to hear her as he shook his head in denial.

"It can't be true. She can't have been...*murdered.*"

Veronica bit her lip, trying to think of something to say. She knew she should be asking Julian questions and jotting down quotes to include in her next update, but she didn't think she could.

The poor guy is suffering and confused. If I take advantage of his vulnerability now, I'm no better than Nick Sargent.

She caught sight of Finn walking toward them with a concerned frown and stepped forward to intercept him.

"You didn't respond to my text," Finn said, holding up his phone. "Is everything okay in here?"

Turning to see that Julian was already walking toward the exit, Veronica ignored the question and scurried after him.

"Julian? Are you okay?"

She caught up to him at the elevator and grabbed his arm, revealing a glimpse of his heart-shaped birthmark before his sleeve fell back into place.

"I thought you wanted to talk."

"I need some time to think," he murmured as the door slid open. "I'll call you later...when I'm feeling better and when you're *alone*."

Veronica looked back to see Finn coming toward them. When she turned around, the doors had closed, and Julian was gone.

"Good job," Veronica snapped as Finn stopped beside her. "You've scared him away. Might as well give up on getting an interview."

Pinning her with a suspicious stare, Finn crossed his arms over his chest. He raised his eyebrows and waited.

"What?" Veronica glared back at him, but she had the sinking feeling that he could see through her act.

"What's the real deal with Julian Hart?" he asked. "You trying to get an interview or a date?"

Veronica's mouth fell open at the blunt question.

"You're crazy," she said, regaining her composure. "I'm trying to give the guy a break. You know, show a little bit of compassion and decency. Maybe that's something you should try."

An elderly couple approached the elevator, and Veronica moved aside to make room, then hurried toward the front door.

"Wait up, Veronica," Finn panted, chasing after her. "Stop acting like an amateur."

Skidding to a stop, she spun to face him.

"I don't think you should be hanging around that guy," Finn blurted out before she could speak. "You're getting too involved, and he's taking advantage of that. Any other reporter would have been asking the hard questions, but you're...not."

Veronica's anger deflated. Finn was right. Something about Julian Hart's story resonated within her. She could see how completely alone he was, and her sympathy for him was making her lose sight of her responsibility.

She was supposed to get a hard-hitting interview that would make viewers tune in. But that approach didn't feel right. Not this time. Veronica looked into Finn's tense face, wanting him to understand.

"It's hard to explain." She struggled to find the right words. "It's just...I feel bad for Julian. I know what it's like to feel alone, and-"

"I get it," Finn replied, his voice softening. "But part of your job is to remain objective. Otherwise, you won't last as a reporter."

Bristling at his words, Veronica shook her head.

"Just because I have a heart, doesn't mean I won't make it as a reporter," she insisted. "Reporters have to understand what people are going through. They have to report the whole story, including the emotional impact of what's happening. Otherwise, it's just a string of facts that anyone could put together."

Finn raised his eyebrows and sighed.

"Reporting someone's pain is different than feeling it yourself. You take on somebody else's pain and you're no longer just telling the story; you become *part* of the story."

"You just don't get it," Veronica said, refusing to back down. "You don't understand how Julian must feel."

Finn's face tightened with anger.

"You're trying to tell a guy who just lost his dad to cancer that he doesn't understand loneliness and pain?"

He didn't give her a chance to respond; he turned and walked through the big glass doors without looking back. Veronica decided not to go after him. She'd managed to upset enough people in the last few hours: Tenley, Julian, her mother, and now Finn.

Turning back toward the bar, Veronica figured it was best for her to be alone for a while. Otherwise, she might screw up something else.

CHAPTER TWENTY-EIGHT

Nessa dug an emergency granola bar out of her purse, tore off the wrapper, and took a big bite as she prepared to turn onto Kingston Road. She'd learned long ago that lunch was never guaranteed. Of course, if things continued as they'd been going this weekend, dinner might have to wait as well.

Stuffing the last sticky bite into her mouth, Nessa parked the Charger along the curb behind the crime scene van and opened the door. She saw Alma loading a box into the back of the van. The senior crime scene technician wore blue coveralls and protective booties, but she'd removed her face mask and goggles.

"Looking for a suspect back there?" Nessa called out, sounding more cheerful than she felt.

Sliding the door closed, Alma turned to Nessa with a satisfied gleam in her eyes. That gleam usually meant she'd found something particularly interesting at a scene.

"Finding the suspects are your job, Chief," Alma teased. "But what I found should help."

"Okay, tell me what you got." Nessa was more than ready for some good news. "I can see you're dying to spill the beans."

Alma nodded and motioned for Nessa to follow her up the front walk. They passed through the thinning crowd of reporters and onlookers to reach the front door. Alma knocked, and a uniformed officer opened the door and waved them inside.

"How's it going, Dave?"

The young officer answered Nessa's question with a thumbs-up as Alma prodded her toward the narrow doorway leading to the kitchen. A hardcover crime scene case was open on the kitchen table. Nessa saw that it held an array of evidence collection bags, protective gear, markers, rulers, magnifying glasses, flashlights, and specimen vials.

"I was able to get several fingerprints off the hot tub." Alma was unable to conceal her excitement. "Quite a few prints, actually. Looked like someone was holding on for leverage."

An ember of hope caught fire in Nessa's chest.

"That's great. I'll cross my fingers the prints turn out to be our guy....and that he's in the database."

"That's not all," Alma said, removing a roll of crime scene tape out of the bag. "I was able to get some prints off the wallet that we found in Portia Hart's purse. I'd been running them through the database when I got the call about this scene and..."

She paused for dramatic effect as Nessa held her breath.

"I just heard back from the lab that we've got a match."

Nessa's heart skipped a beat.

"I told the tech to email the details to Vanzinger with a copy to you and Riley Odell. Figured you'd all want to see that ASAP."

"Great work, Alma." Nessa looked around the little kitchen. "You find anything else around here I should know about?"

Alma reached into the case and pulled out a clear evidence bag. She held it up to the light and Nessa saw that it was packed with prescription pill bottles.

"Looks like Molly Blair was a dealer." Alma shook the bag so that the bottles rattled against each other. "Either that or she had a lot of medical issues."

"So, Molly's death could be drug-related," Nessa murmured. "Maybe Lexi was wrong. Maybe it's not related to Portia Hart at all."

"What do you mean?" Alma asked. "Who's Lexi?"

"She's the girl who found Molly Blair. She had to fight off the killer," Nessa said, lowering her voice. "She's convinced she saw the man who killed Molly Blair at the Riverview Hotel the night Portia Hart died. Said he was running down the stairs dripping wet and that he started chasing her when he realized she'd seen him."

Alma raised her eyebrows.

"So, you're thinking the guy went looking for this girl to shut her up and killed Molly by mistake?"

Nessa shrugged.

"I'm not sure how the creep found Molly, but I believe Lexi's story, and I believe the guy came after her to keep her quiet."

"Well, he definitely wanted to shut her up for good." Alma no longer sounded excited. "Iris said that the poor woman was badly beaten before she went into the water. Whoever killed her didn't bother taking the time to make it look like an accident."

Both women cringed at the remembered image of Molly Blair's battered body floating in the hot tub. Nessa figured she'd be seeing it in her nightmares for months to come.

"Well, one way or the other we need to find out who prescribed all those pills," Nessa said, gesturing toward the bag. "But first, I'm dying to find out who was digging through Portia's wallet."

"Yep," Alma agreed. "Looks like hunky detective Vanzinger was right. You always gotta follow the money."

Surprised by Alma's comment, Nessa felt a stirring of unease. The heightened tension between Vanzinger and Riley Odell was enough to deal with. If Alma made her attraction to the city's newest detective known, the fragile peace in her little police department could be threatened. Perhaps she'd better talk to Vanzinger and warn him that trouble was brewing.

Looks like things around here are about to get a little more complicated.

* * *

Riley was pacing back and forth in the briefing room when Nessa returned to the station. Sticking her head inside the door, Nessa looked around the room, then turned to the prosecutor.

"Where's Vanzinger?"

Riley bristled at the question.

"How should I know, I'm not his keeper."

Nessa raised her hands in surrender and suppressed a sigh.

"The course of true love never did run smooth," she murmured under her breath, wondering how long it was going to take for Riley to forgive Vanzinger. The whole love/hate dynamic was exhausting.

"Did you see the email from Alma?" Riley asked, apparently too caught up in her own thoughts to pay attention to Nessa's mumbling.

"Yes, but I didn't have time to pull up the matching record," Nessa admitted. "Were you able to see who matched the prints?"

Footsteps in the hall announce Vanzinger's arrival.

"You guys see the email from Alma?" he asked, dumping his backpack on the table, and dropping his long, muscular frame into a chair next to Riley.

Nessa was preparing to deliver a sarcastic response when she saw Riley's face. The normally unflappable prosecutor was distraught. All color had drained from her face, and her dark, troubled eyes seemed huge behind red-framed glasses.

"You look...pale, Riley," Nessa said, sliding onto a chair across from the prosecutor. "Are you feeling okay?"

"Well, that's debatable." Riley tried to smile, but her face wouldn't cooperate. "You see, the man who matches these prints is someone I questioned years ago in relation to a theft case. The victim...a wealthy woman in Miami...ended up drowning, so we had to let him go. I knew he'd had something to do with her death, but..."

Nessa's eyes widened as she absorbed Riley's words.

"Who is he?" Vanzinger's voice was hard. "What's his name?"

"Xavier Greyson," Riley whispered, clenching her hands into tight fists on the table. "I knew he was a hustler; a sleazy con man that had stolen money from a lonely woman. But I didn't think...I mean, I didn't know he would *kill her*."

"Of course, you couldn't have known that, Riley," Nessa soothed, startled to see the cool, detached prosecutor heading for an emotional meltdown. "It's not your fault he killed that woman. I'm sure you did what you could."

"That's right," Vanzinger agreed, keeping his worried eyes on Riley's pale face. "None of this is your fault."

Pushing a file across the table to Nessa, Riley took a deep breath and straightened her back. When she looked up a spark of defiance had entered her eyes.

"That's Xavier Greyson's file...or what's left of it."

Nessa opened the folder and stared at the print-out within. The scanned police report contained a complaint of theft filed in Miami Beach back in 2010. The plaintiff was a forty-two-year-old female named Miriam Feldman. Nessa noted a faint checkmark next to the *Widowed* option in the status section of the form.

Scanning the report, Nessa saw that Miriam Feldman had accused her new boyfriend of stealing money from the safe on her yacht. He'd been questioned but hadn't been arrested. A note at the end of the report indicated that the prosecutor's office had declined to proceed with the case due to a lack of evidence.

"Miriam Feldman was found floating in the water off Miami Beach soon after that report was filed," Riley said. "The medical examiner determined that she'd drowned, but he left the manner of death as undetermined. Said he couldn't be sure if it was an accident, a suicide, or a homicide."

Her eyes blazed with remembered anger.

"But I knew it had to be him. I just couldn't prove it." Her voice grew stronger as she spoke. "Then he was gone. He disappeared from Miami as if he'd never existed. Eventually, my boss told me to drop it. Said I needed to move on. So that's what I did."

Nessa's eyes returned to the name of the accused: Xavier Greyson. Was it possible that Portia Hart and Molly Blair had been victims of the same deadly con man that Riley had encountered a decade earlier? If so, how many women had he killed since then?

And what will he do next if he thinks this time he might get caught?

CHAPTER TWENTY-NINE

Vanzinger stared down at the police report, stunned that his instinct to check Portia Hart's wallet for fingerprints had paid off. Xavier Greyson hadn't been satisfied with just taking the life of the rich, glamorous author; he'd had to take the last dollar from her wallet, too. But the heartless con man's greed might very well lead to his downfall.

"I let him go," Riley said, her voice uncharacteristically soft. "I had him...then I let him go free. And look what he's done..."

Concerned by Riley's shell-shocked expression, Vanzinger reached for her hand and squeezed. For the briefest of seconds, he thought he felt her squeeze back. Then she snatched her hand away, looking over at Nessa with an embarrassed scowl.

"You did what you had to do," he said, trying to mask his disappointment. "Unlike the bad guys, we have to play by the rules."

"I should have trusted my gut," Riley muttered, dropping her eyes. "I knew he was a slime ball the minute I laid eyes on him. I should have trumped up some charges or...or done *something*."

Her words hit Vanzinger in the gut. It hurt him to see that the idealistic young woman he'd fallen in love with had become disillusioned over the years. And he hated the fact that his own cowardly behavior had played such a pivotal role. If only he'd handled things differently back then he could have saved her from some of the pain and heartache.

When he'd left Willow Bay without an explanation, thinking it had been the only way to keep her safe from the men who had threatened his life and destroyed his career, Vanzinger had taken her trust and innocence with him. He knew now that no matter what the risks, he should have told her the truth.

But his revelation had come a decade too late. The strained, suspicious look on Riley's face made it clear that she had come to doubt the world and everything in it, especially him.

Feeling the phone in his pocket vibrate, Vanzinger pulled it out. Alma Garcia was calling. His pulse quickened at the thought she might have more updates from the crime scene.

"We managed to run the fingerprints from Molly Blair's hot tub," Alma said without preamble. "And you're not going to believe this."

"All right, let me guess." Vanzinger raised his eyes to meet Riley's guarded gaze. "The prints in the hot tub are a match to the prints in Portia Hart's wallet. They both belong to some creep named Xavier Greyson."

"No fair, Vanzinger," Alma groaned. "I was hoping to shock you."

"Oh, it takes more than that to shock me, Alma."

Riley's eyes hardened, and she looked away. Vanzinger wondered what he'd said to piss her off this time. After he disconnected the call, he sat back in his chair and crossed his thick arms over his chest.

"Greyson's prints were on Molly Blair's hot tub. You add Portia Hart and Miriam Feldman to the mix, and it looks like we got ourselves a serial killer."

"At least we know who he is," Nessa said, looking at Riley. "He can't hide for long now that we know who to look for."

"Actually, I wouldn't be so sure," Riley cautioned. "I never could find a trace of Xavier Greyson in any records or database. At least not the Xavier Greyson I was looking for. So, that could be his real name, or it could just be the alias he was using when we brought him in."

Everyone in the room seemed to deflate at the thought that the name Xavier Greyson was just another one of the killer's cons.

"Based on what we know I think we've got to assume he's running some sort of con on these women," Vanzinger said. "So, he may be using a variety of names and stories to win their trust."

"It's a little more serious than that," Riley said, her eyes blazing. "Xavier Greyson, or whatever his name is, stole Miriam Feldman's life savings and then left her dead body to rot in the ocean. He most likely drowned both Portia Hartman and Molly Blair. He's not just a con man, he's a monster."

Holding his hands up in mock surrender, Vanzinger nodded his head in agreement. He had no doubt that the man who had held Portia Hart and Molly Blair under the water and watched them struggle and die was a monster.

"What I want to know is how he gets these smart, experienced women to trust him." Nessa banged her fist on the table, causing Vanzinger to jump. "He must run a pretty good game."

"He was certainly very attractive," Riley said, "and he tried to ingratiate himself with me when I questioned him. He's quite a good actor. Luckily, I know the type too well to be taken in."

"You mean he tried flirting with you?" Nessa was indignant. "I bet you told him where to go."

Vanzinger swallowed hard at the image of Riley sitting across from a killer. The thought that she'd been face to face with a dangerous criminal scared him, but it also impressed him. No matter how disillusioned Riley might be, she'd never lost her spirit or her will to fight for what was right, no matter what it might cost her.

"What if we broadcast Xavier Greyson's name on the news?" Vanzinger suggested. "Maybe someone will come forward."

"I could talk to someone at Channel Ten and see if they'll work with us on it," Riley said. "Although we still don't have a photo to distribute."

"I plan to ask Alexandra Marsh to work with a sketch artist." Nessa consulted a page in her notebook. "See...it's next on my list."

Vanzinger frowned. Why did Nessa need to keep a separate list?

I'm lead detective on the case, so shouldn't she be working from my list?

He pushed away the voice in his head that told him she didn't trust him to solve the case. It wasn't the right time to listen to his ego.

If Nessa doesn't trust me now, that just means I'll have to do something big to earn her trust. I can start by solving this case.

"I'm not sure we're ready to go public with this guy's name yet," Nessa said. "We'd be showing him our cards, and we might end up spooking him. He could go running for the hills before we have a chance to track him down."

Leaning back in his chair, Vanzinger tried not to show his frustration. He didn't want to contradict Nessa, but he was worried that leaving Xavier Greyson free to roam around might cost another woman her life. He met Riley's eyes and saw that she also looked troubled. As if reading his mind, she turned to Nessa.

"I'll work with Tenley Frost to make sure we have a statement prepared once you give us the okay, Nessa." Riley stood and began gathering her things. "We need to be ready to take this guy down as soon as possible. I want to nail his ass before he can screw with anybody else."

Vanzinger recognized the hostility in her voice. He'd had to deal with it himself for the last few months. It was obvious that Riley remembered the man well, and that she was still holding a powerful grudge. An unsettling question sprang to mind.

Does Xavier Greyson remember Riley, too? Was he still holding a grudge?

CHAPTER THIRTY

L exi stood under the immense oak tree. The sun had disappeared over the horizon, and a blanket of darkness had descended over the neighbor, providing her with cover in the deep shadows along the tree line. Letting the crushed gum wrapper fall from her hands, she moved out of the shadows.

The police cars and crime scene van were gone, as were the throng of reporters and onlookers. Only the yellow strips of crime scene tape remained to mark the tragic events of the day.

Walking north on Kingston Road, Lexi turned into the unlit alley that ran behind Molly's house and followed the back fence to the gate. As she pushed the gate open, Lexi braced herself for whatever, or whoever might come at her. But the dark yard was empty. Closing the gate behind her, she scurried up to the deck.

Yellow tape circled the hot tub, and Lexi crept forward to gaze down into the murky water, half-expecting to see Molly's glassy, lifeless eyes staring back. The dark water was empty.

Lexi's stomach heaved as she turned away, and she bent to retch up a small stream of acidic bile. Her throat burned as she stared down at the spatter of liquid at her feet, surprised she had anything at all left in her stomach.

How long has it been since I've eaten?

Spitting out the foul-tasting bile that coated her mouth, Lexi stumbled to the sliding glass door and pulled weakly on the handle.

To her surprise, the door slid open without resistance. She pushed back the blinds and slipped through.

Blackness enveloped Lexi as she stepped into the chilled air. The crime scene techs hadn't turned off the air-conditioning, and the temperature inside the house was at least thirty degrees cooler than outside. All the blinds were closed, and Lexi felt along the wall, searching for a light switch. Her fingers finally settled on the switch, and she winced as light flooded the room.

Standing in the familiar surroundings of Molly's kitchen, Lexi felt as if she was in a dream. Or maybe a nightmare. It seemed surreal to Lexi that the indomitable woman who had governed her life for the last year was suddenly gone. If she hadn't seen Molly's dead body with her own eyes, she wasn't sure that she would believe it.

Memories of the first time she'd met Molly filled her mind. At first, the woman had seemed glamorous and larger than life, with a fancy car, expensive clothes, and a body sculpted to perfection with the help of multiple plastic surgeons.

Only after Lexi had come to know the real Molly had she seen the ugliness within. All the clothes, make-up, and surgery in the world couldn't give Molly what she lacked. She'd also seen the damage that years of hard living had left behind. The smoking, drugs, and excess left their mark on Molly's face like a curse and were reflected in her dull, listless eyes.

As Lexi looked around the room at what remained of Molly's life, she thought she heard a soft shuffling sound. Whirling around, she saw that the blinds in the sliding glass door were swaying in a gentle breeze that blew in from the still-open door.

Closing her eyes, Lexi allowed the breeze to wash over her face, relishing the respite after the heat of the long, hot day. Taking in a long, deep breath, she decided she was ready to finish her mission.

The secret panel was in Molly's study. Lexi crept down the narrow hall until she reached the little room. She stood in the doorway and felt unsuccessfully along the wall for the light switch. She finally pulled out her cellphone with a shaky hand. She'd use the light from her phone to guide her way.

Aiming the beam toward the wall, she saw that the panel was already open, displaying the starkly empty interior. The army of pill bottles and piles of bags she remembered were all gone.

Crushing disappointment engulfed her, and Lexi sank to the floor, not even trying to hold back her frustrated tears.

Now, what am I going to do? How am I going to get through the night?

She looked down at the phone in her hands, noting that the battery indicator was showing red. She likely only had enough power to make one last call. But who would help her after everything she'd done?

She'd already lost the trust and respect of her friends, and her mother was the only family she had left. Unfortunately, her mother was living on the other side of the state.

And she probably moved there to get away from me and my problems.

So, who else would be willing to help a stranger? Who could she turn to that wouldn't arrest her or judge her?

Shoving a small hand into her pocket, she pulled out the paper with Frankie's number on it. She looked at the wobbly handwriting first with trepidation, then with hope. Maybe he'd really meant what he'd said. She'd seen compassion in his eyes or at least thought she had. What other choice was there?

Tapping in the number before she lost her nerve, she held the phone to her ear. Frankie answered on the first ring.

"Barker and Dawson Investigations."

Lexi hesitated, surprised by the greeting.

"Is this Frankie?"

"Yep, and I bet this is Lexi, right?"

Swallowing the lump that had suddenly formed in her throat, Lexi tried to speak. Her throat was dry and sore, but she eventually managed to force the raspy words out.

"Did you really mean it? Will you help me get into rehab?"

"Yep, I meant it." The relief in his voice matched her own. "So, you still at home? I can come get you now if-"

"Hold on," she said, turning toward a sound in the hall.

"What's going on?"

Frankie's voice faded as she held the phone away, trying to hear. Was that the wind in the blinds again? She should have closed and locked the door. What if then cops were patrolling the place? Maybe they'd noticed the open door and were coming to check.

"Lexi, are you okay?"

Frankie's worried voice sounded far away. She lifted the phone back to her ear, still frowning into the blackness beyond the hall.

"Yes, it's just I...thought I heard something."

Moving into the hall, Lexi headed back toward the kitchen. The blinds swayed in the breeze, and Lexi's allowed herself to breathe.

"It's fine," she said into the phone. "I went back to Molly's house, which I know was a big mistake, but I'm ready to go now."

She braced herself for Frankie's wrath, suspecting he would be outraged that she'd returned to the scene of the crime, but the other end of the line was silent.

"Frankie? Are you mad?"

No response. Her heart sank. She'd gone too far, and now she'd ruined her only chance to get help. Lowering the phone, she checked the display to see if he was still on the line. The phone was dead.

"Shit!"

Jamming the useless phone back in her pocket, Lexi strode across the room. She would go home, charge her phone, and pack a bag. By the time Frankie got to her house, she would be ready to go.

Without warning, two strong hands reached out of the shadows and grabbed Lexi by the throat. The hands were followed by the man from the stairwell. This time he didn't wear a hoodie, or a mask, or sunglasses. This time she could see his cruel, handsome face, and his cold, remorseless eyes.

The man slammed Lexi against the wall hard enough to make her teeth rattle. As she slid to the floor with a whimper, he grabbed a handful of her hair and banged her head against the tiled floor. She felt blood spurt from her nose as he lifted her head to stare into her dazed eyes.

"Who have you told about me?" he asked through gritted teeth. "Have you talked to the cops? What about Riley Odell?"

Unable to form the words, Lexi tried to shake her head instead. She felt the room spin around her as the man put a tight hand around her throat and squeezed.

"Sorry...about this," he gasped out as he knelt over her, "but I can't...have you testifying...against me, now can I?"

Willing herself to fight back, Lexi lifted a weak knee, but the man blocked it with his lean, hard thigh.

"It's not personal you know," he muttered with grim resolve as he raised a big fist. "It's just part of the game."

Lexi raised her eyes toward the door in a last desperate hope that someone would come looking for her. But she saw only the killer's hateful face over her before everything went dark.

CHAPTER THIRTY-ONE

Gracie's tail wagged with joyful abandon as she followed Hunter through the parking lot. She stopped next to his black Audi sedan and waited for him to open the door. The big white Lab had only been living with him for a few days, but Hunter felt as if the cheerful dog had always been by his side.

As Gracie jumped into the passenger seat, Hunter wondered what he was going to do once Finn moved on. How could he give up Gracie, again? He still remembered the pain of leaving her with Jordie the first time. But he'd had no choice. Both he and Gracie were suffering from PTSD and needed care. Luckily for Gracie, Jordie had been there to help her recover.

It had taken Hunter a bit longer, but he'd also found his way through. And now they were whole and back together, but he knew it couldn't last. Finn needed the dog more than he did. The boy had lost his father. Hunter couldn't ask him to give up his dog as well.

After securing the seatbelt around Gracie's solid body, Hunter started the car and sped out of the lot. He was restless, so he rolled down the windows and steered the car toward the highway, wanting time to think, and giving Gracie a chance to enjoy the breeze.

Speeding through the city, his mind filled with worries about the stations' financial difficulties and guilt that he hadn't been straight with Veronica. His thought about Veronica Lee didn't improve his mood. His guilt over misleading her about the station wasn't the only thing that bothered him.

The knowledge that he was growing too protective of his newest reporter, and dangerously close to being emotionally involved, had been eating at him. Switching lanes and stepping on the gas, Hunter wondered when things had changed.

Somewhere along the way Veronica had stopped being the green, weather girl he'd hired, and had become a truly talented reporter. She'd also started showing up in his thoughts on a regular basis, and he hadn't been able to get her out of his mind for long.

Maybe I should start dating again. Perhaps a distraction will help.

He pictured Tenley Frost's beautiful face. Now that he was no longer her boss, and she worked for the City of Willow Bay, there was no ethical reason to prevent him from asking her out on a date. He was pretty sure she would be willing since she'd made it crystal clear over the years that she found him attractive.

But he'd made it a point never to cross the line with his employees, no matter how willing they might seem, and it had never been a problem to resist the temptation before.

So, why am I tempted to cross that line with Veronica, now?

What was it about Veronica Lee that was different? Of course, she was attractive, but he'd dated many beautiful women in cities around the world. Sexy, smart women that had never really known him, and had never managed to touch his heart.

With Veronica, it felt different. The attraction wasn't just physical. There was something about her unjaded, curious attitude that was refreshing. He felt better when he was with her. As if her positive energy rubbed off on him somehow.

Pulling into a gas station to refuel, Hunter wondered what effect he had on her. He couldn't be sure how she felt about him, but he knew that Veronica had a big heart and that she was drawn to people that seemed to need help. So, while his instincts told him the attraction was mutual, he feared she was drawn to the damaged part inside him. The part that had broken into a million pieces back in Kabul, and which he was still trying to put back together.

It wouldn't be fair to saddle her with his issues and problems, even if he wasn't her boss, and even if they were in a position to see what might happen between them.

So, I need to stay away, at least emotionally. For her sake, and my own.

As he finished filling the tank and climbed back in the car, Hunter wondered if Veronica had gotten her interview with Julian Hart yet. It would be a big scoop for the station; viewers would surely tune in to hear what Portia Hart's reclusive brother had to say about his sister's tragic death. And Veronica would be just the right reporter to handle the interview with compassion.

He thought of the comment he'd overheard Finn say earlier in the day about Veronica getting involved with a subject of one of her stories. Had he been talking about Julian Hart. Could Veronica be interested in more than just Julian's sad story?

Picturing the downcast figure he'd seen in Channel Ten's parking lot that morning, Hunter assumed the tortured artist routine had gotten to her. Being a billionaire probably didn't hurt either. He couldn't blame her really, but he didn't like to think of Veronica getting mixed up with a family that seemed to be cursed.

Maybe having all that money was a curse and not a blessing. Portia and Julian Hart's life of excessive money and angst certainly hadn't seemed to end in a happily ever after.

Turning to Gracie, Hunter decided he wasn't ready to go home.

"How about we do a little investigating of our own, girl?"

Gracie looked out of the window with eager eyes as Hunter headed the car toward Kingston Street.

* * *

Hunter drove down Channel Drive looking for Kingston Road. He noticed a blue Toyota coming the other way, absently noting the *Willow Bay Quick Rides* decal on the window.

Spotting the crime scene tape across the front of the house, Hunter circled the block, wanting to check out the whole scene before going any closer. The house looked dark and deserted from every angle, and Hunter decided to park the Audi and let Gracie stretch her legs. The walk would give him a perfect excuse to nose around without drawing undue attention.

Gracie trotted beside Hunter as he walked past the house. She pulled him toward a big oak tree and stopped to mark it as her territory. As Hunter waited, he noticed the silver gleam of a discarded candy wrapper on the sidewalk. As he bent to pick it up, muffled footsteps sounded behind him and a man stepped out of the shadows.

"Nice looking dog," a gruff voice called out. "That one of them rescue dogs? My grandson tells me I need to get one of those now that old Spike is gone."

Hunter watched as the man approached with the help of a cane. His bespectacled face was wrinkled with age, but his eyes were sharp behind his thick lenses.

"This is Gracie," Hunter said, looking down at the Lab with affection. "And I guess you could call her a rescue dog. A friend of mine brought her back from Afghanistan a while back. She was just a skinny little thing then."

The man seemed to contemplate the information, then nodded, as if he approved.

"I was in the army myself. About a hundred years ago."

Hunter smiled and shook his head.

"Oh, I wasn't in the military. I was a reporter. Now I work at a local news station."

The man's expression changed. His forehead collapsed into wrinkles.

"You aren't with that Channel Six, are you?"

"No. I'm the station manager at Channel Ten."

"Yeah?" The man cocked his head and grinned. "Well, you're lucky, cause I like your show. That new girl you have is a breath of fresh air. Not all fake like that Nick Sargent on Channel Six."

Hunter felt a twinge of satisfaction.

"You're not a fan of Nick Sargent, Mr...?"

"Trout. Otis Trout," the old man said. "But you can just call me Otis."

"And I'm Hunter Hadley, but you can call me Hunter."

The old man stared at him, his eyes suddenly suspicious.

"You related to the Mayor?"

"I'm his son, actually," Hunter admitted. "But that doesn't mean I agree with his policies."

"I should hope not, young man," Otis sniffed. "The younger generation is supposed to be smarter than the old one. Hopefully, you're a right bit smarter than your father."

Holding back a smile, Hunter tried to change the subject.

"So, why don't you like Nick Sargent?"

"He's a phony, that's why. He acts like a choir boy on the news, but I've seen him sniffing around here after all them young girls Molly used to bring around."

Hunter stared at the older man, too surprised to speak.

"I mean, in my time I liked the ladies as well, but them girls are way too young to be hanging around with the likes of him."

"You must be mistaken, Mr. Trout." Hunter tried to keep the lighthearted tone in his voice. "Whoever was coming over here probably just looks like Nick Sargent."

Otis snorted in disdain.

"I'm not senile, and I'm not blind." He thumped his cane on the sidewalk for emphasis. "Besides, I heard Molly call him by his name plenty of times. That man was hanging around here like a bad smell."

Deciding it would be futile to argue, Hunter held his tongue. If the old man thought he'd seen Nick Sargent at Molly Blair's house, who was he to say otherwise? Willow Bay was a small town, and there weren't many men in town who would easily be mistaken for the handsome reporter.

Besides, the possibility that Nick Sargent had a connection to the murder scene intrigued him. He'd been a reporter long before he'd become the station manager. Perhaps it was time for him to put his investigative skills back to use. He'd been out of the game for too long. This was the perfect opportunity to jump back in with both feet.

As he watched Otis Trout tottered back into the shadows, Hunter mapped out a plan. Investigating a reporter at his rival station was a sensitive operation. If someone found it would look like he was trying to sabotage the competition. And even if Nick had been hanging around Molly's house, that in itself proved nothing. It certainly didn't prove murder.

But the accusation that Nick had been hanging around with young girls, possibly even underage girls, was disturbing in itself. It couldn't hurt to do some digging. At the very least he could discredit the old man's story. At most, he might end up with a major scoop.

Once he and Gracie were back in the car, Hunter pulled out his phone and scrolled to a number saved in his contact list. He hadn't felt the need to call Nessa Ainsley since the whole Boyd Faraday fiasco, but maybe it was about time he reached out to the new chief of police. She wasn't a big fan of his dad, but then, neither was he.

Nessa answered the phone on the first ring.

"Hunter, how are you?"

"Confused," he answered, smiling at the southern twang in her voice. "I just heard something that I think you'll want to hear."

CHAPTER THIRTY-TWO

Veronica sipped her glass of sparkling water and checked her watch. She had remained at the Riverview Hotel after Finn had stormed away in hopes that Julian would call her back and agree to the interview. But when her phone finally rang, she hadn't recognized the number. It had been Riley Odell calling to say she had a potentially huge story to share.

After arranging to meet at the hotel bar, Veronica had ordered the bubbly, non-alcoholic drink and claimed a quiet table in the corner. She now sat in anxious anticipation, wondering what the big news was, and why the prosecutor had decided to call her.

"You need another drink?"

Benji appeared by her elbow, a tray in one hand, and a dishtowel in the other. His long dark hair was slicked back into a small ponytail, and he was sporting a light five o'clock shadow. With his white button-up shirt and black pants, Veronica decided he could pass for one of the Chippendale's dancers she'd seen on her one and only trip to Las Vegas. All he was missing was the bowtie.

"No, I'm good, thanks." Veronica looked over his shoulder toward the door. "I'm kind of expecting someone, so I'll wait to see what they want before I order anything else."

Benji nodded. He moved on to the bar and set down his tray, then began using the towel to wipe off the empty tables.

"I guess Sunday nights must be pretty slow," Veronica said when he reached the table next to hers.

"Yeah, most nights are slow around this town."

He stopped next to her and leaned against the table, his arm only inches from hers. "Nothing like the places I've worked in Miami and Key West. They were always busy. Always a party going on."

Veronica leaned back, inching away from the thick scent of cologne that hovered around the bartender.

"So, why'd you come here, then?" Veronica asked, unable to break her reporter's habit of asking a million questions. "Why not stay where you were?"

Benji shrugged his broad shoulders.

"I guess I like variety." His mouth spread into a wide smile. "I get bored doing the same things, you know?"

Resisting the urge to roll her eyes, Veronica nodded and gulped down the last of her water.

"I think I will take that other drink now," she said, eager for him to leave. "And then I need to prepare for my meeting."

She reached inside her bag for the notebook she usually carried, but it wasn't there. She looked around for a spare piece of paper as Benji returned with her water.

"It's on the house."

Veronica offered up a weak smile.

"Oh, thanks. That's sweet."

Her eyes widened as she saw Riley Odell come through the door.

"Oh, and do you have any paper I could use?" she asked Benji. "I need to make some notes."

Benji picked up a *Special of the Day* menu and flipped it over. The back was blank. He shrugged off her thanks and walked away just as Riley slid onto the barstool across from her.

"I'm glad we've got the place to ourselves," Riley said, looking around at the empty stools. "Because I'm not ready to go public with what I'm about to tell you just yet. I need you to swear you'll keep the information off the record for now."

Veronica's heart sank.

"So why are you telling me then?" she asked, trying not to sound as annoyed as she felt.

"I'm telling you so that you'll be ready to run a special report when I give the go-ahead," Riley replied. "I have to wait until I get approval from the chief of police and the media relations officer."

Veronica grimaced at the mention of Tenley Frost, but she nodded her understanding.

"Okay, I get it. I won't release anything until I get your say-so. Now, what's this big news?"

Riley took a deep breath and leaned in just as Benji appeared behind her with his tray.

"Can I get you a drink, ladies?"

Veronica shook her head, and Riley waved the bartender away without looking up. When he'd gone, she continued in a low voice.

"We've linked the murder of Portia Hart and Molly Blair to the same man. A man that has been questioned before in relation to another murder back in 2010."

Struggling to keep her composure, Veronica gaped at Riley.

"Portia Hart was murdered by a *serial killer*?"

Riley held a finger to her lips.

"Shh! We're trying to keep this under wraps for now, remember?"

Veronica nodded and began writing down notes on the back of the menu as Riley began to explain what they'd found out.

"He's in the system under the name Xavier Greyson."

Scribbling down the name, Veronica was already planning out the report she would produce, and the appeal they would make to the community for information about the killer.

"Do you have a photo of this Xavier Greyson?"

"We're trying to get a composite sketch," Riley said. "We didn't get a mugshot because he was never officially arrested, but we were able to get his fingerprints and match them to all three crime scenes."

"A composite sketch? Does that mean you have a witness that has seen the guy's face? Someone that can identify him?"

Riley bit her lip, then nodded.

"But I can't share her name with the media."

"I understand," Veronica assured her, "just send me the sketch when it's ready, and I'll start working up the report first thing tomorrow morning."

Veronica was already picturing the special segment she would create. Channel Ten would be the first station to display the image of the man who had killed Portia Hart, and she would be the reporter who broke the story.

"Listen, I better go," Riley said, looking at her watch. "Just promise me you'll keep this to yourself until you hear back."

"I will," Veronica agreed.

She stood and watched as Riley hurried out the door. Before she could turn back to the table, she saw Julian Hart walking through the lobby. Spinning around, she almost knocked over Benji, who had already started to clear the table.

"Oops, sorry." She shoved the menu with her notes into her bag and slung the bag over her shoulder. "We're all done here...thanks!"

Grabbing a twenty-dollar bill from her wallet, Veronica dropped it on the table and dashed out into the lobby. Julian was waiting by the elevator holding a paper grocery bag. He looked startled to see her.

"Julian, I thought you were going to call me." She pointed to two chairs in an alcove. "Did you still want to talk?"

"I've been working on a new sketch. I guess I lost track of time." The elevator doors slid open. "Why don't you come up?"

Not wanting to lose her opportunity for a second time, Veronica stepped on the elevator and rode with Julian in silence to the fourteenth floor. She followed him off the elevator and down the hall. He stopped and waved his key card outside Room 1410.

Veronica stared at the door to Room 1408 with wide eyes. How could Julian bear to be right next to the room where his sister had been murdered? The realization that might know the name of the man who had been in that room, and who had killed Portia Hart, sent a shiver down her spine.

Would she be able to interview Julian about his sister's death and not reveal what she knew? It felt wrong on too many levels.

"Come on in," Julian said, carrying his bag into the suite. "I'll just put this down on the bar."

Veronica hesitated just inside the door as her mother's voice sounded in her head, warning her against strangers.

Reaching into the bag, Julian pulled out a bottle of wine and a small container of fresh fruit. He gave Veronica a self-conscious smile, then picked up the corkscrew.

"Would you like a glass?" he offered, once the cork was out. "I'd rather not drink alone, although I often do. Portia used to bug me about it. Said I was becoming a *closet alcoholic*."

His smile wobbled, and he turned his attention to pouring the wine into two stemless wine glasses imprinted with the Riverview Hotel logo. He held a glass of the dark red liquid toward Veronica.

"I don't drink while I'm working," she said, reluctantly taking the glass. "And I shouldn't be in your room without my cameraman."

"What do you think of my sketch?" Julian asked, ignoring her protests as he pointed to a sketch pad on the table. "I started this the day before I got the call about Portia."

Veronica's eyes moved to the table; she was immediately captivated by the colorful drawing. Stepping closer, she studied the beautifully detailed beach scene, where a blazing sun was setting in the distance as two children played in the surf. She glanced up at Julian, intrigued by his ability to convey so much emotion with a piece of paper and a few colored pencils.

"Me and Portia," he said, nodding at the figures on the paper. "We grew up on the coast. We were so close back then."

Julian walked to the window and stared down at the river.

"My sister and I both suffered after my parents died, but we had each other. At least we did at the beginning."

"Did something happen to change that?" Veronica asked,

Julian paused as if carefully considering his next words.

"Can I tell you something off the record?"

His question made Veronica's stomach drop, but she nodded, knowing she had no choice but to respect his request. She'd crossed a line when she'd entered his room, moving from a public forum to a private conversation. She wouldn't be able to use anything Julian Hart told her without his express permission.

"My sister made some very bad investments a few years back. She ended up losing most of her inheritance." He paced across the room, stopping in front of her. "It put a strain on our relationship, as I'm sure you can imagine."

Actually, Veronica couldn't imagine inheriting and then losing a billion-dollar fortune, but she nodded in agreement anyway.

"I always thought she wrote *Simply Portia* to justify her scaled-back lifestyle, but it ended up being a self-fulfilling prophecy," Julian said. "Living more simply did seem to make her happier. Lately, she didn't seem to care about the money at all. But maybe that was all just an act. Maybe it all got to be too much."

Veronica blinked.

"So, you still think she killed herself?"

"I think it's a possibility, although I guess it could have been an accident. She wasn't used to taking drugs, or even medicine. She liked natural remedies. Maybe she didn't know what would happen."

"You don't think someone was...involved with her death?"

"Who would want to kill Portia? Everyone loved her."

Julian's tone was defiant as he took a long sip from his wine glass.

Veronica opened her mouth then closed it again. She couldn't tell him what she knew, and she couldn't bear to watch him agonize over the possibilities. Picking up her bag, she handed him her untouched wine, determined to leave before she said something she'd regret.

"Please, don't leave yet."

His voice was an anguished plea as he reached out to catch her hand and caught the strap of her bag instead. The bag fell open, causing the contents to tumble to the floor.

"I'm sorry...I didn't mean to..."

Kneeling, he began to pick up the things she'd dropped. His hand fell on the menu with Veronica's handwritten notes, his gaze lingering on Portia's name, and the name of her suspected killer. He held up the paper, lifting disbelieving eyes to Veronica.

"What's this? Some kind of sick joke?"

Grabbing the paper, Veronica pushed it back into her bag and turned to leave, but Julian jumped up and shoved his hand against the door before she could pull it open.

"Is it true? Do the police think Portia was killed by a *serial killer?*"

His voice was thick with the need to know. As she exhaled, trying frantically to think of a response, her cell phone buzzed in her pocket. She grabbed for it, hoping for some kind of rescue. She saw instead that her mother had sent a text.

Come home, Ronnie. It's dangerous to be out so late.

Dropping the phone back in her pocket, Veronica forced her voice to remain steady and calm.

"That's my cameraman. He's waiting downstairs for me."

Julian's face had taken on a haunted expression. He let his hand fall to his side.

"Go ahead then...leave." He gestured to the door. "You got what you came for, so go."

Veronica hesitated, tempted to tell him the truth. He was Portia's brother after all. He deserved to know, didn't he?

Pulling open the door, Veronica stepped into the hall. There was no other choice. Her first responsibility was as a reporter. If she violated her agreement with Riley Odell, she would put Channel Ten's credibility and reputation at risk. Hunter had trusted her, and she couldn't let him down.

As she waited by the elevator, Veronica looked down the hall. Julian Hart stood silently at the door to Room 1410, his face hidden by shadows. The image of the ghostly, solitary figure stayed with her as she headed home.

CHAPTER THIRTY-THREE

Nessa poured herself a second cup of coffee and headed for the interview room. She'd canceled the department's standing Monday morning briefing so that she and Vanzinger could interview Julian Hart. She wanted to catch him before he decided to leave town. Hopefully, he'd be able to shed some light as to how his sister had gotten caught in Xavier Greyson's web.

Stepping into the hall, she nearly spilled her coffee as she swerved to avoid the big figure barreling toward her.

"In a hurry, Jankowski?"

She was pleased to note that her ex-partner looked good. His thick blonde hair was neatly styled, his face freshly shaved, and he wore a baby blue shirt with the sleeves rolled up to reveal his strong, tan forearms.

It looked like he was finally figuring out how to cope after the rough year he'd endured and was getting back to normal.

"I'm going over to Kingston Road to finish interviewing Molly Blair's neighbors," he said, still moving toward the exit. "I'll take Officer Ford with me, so it goes quicker. Should be back before noon."

Continuing down the hall, Nessa stopped outside interview room three, knocked softly, then opened the door. Vanzinger sat on one side of the wooden table, and Julian Hart sat on the other.

"Good mornin', Mr. Hart, good mornin', Detective."

She sank onto the chair next to Vanzinger and set the coffee in front of her. She studied Julian's impassive face as she cradled her cup, wondering how to start the interview, but Vanzinger had already beaten her to it.

"We were just discussing the inheritance Julian and Portia were left by their father," Vanzinger explained. "I was trying to get a feeling for Portia's financial situation."

Irked that Vanzinger had started the interview without her, Nessa summoned her sweetest southern smile. This was Vanzinger's case after all. She was just guiding and assisting.

"I don't see what our inheritance, or our finances, have to do with my sister's death," Julian said, crossing his arms over his lean chest. "And I don't know why I should divulge our personal financial information to you."

Reminding herself that Julian Hart was in mourning, Nessa forced herself to count to five before answering.

"Mr. Hart, we aren't trying to cause you undue pain or inconvenience. We just need to understand what was happening in your sister's life leading up to her death so we can figure out exactly what happened to her, and why."

When Julian didn't respond, Nessa leaned back in her chair and sighed. No use delaying the inevitable.

"Mr. Hart, we've requested a warrant to access your sister's bank accounts, but that could take another day or two if the judge isn't in a good mood." Nessa met and held Julian's gaze. "I was hoping maybe you could go ahead and tell us what we're likely to find."

An awkward silence followed, then Julian emitted a heavy sigh.

"My sister wasn't great at finances, and she wasn't the best judge of character," he said, looking at his hands, which were clenched into fists on the table. "She made some disastrous investments in some very dubious start-ups. She ended up losing most of her inheritance."

Hiding her shock, Nessa glanced at Vanzinger to gauge his reaction. He stared back with wide eyes.

"So, your sister was broke?" Vanzinger's voice betrayed his surprise. "Is that what you're saying?"

"No, I wouldn't say she was *broke*." Julian ran a distracted hand through his hair. "But her net worth was substantially reduced."

He thought for a minute, as if deciding how much to say.

"Although recently things were improving. I'd helped her settle all outstanding debts, and she'd started receiving royalties from her book. She even had a million-dollar advance for another book deal."

"So, she was a millionaire, not a billionaire?" Nessa tried to rein in her sarcasm. "Is that what you mean when you say she was having financial difficulties?"

Julian shrugged.

"I'm not sure how much money she had. We've lived separately for many years and have our own accounts. But from what she'd told me, she was regaining control of her finances."

"So why would she take out an insurance policy and name you as the beneficiary?" Vanzinger asked with a puzzled frown. "If she was *reduced financially* and you kept hold of your great big inheritance, why would she need to do that?"

Shaking his head in confusion, Julian seemed to be lost for words.

"What insurance policy?" he finally managed to say.

Nessa studied his reaction, sure that he was genuinely stunned.

"We're still trying to get all the details, but someone claiming to be from Sterlington Trust Insurance Group is investigating your sister's death. He says she had a policy, and that you're the sole beneficiary."

Julian narrowed his eyes.

"What do you mean *claiming* to be from this insurance company?"

Glancing at Vanzinger, Nessa nodded.

"We aren't sure this guy is legit," Vanzinger admitted. "But we're checking it out just to be sure."

"Portia was easily led and persuaded to invest money," Julian said. "This was probably another such unfortunate situation where she was misled by some shady character."

Nessa wondered if Xavier Greyson had been one of the shady characters that had taken advantage of Portia's trusting nature.

"So, you had no expectation of benefitting financially from your sister's death?" Vanzinger asked.

The blunt question hung in the air; Nessa waited for the explosion.

"I have more money than I'll ever need or ever wanted, Detective. So, if your little theory is that I played some part in my sister's death for financial gain, you're dead wrong."

"Okay, I hear you," Vanzinger replied, unfazed by the outburst. "But what about the pills we found in her hotel room? Why didn't you tell us they were yours?"

Banging both fists on the table, Julian glared at Nessa and Vanzinger, his cheeks red and his eyes blazing behind his glasses.

"That's ridiculous. Why would I give Portia pills? She never took any drugs. She even told me I should give up my pain pills because they were addictive. Why would she..."

The blood drained from his face and he sat very still.

"Wait...how do you know they were mine?"

"The prescription on the bottle was in your name," Nessa said. "It was a prescription for Oxycodone. The bottle was empty."

Slumping back in his seat, Julian once again clenched his fists.

"Portia must have taken them the last time she visited me in Hart Cove. She had occasionally struggled with depression."

He looked at Nessa as if seeking absolution.

"She couldn't have known the pills were for pain, not anxiety. I should have secured them...I should have-"

"Why are you taking Oxycodone, Mr. Hart?"

Nessa's question cut through Julian's recriminations, and he turned to her as if in a daze.

"I was injured in the plane crash that took my parents' lives. My injuries resulted in chronic pain."

"And your sister?"

"She was in college at the time, so she was spared the ordeal."

"That seems a little unfair," Vanzinger said. "Portia escaped injury and then blew her part of the family fortune. Then after you bail her out, she goes out and becomes a celebrity and leaves you all alone. Did that piss you off?"

Julian stood, his whole body shaking with rage.

"Portia was the only family I had left. The only person in the world I loved. Now she's gone, and I have...no one. And you think I played some kind of role in her death?"

"No, Mr. Hart. I'm sure Detective Vanzinger isn't suggesting that," Nessa called out as Julian strode to the door. "But we do need to know if you can think of anyone would have wanted to hurt her."

But Julian Hart didn't hear her; he was already gone.

* * *

Nessa decided to walk the few blocks to City Hall. She and Riley Odell needed to plan out their appeal for information on Xavier Greyson, and the walk would give her a chance to clear her head.

But by the time she'd reached the corner, her blouse was sticking to her clammy skin, and she was wondering if she'd made a mistake by venturing out into the stifling summer heat.

Waiting for the light at the crosswalk to turn green, Nessa saw a sleek black Audi pull up to the curb. The tinted window rolled down to reveal Hunter Hadley's handsome face.

"You got a minute, Chief Ainsley?" he called out. "I need to talk to you about the Molly Blair case."

Nessa leaned in the window, relishing the sweet cold air blowing from the car's vents.

"If you've got air conditioning, I've got time."

Nessa opened the door and slid into the passenger seat. She was surprised to see a furry white face peering over the seatback.

"Well, hello there, cutie." She reached back to scratch the dog's soft fur. "Who have you got here, Mr. Hadley?"

"That's Gracie," Hunter said, smiling back at the white Lab. "She's my house guest for the time being."

Reaching out to adjust the air vent, Nessa closed her eyes and let the air blow her red curls back from her face.

"I found some interesting information when I was at the Kingston Road crime scene last night. I thought you'd want to hear it."

"What I want is to get to City Hall," Nessa said. "But if you drive me there, I'll listen to your news on the way."

Hunter signaled his agreement by steering the car back into traffic. He wasted no time in sharing his big news.

"One of Molly Blair's neighbors saw Nick Sargent at her house."

Nessa frowned.

"Okay...so what? Every reporter in town was there yesterday."

"No, he was there before Molly Blair was killed. Apparently more than once. The neighbor seemed to think he was coming regularly to visit the young girls that hung out at Ms. Blair's house."

Recalling the tearful confession Lexi Marsh had made the day before, Nessa felt a stir of unease.

"Molly ran an escort service and I was...one of her girls."

"That's not all," Hunter continued, pulling up to the curb outside City Hall. "I have information that Mr. Nikolai Sokolov was a guest at the Riverview Hotel the night Portia Hart died."

Nessa raised one eyebrow and cocked her head.

"Who's that?"

"Nick Sargent," Hunter said. "Nikolai Sokolov is his real name. He just uses the name Nick Sargent professionally."

"How did you get that information?"

"I have my sources. Let's just say I got a look at the guestlist for that night. I was looking for people to interview for the show. Needless to say, his name stuck out."

Nessa stared at Hunter, unsure how to handle the unexpected revelation. She'd never had a reporter provide incriminating information on another reporter.

"I think you need to spell it out for me," she said, reaching for the door handle, "because I'm already late for my meeting. Just what is it you're trying to say?"

"That something doesn't smell right, and that I'll be looking into Nick Sargent's recent whereabouts. I just wanted you to know in case you wanted to investigate him yourself or ask him about it."

Hunter offered Nessa a sardonic smile.

"As you can imagine, he's not likely to grant me an interview."

As Nessa climbed out of the car, she wondered if the popular, clean-cut Nick Sargent could somehow be involved with the Portia Hart and Molly Blair cases.

The forensic evidence links both deaths to Xavier Greyson. So where would Nick Sargent, or Nikolai Sokolov, fit in?

Unable to come up with a quick answer, Nessa hurried toward the entrance to City Hall. Maybe Riley Odell could make sense out of Hunter's tip-off.

After all, he was an experienced reporter, and she trusted his instinct. And based on what he'd found out about the Channel Six reporter, she'd have to look into it.

But first, she and Riley needed to decide what to do about Xavier Greyson. At least three women they knew of had died at his hands, and there could be more victims out there that had never been found. If they didn't find him soon, there was no telling who would be next.

CHAPTER THIRTY-FOUR

Riley was just leaving City Hall when she saw Nessa climb out of a black Audi sedan and hurry toward the building. She waited for the chief of police to approach, curious as to the owner of the sleek car, but anxious to get going.

"Does Jerry know you're driving around town with another man?"

Nessa stopped short, catching sight of Riley with a startled laugh.

"Jerry knows I don't have enough free time to start an affair," Nessa replied, checking her watch. "And speaking of time, aren't you and I supposed to be meeting right about now?"

"There's been a slight change in plans."

Gesturing for Nessa to follow her, Riley marched across the courtyard toward the sidewalk. She stopped at the intersection and turned to Nessa.

"I got a tip that Maxwell Clay is at Barker and Dawson's Investigations over on Townsend right now." She looked both ways, then darted across the street even though the crosswalk light was still flashing red. "It's only a few blocks away."

Her words seemed to spur Nessa to walk faster, and ten minutes later they were at the threshold of Willow Bay's newest private investigation agency. Frankie Dawson and Pete Barker stood over a man in a straight back chair. Riley assumed the interrogation had already started.

"Maxwell Clay?"

The man nodded, and Riley felt a strange surge of disappointment at the man's ordinary appearance. She noted the sheen of perspiration on his pasty forehead and the damp strands of thin grey hair he'd combed over to hide his receding hairline.

He's definitely not a cool, confident con man like Xavier Greyson.

"I'm Riley Odell with the state prosecutor's office, and that's Nessa Ainsley, Willow Bay's chief of police. We'd like to ask you a few questions about your relationship with Portia Hart."

Clay stood and adjusted his suit jacket, then offered Riley his hand. Something about the man reminded her of a used car salesman. She ignored his hand and waved him back into his chair.

"Mr. Clay, I understand that you misrepresented yourself to Mr. Barker and Mr. Dawson here, and made false claims about your employment at Sterlington Group Insurance."

It was a statement, not a question, but Clay didn't seem to notice. He just stared at Riley with growing dismay, and she bulldozed on, confident he would be easy to break.

"Just what were you hoping to accomplish with your lies, Mr. Clay? And what is the nature of your relationship with Ms. Hart?"

"Relationship?" Clay shook his head in denial. "There's no *relationship*. One of my agents sold Portia Hart an insurance policy through my agency in Hart Cove. That's the extent of my relationship with Portia Hart. I've never even met her."

Riley watched as a trickle of sweat worked its way down Clay's cheek. There was no doubt he was hiding something, but what?

"So why tell Mr. Dawson that you worked for Sterlington Trust? And why were you trying to investigate Portia Hart's death?"

"I was simply trying to find out if Portia Hart had...had taken her own life, or not. There are terms in...in the...the policy that-"

Stepping closer, Riley interrupted the man's blathering. It was time to end Clay's pointless charade.

"What policy, Mr. Clay? I've contacted Sterlington Trust and they claim the life insurance policy purchased by Portia Hart was canceled over three years ago. They have no intention of investigating or paying out a claim."

Clay opened his mouth, then closed it again. The trickle of sweat finally reached his chin and dripped onto his shirt collar.

"What's your game, Mr. Clay?"

Dropping his head into his hands, Clay remained silent. Riley looked over at Nessa, who shrugged. Pete Barker however wore a suspicious frown. He raised an eyebrow to Riley, silently asking permission to join the interrogation. Riley nodded, eager to see Barker's decades of experience as a police detective in action.

"Mr. Clay, I'm Pete Barker...Frankie's partner." Barker leaned against the wooden desk next to Clay and sighed. "I have a feeling I know what's going on here."

Clay raised his head and looked up at Barker but didn't speak.

"I think your agent really did sell Ms. Hart an insurance policy, and I think it was one of the biggest policies your agency had ever handled." Barker cleared his throat and paused. "Which is probably why you were tempted into making a very bad decision. Am I right, Mr. Clay? Did you make a bad decision?"

Nodding mutely, Clay tried to clear his throat.

"Frankie, get Mr. Clay some water."

Barker's partner ducked into the back room, returning with a bottle of water. He unscrewed the cap and held it out to Clay, who took it and held it to his lips with a shaky hand.

"Okay, Mr. Clay. It's time to come clean. You tell us exactly what you've done, and we can put this all behind us."

The room was quiet as Clay took another sip.

"Portia Hart bought a large policy through my agency over five years ago. She would send her premium payments to our office, and we then submitted payment to Sterlington. It's a service we offer our best clients."

Clay spoke in a low voice; Riley had to lean forward to hear him.

"The agency started having...financial problems. One month I decided to use Portia's premium to pay some bills. I thought I'd send the payment to Sterlington later in the month. That was the start. Eventually, I let her policy lapse, but I...didn't mean for it to happen."

"You kept accepting the premiums payments, didn't you?" Barker asked, his voice soft. "You took her money and you never told her that the policy had been canceled."

Wiping his forehead with the back of his hand, Clay nodded.

"So, why'd you come forward now that she's dead?" Frankie asked, his face a mask of confusion. "Why not just lay low?

Riley thought she knew the answer to Frankie's question.

"You thought Julian Hart knew about the policy, didn't you?" She said, working it out in her head as she spoke. "You thought if you could prove Portia had committed suicide, Julian wouldn't bother trying to file the claim.

A flush of color washed over Clay's face, but he didn't respond.

"You were hoping Julian Hart would never find out the policy had been canceled. That way your fraud wouldn't be exposed."

Shaking his head in denial, Clay rose from his chair.

"It wasn't fraud," he insisted. "I was going to reactivate the policy once I got back on my feet. If she hadn't died, no one would have ever known...everything would have been fine."

Riley turned away from the man's desperate attempts to explain. She wasn't interested in solving an insurance fraud case. At least not right now. She would report Maxwell Clay's crimes to the authorities in Hart Cove and they could deal with him.

Right now, she had a much bigger case to solve, and Maxwell Clay had wasted too much of her valuable time already. She was sure

Nessa would agree that the pathetic insurance agent could be crossed off their list of suspects in Portia Hart's death.

* * *

Riley and Nessa stared at the computer screen in stunned silence. The warrant had been issued for Portia Hart's bank accounts, and the bank had provided Riley with a printout of Portia's recent transactions and current balances in a variety of accounts.

"Cole and Cooper have more in their little money jar than she has in the bank." Nessa sounded dazed. "What the heck happened?"

Scanning through the transactions, Riley saw that several large transfers had taken place on Friday. She clicked on the transaction, but the door to her office banged open before she could see where the money had gone.

Her assistant stood in the doorway wearing a panicked expression.

"You're gonna want to see this right away."

Riley followed the sound of raised voices out to the lobby where the television was tuned to Channel Six.

Nick Sargent stood in front of the Riverview Hotel as a *Breaking News* banner scrolled across the bottom of the screen.

"For those of you just joining us, sources have confirmed that a suspect has been identified in the tragic drowning deaths of celebrity author Portia Hart and local resident Molly Blair."

Watching in transfixed horror, Riley felt Nessa stiffen beside her. They both watched helplessly as Xavier Greyson's name was splashed across the screen.

"Xavier Greyson has been named as the top suspect in the deaths which have terrorized the Willow Bay community during the last forty-eight hours."

Nick's face was filled with grave concern, and his voice was somber as he spoke directly into the camera.

"And now some residents are asking why the Willow Bay authorities refused to release the name of this dangerous criminal and are demanding answers as to what is being done to find him."

A big hand fell on Riley's shoulder. She spun around to see Tucker Vanzinger's angry face. He looked ready to burst, but she put up a hand to silence him. Pulling him by one thick arm, she led Vanzinger back toward her office, urging Nessa to follow.

"Who could have leaked this?" he demanded as soon as they were behind closed doors. "Who else knew about Xavier Greyson?"

"There's only one person I shared the news with," Riley said, feeling sick to her stomach. "I told Veronica Lee the details last night so she could prepare the special report once I gave her the go-ahead."

Nessa frowned and shook her head.

"But Veronica works for Channel Ten, doesn't she? Why would she share the information with a competitor?"

"I don't know," Riley said, grabbing her purse and keys off her desk. "But I'm going to find out."

"Hold on, there, Riley, you don't want to make this even worse."

Reaching for her hand, Vanzinger tried to slow her down, but Riley pulled away and wrenched open the door.

"Now Xavier Greyson will know we're looking for him before we're prepared to act."

Her anger rose as she heard the fear in her own voice.

"He'll get away, and there's no telling who else might get hurt."

CHAPTER THIRTY-FIVE

The constant vibration underneath Lexi sent bolts of pain shooting through her aching head. Her eyes fluttered open, but she couldn't see anything in the utter darkness around her. She was wedged onto her right side, and as she tried to sit up, her head hit something hard.

Falling back against the soft carpet, another rough jolt beneath her sent her head spinning, and she thought she might black out.

Has there been an earthquake? I didn't know Florida had earthquakes.

As the fog of pain began to clear, she raised a weak hand and felt smooth, hard metal above her. She tried to move her other hand, but it was wedged in tightly between her body and the carpeted surface beneath her. Wiggling her arm free, she felt around her with growing panic, not wanting to acknowledge what was happening.

I'm in the trunk of a car. Someone's locked me in the trunk of their car.

The terrifying events of the previous day came flooding back.

The man that chased me on the stairs and who was standing in the crowd. It's him. He killed Molly, and now he's got me.

Fear knifed through her, overriding the pain in her head. She tried to scream but found that she couldn't make a sound. Her throat and mouth were completely dry. And there was so little air in the confined space that she couldn't draw in a full breath.

Forcing herself to stay still, she sucked in tiny gulps of air and listened. She could hear the whooshing sound of the wheels on the road, and the smooth hum of the car engine. And was that the faint sound of music?

Where's he taking me? Why not just kill me at Molly's place?"

The soft music was suddenly interrupted by a loud voice.

"Breaking news today in the death of Portia Hart. An unnamed state official has named Xavier Greyson as a person of interest. Greyson is thought to have information about Portia Hart's death, as well as information about the violent death last night of Molly Blair, a Willow Bay resident who was attacked in her own backyard."

Xavier Greyson?

Lexi had never heard the name before. She wondered if that was the name of the man that had thrown her into the trunk of the car. If the police knew who he was and that he killed Molly, would they know he'd taken her, too?

Does anyone even know I'm gone? Are they looking for me?

"Greyson has also been linked to a suspicious death in Miami back in 2010. Anyone having knowledge of Mr. Greyson should immediately contact authorities."

Listening to the voice with growing horror, Lexi tried not to cry. That would only use up the little oxygen she had left. But the knowledge that the man called Xavier Greyson had already killed three other women terrified her.

If he killed them, there's nothing to stop him from killing me.

She stifled a sob and tried to listen to the reporter's voice. Maybe he would mention her next. Maybe they did know she was gone and they were looking for her even now.

"For more on this story, watch Channel Six news at noon. Reporting live for Channel Six, this is Nick Sargent."

The familiar name sent a ripple of revulsion and fear down Lexi's spine. Regret at her own stupidity washed through her. Memories of the last time she'd heard that voice made her stomach heave.

Lexi stopped outside the door to Room 1025 and hesitated, adjusting her long, pink wig, tempted to flee back down the hall. She cringed at the thought of the task that lay ahead. But it was what Nikolai want, and Molly would be furious if she let him down.

All the girls who worked for Molly dreaded being picked by the cruel man for one of his special jobs, but he held sway over their lives, and they all had to do their part to keep him happy. Molly had warned them that Nikolai would stop supplying her with the pills and powder if they didn't.

Taking a deep breath, Lexi knocked on the door and waited. She jumped when the door opened to reveal a heavyset man in a bulky white hotel robe. He had thinning gray hair and dark, bushy eyebrows.

"About fucking time." He stood back to let Lexi enter, and she pushed the door closed behind her. "I don't have all night, you know. My wife will be calling the cops looking for me."

"Sorry, the service just called me an hour ago." Lexi tried to smile. "I got here as fast as I could."

The man untied his robe and let it fall to the floor. Lexi tried not to look at him as he sat on the bed wearing only a pair of white boxers.

"We need to settle the money first," she said, trying to remember exactly what Nikolai had told her. "Then we can have some fun."

Shaking his head in frustration, the man stood and crossed the room. He picked up a pair of pants that had been draped over a chair and dug in the pocket for his wallet. He opened it and counted out three one-hundred-dollar bills and threw them on the table.

"You can put them right here." Lexi lifted her short skirt to reveal a lacy garter belt. "Don't worry, I won't bite."

Posing seductively, she made sure her pink braid hid most of her face as the man approached with a nauseating leer. He was close enough for her to smell his sour breath as he bent to tuck the bills into the garter belt. She glanced toward the door, worried she'd gone too quickly, but she then saw it swing open just as planned.

A bright flash momentarily blinded her as a man in a ski mask stepped into the room and pointed a long-lensed camera at the man in front of her, who had frozen in place with his hands on her garter belt.

"What the hell are you doing?" The big man's voice boomed through the quiet room.

The masked intruder put a long finger to his lips.

"I wouldn't want to draw attention to this if I were you, Mr. Murray. Your wife might be curious to know why you were here...with her."

The man glared at Lexi, and she recoiled at the fury in his narrowed eyes. He lunged toward her, but the masked man stepped forward and stuck a hard fist in the big man's paunch.

"Go on," the masked man said to Lexi. "I've got what I need."

He pushed her into the hall and slammed the door shut behind them. Ripping off the ski mask, Nikolai pointed to the stairwell.

"Now, get out of here before someone calls security."

But before she could leave, he gripped her arm and pulled her against his chest. His voice was a low growl in her ear.

"And if you know what's good for you, you'll never speak of this to anyone. You understand?"

Lexi nodded, and he shoved her toward the exit. She looked back as he opened the door to a room further down the hall and disappeared inside. Pushing the exit door open, she started walking down the ten floors to the side exit. She looked up when she'd heard a sound on the stairs above her and saw the angry face of a man in a dark hoodie. Her fight or flight instinct kicked in, and she began to run.

The car jerked to a sudden stop, causing Lexi's head to bump against the floor, bringing her mind back to the painful reality inside the cramped trunk.

Struggling to move her legs, which were stiff and cramped from being wedged against the trunk lid, Lexi felt one shoe slide off. She tried to stretch her leg out, but the trunk wall blocked it. Bending her knee, her foot connected with something soft and pliable behind her. She used her toes to explore, trying to make sense out of what she was feeling.

Twisting to the left, Lexi managed to reach back and feel the bulky object behind her. Her fingers came away wet and sticky.

What is that?

Suddenly she realized what the metallic odor inside the trunk was.

It's the stench of blood.

Lexi reached out again, her numb fingers brushing against a fall of soft hair. Stretching her hand further, her fingers settled on cold, unyielding flesh.

It's a body. I'm in the trunk with a dead body.

As the car started to move again, Lexi Marsh began to scream.

CHAPTER THIRTY-SIX

Xavier saw the flashing lights in his rearview mirror and looked toward his backpack, debating whether he should go ahead and pull out the Glock. Instead, he put his foot on the brake and brought the blue Toyota sedan to a halt by the side of the road. The cruiser whizzed by him and raced out of sight.

Shaken by the close call, Xavier decided he needed to come up with a plausible story in case he did get pulled over. He'd have a hard time explaining how he came to be in possession of the vehicle registered to Constance Volkson. Looking at the identification card clipped to the dashboard, he smiled.

I doubt the cops will think I'm a blonde, blue-eyed woman from Chicago.

And he'd have to do some explaining about the decal. After he'd gotten the talkative Connie out of the way, he'd decided to leave the *Willow Bay Quick Rides* decal on the windshield, hoping it would make his presence less suspicious as he finished up his business in Willow Bay. Now he wondered if the ride service decal might lead to awkward questions if the cops did stop him.

Figuring it wouldn't be long before they discovered that Connie and her car were missing, Xavier decided he'd better go ahead and dump the car. Of course, the bodies in the trunk would need to be disposed of, too.

Luckily, Mosquito Lake should provide the perfect cover. He'd let the Toyota roll into the murky lake beside the taxi, and then the car and the bodies within would be out of sight and out of mind.

Accelerating past the airport exit, Xavier tried to think through the rest of his plan. After he disposed of the car and its unwanted cargo, he would find a ride back to the hotel garage where he'd parked his car. Now that he'd eliminated all witnesses, he was free to begin the next phase of his plan.

He began looking for the turnoff to the lake. Slowing as he approached the side road, he saw the blue and red lights of a police car flashing through the foliage. He steered the sedan past the road, craning his neck to see what was going on.

A tow truck was pulling a car out of the lake. The car was covered in algae and weeds, but the yellow paint beneath was clearly visible. Someone had found the taxi, and they would unquestionably open the trunk to see what was inside.

Xavier rammed his foot down on the gas, suddenly sure he would be stopped and questioned, and that his cargo in the trunk would be discovered. But no one noticed the Toyota driving by, and no one stopped him. After he'd driven a few more miles, he decided to turn around. He needed to get out of town quickly; panicking now would be the worst thing he could do.

But as he mapped out an alternative route back to Willow Bay, he couldn't help but worry. The whole world seemed to be falling apart along with his plan. He knew he still had a chance to make it work, but his confidence was taking a blow with every misstep.

Feeling the tension building inside him, he tried to remember the rules his father had drummed into his head when he was growing up.

Whatever happens, keep your cool. Never let 'em see you sweat, and never quit in the middle of a game. That's the sure way to end up a loser.

Thinking about his father made Xavier moody. It also made him determined to prove he could run a bigger con than his old man. He'd looked up to his father for years, but now he was on his own, and this was his chance to uphold the family tradition and raise the stakes to a level his father had never even dreamed of.

Sure, he'd already scored all the money in Portia Hart's account, but the haul had been much less than he'd need to disappear into a life of ease. In order to fulfill his dream, he'd have to have more. He banged a fist against the steering wheel as he thought of all the money Portia had thrown away.

The stupid bitch screwed up my plan. What a fucking waste.

When he'd seen Portia Hart at the resort in St. Barts he'd been impressed. She was single and attractive, and the Cartier watch she wore on her elegant wrist cost more than a new BMW.

And once he'd found out who she was, and what her net worth was estimated to be, he was convinced she was the whale he'd been training to catch all his life.

From that moment on he'd played the perfect game. First choosing a lounge chair close enough to show off his tan torso and chiseled six-pack, and then proceeding to ignore her for the majority of the day.

Arranging an accidental meeting at the pool bar had been easy, and she'd bought his carefree wanderer act hook, line, and sinker. By the end of the first evening, he was in her room toasting to her health. By the end of the first week, he was in her bed, toasting to their new life together.

He was ashamed to think how he'd even allowed himself to imagine he really could be in a relationship, at least for a while. Portia Hart had been beautiful, rich beyond belief, and easy to manipulate. What more could he ask for?

It was only after he'd traveled with her to New York, and overheard her on the phone with her accountant, that he'd gotten suspicious about her financial situation. He'd been devastated when he'd finally gotten the chance to look at her bank account statement and realized the truth about her finances.

If I had a heart, she would have broken it. Luckily, I take after my father.

But eventually, his father had played one too many games. He hadn't known when to stop, and he'd gotten caught. Xavier wouldn't let that happen to him. He wanted to go out on top, and he knew it was time to retire, but he'd need to find one last target to do it in the style he had always imagined for himself.

A few million bucks would get him through the first year or two, but he had his heart set on billions. There was only one person he knew of that had billions of dollars in the bank. It was the one person who should have stopped Portia from wasting her inheritance. The one person who would never appreciate the good life that kind of money could buy.

Bringing his attention back to the road, Xavier decided to take care of first things first. He would find a place to dispose of the bodies in the trunk, and then he would head to Hart Cove. It was time to make the next move in his final game.

CHAPTER THIRTY-SEVEN

Veronica stood with the Channel Ten news crew staring at the television mounted on the wall. Nick Sargent's special report on Portia Hart's suspected killer was airing for the second time, and she was having a hard time controlling her anger.

How dare Riley Odell dangle the story in front of me and then hand it to Nick Sargent to break? Did I say or do something wrong?

Focused on Nick Sargent's smug face, Veronica didn't hear the door to the newsroom open.

"I need to talk to you...*now.*"

Veronica turned to see Riley Odell standing behind her. The prosecutor's normally cool, guarded expression had slipped. Her face was tense; she looked as hurt and angry as Veronica was feeling.

Hunter stepped between them and held up a placating hand.

"Why don't you both go in my office where you can talk privately." He guided them to the door, then closed it behind them.

Veronica turned to Riley with a confused frown.

"You said you'd let *me* break the Xavier Greyson story, and then you gave it to Nick Sargent. Why?"

Riley raised her eyebrows as if shocked by the accusation.

"You said *you'd* keep it off the record until I gave you the okay, and now it's all over the news and we're not ready."

"Are you saying that you didn't give Nick Sargent the same information you gave me?" Veronica asked.

When Riley shook her head, Veronica rushed to her purse and pulled out the menu with Xavier Greyson's name written on the back.

"I haven't told a soul, not even Hunter," Veronica said, staring at the paper in her hand. "I swear...I had it with me at the hotel and then I went home. I never told anyone about it."

Riley studied her with narrowed eyes as if trying to decide if she was telling the truth.

"Could someone have seen your notes?"

Veronica remembered shoving the paper in her purse in the bar. The only person around had been Benji, the bartender. Could he have seen the notes, or even overheard their conversation?

And then there had been the incident in Julian Hart's hotel room. He'd seen the notes when her purse had spilled open. He'd seen what she'd written, but he'd been devastated. Would he really go to Channel Ten and share the information about his sister's killer with Nick? It seemed highly unlikely.

"I guess the bartender could have seen it when he was delivering the drinks and clearing the table," Veronica admitted. "And then...well, Julian Hart saw them when I went up to his room."

"You went up to his room? When?"

Swallowing the lump that had worked its way into her throat, Veronica tried to find the right words. Words that wouldn't make her sound quite so bad.

"I'd asked Julian for an interview," Veronica explained, keeping her voice calm. "He suggested we do it in his hotel room."

"Okay, so what exactly did you do with him...*in his room?*"

Veronica stared out through the glass walls of the office, watching as Hunter and Finn gazed up at the television, both men apparently transfixed by what should have been her story.

"Nothing happened, Riley," Veronica said, knowing she'd probably turned an embarrassing shade of red. "I was only there for a few minutes, but my purse fell open and Julian saw my notes. He was actually pretty upset. I can't imagine he would-"

"How could you have been so careless," Riley fumed, shaking her head in frustration. "Now Xavier Greyson has fair warning. He might go to ground. He might panic and hurt someone else. Whatever happens, we no longer have the element of surprise."

She put her hand on the doorknob, then stopped, looked back at Veronica's crestfallen face, and sighed.

"I'm sorry to be so harsh...I'm sure it wasn't intentional. But I've gotta let Nessa know what happened. We'll need to decide what to do to try to bring in Xavier Greyson before he can hurt anyone else."

Veronica stared after Riley, hating the feeling of helplessness that washed over her. Somehow, she'd allowed the story to leak, and now Riley and Nessa would have to fix her mistake.

"You okay?"

Hunter stood outside the door, studying her stricken face.

Veronica shook her head; her throat was too tight to speak as Finn walked up and joined them. He turned to see the front door close behind Riley, then pointed to Nick Sargent on the television screen.

"Did her blow-up have something to do with Nick's big story?" he asked. "Cause I'm not sure how that could be your fault."

Dropping her eyes, Veronica felt a flush of shame heat her cheeks.

I shouldn't have sent Finn away yesterday. If I'd acted professionally, none of this would have happened.

Swallowing hard, she decided it would be easier to just tell them the whole story now, rather than wait for them to figure it out on their own. She waved Hunter and Finn into the office, then sank into a chair across from his desk.

"Riley Odell met me last night at the Riverview Hotel and gave me information about a man she suspects killed Portia Hart and Molly

Blair. She asked me to keep the information to myself until she was ready to release a public appeal."

"I'm assuming the man is Xavier Greyson; the same man that Nick Sargent is reporting on this morning?" Hunter's forehead creased into a frown. "And somehow the information Riley gave you got leaked to Nick?"

Nodding miserably, Veronica knew she had to tell him the rest.

"After Riley left the hotel, I only saw two people. So, I'm guessing one of them had to have shared the information."

"Okay, so who are they?" Finn's voice was eager as if he was ready to hunt down whoever Veronica named.

Veronica glanced at Hunter, but he still wore the same frown.

"Well, we met in the hotel bar, and there was a bartender there that keep hovering around. He handed me some paper to use and was clearing off the table as Riley was leaving."

"So, you think he might have seen the notes?"

Shrugging, Veronica tried to remember anything unusual about Benji's behavior, but nothing specific came to mind.

"I'm not sure," she admitted. "I left quickly because...well, I saw Julian Hart in the lobby. I followed him to the elevator and asked for an interview and he suggested I go up to his room."

Both men stiffened, and Hunter's frown deepened.

"I hope you didn't go into his room alone." Finn sounded incredulous. "That could compromise the whole story...not to mention put you in a potentially dangerous situation."

"I wasn't there for long," Veronica protested, ignoring Finn's disapproving scowl. "And nothing happened out of the ordinary other than...well, other than I dropped my bag and my notes fell out."

Running a hand through his unruly hair, Hunter walked to the window and looked outside. Veronica felt the impulse to apologize, but her last bit of pride stopped her.

"I was trying to chase down a story. Get a big interview," she insisted. "I didn't do anything *wrong*. At least, I didn't mean to. But now Nick has stolen my scoop, and Riley thinks we've given Xavier Greyson a head start. She's pretty worried..."

Hunter didn't seem to be listening. He continued to stare out the window with a grim expression. Finally, he turned to face them.

"This is the last thing we need." Hunter's jaw was clenched, and his voice tight. "This station is already having trouble keeping advertisers. If there are questions of our integrity...or if we aren't able to break the latest news...that will only make it harder."

Unease ignited in Veronica's stomach.

"You see...the station is up for sale," Hunter admitted, not meeting Veronica's eyes. "I've tried to get the board to hold off, but the chairman called me this morning. He's got a buyer lined up, and I wasn't able to change his mind. All this will only confirm to him he's made the right decision."

Jumping up from the chair, Veronica crossed to stand in front of Hunter, unable to believe what she was hearing.

"When did this happen? When I asked you on Saturday about the station, you said that it was going to be okay."

The regret in his eyes confirmed her fear. He'd lied to her. He'd told her what she wanted to hear because he couldn't trust her with the truth. And she couldn't say she blamed him. Look what had happened when Riley had trusted her.

"I'm sorry, Veronica. I was hoping to talk the board out of selling. I'd hoped to find some new advertisers but...well, it didn't work out."

"That's the theme of the day," Veronica said numbly. "Nothing seems to be working out."

Putting a hand on her arm, Hunter stepped close enough for her to feel the heat of his body and smell the faint scent of his cologne.

"A new owner doesn't mean things have to change, at least not for you. They may want to bring in new management, but they'll need good reporters."

His words cut through her. Based on what had happened in the last twelve hours, she obviously wasn't a good reporter, and a new station manager would want only the best.

An ache started up in her chest at the thought of working at Channel Ten without Hunter. Desperate to hide the tears that had pooled in her eyes, Veronica turned and rushed toward the door.

"Wait, Veronica...please, stay. We'll work this out."

But Veronica knew it was no use. She could no longer trust herself to make the right decisions, and she couldn't trust Hunter to tell her the truth. She grabbed her bag and headed out to her Jeep, her mind reeling at the thought of never coming back.

It's all over. Just like that, everything I've worked for is over.

* * *

Veronica steered the red Jeep toward downtown. She didn't want to go home; she couldn't face her mother. And she needed to find out who had leaked the Xavier Greyson story. If her reporting career was at an end, she deserved to know how, and why.

The Riverview Hotel's lobby was quiet. The police were gone, and most of the reporters covering the Portia Hart story were camped outside City Hall, hoping for an official statement about the murders.

Approaching the reception desk, Veronica saw the hotel manager chatting with the desk clerk.

"Sorry to bother you, Mr. Robinson," she said, glancing at his nametag. "I'm hoping to speak to Julian Hart. Can you call up to his room for me?"

Dennis Robinson offered a perfunctory smile and shook his head.

"I'm sorry, dear, but Mr. Hart checked out this morning." He lowered his voice and leaned forward. "Poor boy was torn up when he heard the news. They're saying his sister was a victim of a serial killer. He was probably in shock, as I'm sure you can imagine."

Disappointment surged through Veronica at the thought that she wouldn't have the chance to talk to Julian. She felt a twinge of guilt as she recalled how lonely he'd looked when she'd left him the night before.

Dennis looked over her shoulder and stiffened. He excused himself and stalked toward the bar. Veronica turned to see him approach Benji, who was holding a big duffle bag and wearing a smug smile.

The bartender had swapped his uniform for a pair of faded jeans and a form-fitting white t-shirt that clung to his muscled torso. She watched as Benji accepted an envelope from the manager's hand.

As Dennis walked away, Benji waved at Veronica and headed toward the exit. She scurried after him, her suspicion growing.

"You're quitting?" she asked, nodding at the duffle bag.

"Yeah, I came into an unexpected windfall last night," he said, offering her a wide grin. "Enough for me to head down south. This was never meant to be a permanent gig anyway."

The image of Benji hovering behind her the night before flashed in her mind. She felt her pulse quicken in anger.

"It was you, wasn't it? You read my notes, and somehow you passed the information to Nick Sargent."

Pulling out his phone, Benji tapped on the screen. An amused smirk appeared on his face as he held the phone toward Veronica.

"You really are clueless, aren't you?"

She gaped at the picture of the menu on the tabletop. Her handwritten notes were perfectly clear and legible.

"Why would you do that?" Veronica shook her head in disgust. "I mean, that information is sensitive, and it's devastating to the victim's family."

"You mean like Portia Hart's wimpy brother? The guy that hung around here looking like he wanted to kill himself all the time?" Benji snorted. "Believe me, he's got bigger problems than me making a little green off a story. In fact, I'd put money on him turning up dead just like his sister. That kind of shit runs in the family."

Grabbing Benji's phone from his hand, Veronica spun and hurried toward the exit. She dropped the phone into the fountain outside just as Benji came charging after her. As he splashed into the water after the phone, Veronica headed back to her Jeep.

She didn't let the tears fall until she was sitting safely in the driver's seat with the doors locked. She'd ruined everything. The investigation into Portia Hart's death. Her chance of being a respected reporter. Even her relationship with her mother.

Wiping away tears with the back of her hand, she caught sight of her red, swollen eyes in the mirror. The image shocked her. Why was she allowing herself to wallow in self-pity? If anyone was hurting now it was Julian Hart. He was the one who was grieving and totally alone in the world. Benji's words replayed in her head.

"The guy that hung around here looking like he wanted to kill himself all the time? I'd put money on him turning up dead just like his sister."

Would Julian try to hurt himself? She thought of the beautiful sketch he'd drawn. A picture of himself and his sister in happier days. An image of a time long past that must haunt him.

Pulling out her phone, Veronica scrolled through her messages and found the text Julian had sent her the day before. She would send him a message. Just to check in and make sure he was okay.

You checked out of the hotel. Are you okay?

She waited, not sure if she expected a response or not. His reply popped up almost immediately.

I know what happened now. There was no reason to stay.

She resisted the impulse to reply that he could stay for her, that she would be there for him. He deserved the truth, and the truth was, she was head over heels for Hunter. After everything that had happened today, she knew that now, even though now was too late.

But it was obvious that Julian was in desperate need of a friend. Maybe she could still make things right.

If you need a friend, let me know.

She waited for a reply. After a long pause, a response popped up.

I need to make arrangements to bury my sister. Nothing else matters now.

The despondent tone of his text worried her. She tried to think of something comforting, but her mind went blank. Finally, she typed out a reply and pressed send.

Things will get better. Just hang in there.

She re-read her text and grimaced, wishing she had thought of something more original than a cliché off a motivational poster. When no response came back, Veronica decided to call him. She couldn't leave it like that.

As the phone rang again and again without answer, Veronica began to worry that Benji's dire prediction may have been right. Perhaps Julian was on the path to a tragic end, just like his sister. And unless she thought of something fast, no one would be there to save him.

CHAPTER THIRTY-EIGHT

The phone on her desk wouldn't stop ringing as Nessa tried to concentrate on what Riley Odell was saying. She jabbed at the *Do Not Disturb* button and raised her hand to stop Riley's ongoing rant, but the prosecutor didn't seem to notice.

"We're both going to be hung out to dry if we don't give Tenley Frost and Mayor Hadley an update within the next hour."

Nessa opened her mouth to respond, but Riley wasn't finished.

"Every reporter in the state is standing outside City Hall waiting for an official release, and most people around here are scared to death that we've got a killer on the loose."

Surprised at the rare show of emotion from the normally cool and collected prosecutor, Nessa tried to curb her own instinct to panic. She'd wanted the job as chief, and now she had to own it, along with all the problems and headaches that came with it.

"We'll get them their update." Nessa kept her voice calm. "But let's walk through what we know first to make darn sure what we're giving them is accurate. We don't need any more screw-ups."

Riley nodded, then she slumped back into her chair, apparently drained of her anxious energy, at least for the moment.

"And we need all the brainpower we can get." Nessa picked up the phone receiver and punched in Vanzinger's extension.

"Can you and Jankowski come to my office?" she asked, once Vanzinger picked up. "I need your help."

Minutes later the two big detectives appeared at her door. She stood and waved them all toward a round table by the window.

"Okay, so we need to give an update to the media, the mayor, and the public." She looked directly at Vanzinger. "Detective, you're supposed to be leading the case, and I'm aware I've been stepping all over it. I guess I'm still trying to figure how this chief thing is gonna work."

"I understand, Nessa." A flush of color painted Vanzinger's cheeks. "I'm still getting used to being back in the department myself. I'm just happy to be part of a team that's trying to do the right thing, even if we aren't perfect."

"Speak for yourself, Tucker." Jankowski's sarcastic tone lightened the somber mood in the room. "Now, what are we giving to Tenley Frost? She's the first one we need to update."

Taking out her notebook, Nessa turned to the last page.

"I've been going through all the evidence again, and something just doesn't seem to fit." She looked at her list with a frown. "Our theory is that Xavier Greyson's motive to kill Portia Hart was her money, right?"

"Right, that was our theory before we found out she'd lost most of her money," Riley said. "I mean, everyone thought she was a billionaire. Greyson probably thought he'd found the mother lode."

"Maybe that's why he killed her," Vanzinger offered. "Maybe he found out she wasn't as rich as he'd thought, and he got mad."

Nessa shrugged. She doubted any of them could ever completely understand imagine Xavier Greyson's motive.

"Well, someone cleaned out her accounts, and I'm assuming it was Greyson," Riley added. "Royalties had started rolling in, then as of Friday, it was all transferred to an offshore bank."

"Friday, huh? The same day she was killed." Vanzinger leaned back in his chair. "I'd say he wanted to have the weekend to finish Portia off before she noticed the money was gone."

"But why now?" Jankowski questioned. "Why in Willow Bay?"

Nessa thought back to her conversation with Jane.

"People around Portia were getting suspicious. Her agent was asking questions, and sooner or later her brother was gonna find out she was spending money on a new man." Nessa warmed to her theory. "Xavier had to have known it was just a matter of time before his cover would be blown. Maybe he wanted to end it in a small town where no one knew either of them."

"So, killing Molly Blair and attacking Alexandra Marsh...that was just him trying to get rid of any witnesses?" Jankowski asked.

Before Nessa had a chance to answer, she heard a knock on the door. A second later Andy Ford stuck his head into the room. The young officer's eyes widened at the group gathered around the table.

"Sorry to interrupt, Chief. But a fisherman out on Mosquito Lake got his hook caught on something." Andy shifted uncomfortably as if he hated to be the bearer of bad news. "Ended up being a taxi that had been reported missing on Saturday. We towed it out and found two bodies in the trunk. A male and a female."

"Shit!" Nessa slapped her hand on the table. "Do we know who they were? Any idea how long they were in there?"

"Bayside Taxi reported a cab and driver missing. They said the driver dropped off a passenger at the Riverview Hotel on Saturday afternoon, and then just dropped off their tracking system."

All eyes turned to Nessa at the mention of the Riverview Hotel.

"We better get down to Mosquito Lake," Nessa said. "I have a real bad feeling about this."

* * *

The taxi hadn't been in the water for more than forty-eight hours, but it looked as if it had been brewing in the murky water for months.

Algae, clumps of pondweed, and streaks of slimy green muck covered the car as it sat baking in the summer sun.

Nessa stood on the bank of Mosquito Lake next to Vanzinger and Jankowski. She circled to the open trunk and peered inside, gasping as her eyes fell on the neon pink dress. It was wet and smeared with mud, but she recognized it as the one Jane Bishop had been wearing on Saturday. The body's thatch of white hair confirmed her fears.

"That's Jane Bishop, Portia Hart's agent," Nessa said, unable to tear her eyes away. "She was at the station just the day before yesterday. She knew Portia had been killed..."

Spinning around, Nessa ran for the edge of the lake. She bent over just as the remains of her morning coffee spewed into the dark water. She wiped her mouth on the back of her hand.

"Sorry about that," she murmured, looking up at Vanzinger, who had come to stand beside her. "I haven't done that in years."

"I feel like upchucking every time I see a dead body," Vanzinger muttered. "I think most decent people do."

The queasy feeling in her stomach remained as Nessa made her way back to the trunk. She wasn't done yet. Her first thought had been for Jane Bishop, but she now needed to find out who the other victim had been.

Forcing herself to look inside, Nessa saw that a man lay underneath Jane's pitiful remains. The frozen grimace on his face was visible through the grimy plastic bag that covered his head.

"I guess we've found the taxi driver that was reported missing," Nessa said, noting the wedding ring on the man's limp hand. "At least we'll be able to let his family know what happened."

Jankowski stared into the trunk with a stony expression.

"But will they ever be able to understand *why* it happened?"

The anguish in his voice was palpable. Nessa reached out and put a hand on his arm, knowing he must be thinking of Gabby. He'd found the battered body of his ex-wife only months before, and the sight of the senseless carnage in the trunk had likely conjured painful memories. The sound of wheels on gravel caused Nessa and Jankowski to turn around. A black Audi was bumping down the road toward them.

"What's he doing here?" Nessa asked as Hunter stepped out of the sedan, followed by a white Labrador retriever.

"How the hell did he find out about this?" Jankowski's face tightened into an angry scowl. "The last thing we need is the press contaminating the scene before we've had a chance to secure it."

"I've got this," Vanzinger said, jogging toward Hunter.

Holding up a big hand, he called out in a commanding voice.

"Halt right there, Mr. Hadley. This is an active crime scene."

The loud shout coming from the advancing detective startled the white Lab, who skittered back toward the Audi and huddled beside the back tire. Vanzinger skidded to a stop a few yards away.

"It's okay, Gracie," Hunter soothed, glaring over at Vanzinger as he knelt by the trembling dog. "I won't let anybody hurt you, girl."

Nessa took a few careful steps forward, then stopped, not wanting to scare the traumatized animal. She remembered the friendly Lab from the day before.

"Hi, Gracie." Nessa inched closer, holding out a hand. "Remember me? We meet yesterday."

Watching her with cautious eyes, Gracie didn't move.

"She has PTSD." Hunter stroked the dog's white fur with a big hand. "She was with me in Kabul when there was an...an incident. Let's just say she doesn't like loud noises and shouting."

"Sorry about that, man," Vanzinger said, maintaining his distance. "But this is an active scene and we're stilling trying to secure the perimeter."

Hunter looked past Nessa and Vanzinger to the taxi. His eyes gleamed with interest, but he dragged his gaze back to Nessa.

"I heard the call on the police scanner," he admitted. "Gracie and I were already in the car so I thought we might as well–"

"You thought you'd try to cash in on someone's grief?" Jankowski snapped, walking up to stand beside Vanzinger. "How typical."

Hunter ignored Jankowski's insult. He kept his eyes on Nessa.

"Have you looked into the info I gave you on Nick Sargent?"

Nessa shook her head. The task of following up with the Channel Six reporter was on her list, but she hadn't had the chance to get to it yet. She turned to Vanzinger and Jankowski to explain.

"Nick Sargent stayed at the Riverview Hotel the night Portia Hart died, and a witness in the neighborhood placed him at Molly Blair's house before her murder."

Vanzinger cocked an eyebrow.

"You mean that reporter on Channel Six?"

Nessa nodded, then turned back to Hunter.

"We've got our hands full, as you can see, but as soon as I get the chance, I'll pursue it," Nessa assured him. "We've got a witness that saw the man who killed Molly Blair. I'll see if she can identify Nick."

Hunter didn't look convinced, but he opened the passenger door for Gracie and waited for her to jump in.

"Our van will be out here pretty soon," Hunter said, walking around to the driver's side. "Along with Channel Six, I imagine. The public has a right to know what's going on in this town."

As the sleek black car departed, Nessa called over to Andy Ford, who still stood guard by the taxi.

"Andy, I need to talk to Lexi Marsh. Can you bring her down to the station later this afternoon once you're done here?"

"Oh, I guess you haven't heard then." Alarm filled the young officer's freckled face, and he couldn't quite meet her eyes.

"Heard what, Andy?"

"We lost Lexi Marsh, Chief," Andy admitted. "We haven't been able to locate her since yesterday afternoon."

"She's been missing for twenty-four hours?"

Recalling Hunter's suspicions about Nick Sargent, Nessa glared at Andy, hoping it wasn't already too late.

"Call Eddings and tell him to bring Nick Sargent in for questioning right away," she ordered, her voice urgent. "Track him down and put him in an interview room until we can get back to the station."

She thought for a minute, then pulled out her phone. There was one person who might be able to help find Lexi Marsh.

"Frankie? This is Nessa. I think we're gonna need your help."

CHAPTER THIRTY-NINE

Thunder clouds had begun to gather in the east when Frankie and Barker arrived at the modest apartment complex on Channel Drive. Lexi's apartment was on the ground floor, and it looked the same as all the other drab units. The doors and windows were closed, and there was no sign that anything was amiss.

"Lexi? It's me, Frankie."

Knocking on the front door, Frankie wondered if Lexi was holed up inside, too stoned, or maybe too scared of the police, to answer. When the door remained closed, and he heard nothing from inside, he tried again, in a louder voice.

"Come on, Lexi. I just want to know you aren't dead in there."

Barker dropped a big hand on Frankie's shoulder.

"Let's go check around back," he suggested. "If there was a patrol car out front, I'm guessing that's the exit she'd have taken."

The back of the apartment building faced an uneven parking lot. Frankie saw that each unit had one small window. He counted across until he found Lexi's window, which appeared to be closed.

Striding across the patch of rough grass, Barker put a finger under the window frame and pulled. The frame popped out and tumbled to the ground. Barker put his hands on the window and looked back at Frankie.

"You ready to go in if this opens? Cause I doubt I'll fit."

Frankie automatically nodded, but his heart began to thump in his chest. He was suddenly sure that Lexi Marsh's dead body would be waiting for him in the apartment. A clap of thunder overheard sent him scurrying toward Barker.

"Okay, here it goes."

Barker slid the window up without any effort and stepped aside.

Leaning his head through the open window, Frankie called out.

"Lexi? It's me, Frankie. You okay in there?"

The air in the apartment was stifling. He pulled his head out and looked back at Barker.

"Man, it's fuckin' hot in there. The air conditioning must have been shut off for a couple of days."

"You go in and look around." Barker gestured to the open window. "Just be careful and I'll meet you at the front door."

Gripping the windowsill, Frankie hoisted his long, thin body up and over the ledge. He twisted around and lowered his feet onto the carpeted floor. Looking back, he saw that Barker was already gone.

The room was dim, and the air was even hotter than Frankie had imagined. He was dripping with sweat before he'd reached the bedroom door. His hand grazed a light switch in the hall, and he turned it on, illuminating the apartment's shabby interior.

His eyes darted around the room, expecting to see Lexi's limp body at any minute. But the room was empty. He surveyed the few pieces of furniture in the living room, then moved to the tiny kitchen. The refrigerator was empty, and the trashcan held only a crumpled cigarette pack and a discarded pill bottle.

Pounding on the front door reminded him that Barker was still waiting outside. He crossed to the door and turned the deadbolt.

"I thought you might have fallen asleep in there," Barker looked past Frankie into the apartment. "What did you find?"

"I found out this poor girl needs some help," Frankie said. "Look at this place. It's fucking depressing."

243

"Well, we gotta find her first, before we can help her."

Barker pushed past him, opening closet doors, and looking under the bed and the sofa. After a few fruitless minutes, he walked back to the front door.

"Okay, she's not here," he said, his voice grim. "And from the looks of it, she never really settled in, like she didn't plan to stay here long. Maybe she just decided it was time to move on."

As Barker turned to leave, Frankie hesitated. He looked back at the bleak room, then crossed to the trashcan. He bent and pulled out the crumpled cigarette pack. Looking inside, he saw two broken cigarettes had been left in the pack. He wondered how hard it had been for Lexi to throw them away.

She was trying to do better. She hadn't given up yet. Neither will I.

* * *

Frankie hated to go back to Nessa with bad news, but he had to let her know that Lexi was still missing as soon as possible. Maybe she could put out a missing person bulletin, although he had little hope that it would do any good if some psycho really had taken her.

Pushing through the doors of the WBPD, Frankie saw that the lobby was empty, except for the uniformed cop sitting at the front desk. He followed Barker up to the counter and waited while the ex-detective asked if Nessa was back yet.

"No, the chief is out at a scene," the desk sergeant said, nodding to the waiting area. "You can have a seat and wait if you like."

Frankie folded his long body into a wobbly metal chair while Barker paced back and forth in front of him.

"Will you sit down, man? You're making me dizzy," Frankie complained. "It's not gonna do any good to–"

He stopped in mid-sentence as the front door banged open and a tall man with thick black hair and a smooth, clean-shaven face stalked into the room. A uniformed officer followed him inside, looking toward the desk sergeant with nervous eyes as if he might need help with the obviously irate man.

The tall man looked familiar, but Frankie couldn't place him. Barker caught Frankie's eye and murmured, "That's Nick Sargent."

Frankie frowned, clearly confused.

Sinking in the chair next to him, Barker tried again.

"That's the reporter at Channel Six, Nick Sargent."

The reporter strode to the front and leaned over the counter.

"I've been summoned here by Chief Ainsley," Nick said, his voice rising with indignation. "And I don't have all day."

"I'm here, Mr. Sargent, now please lower your voice."

Nessa stood in the doorway, flanked by detectives Vanzinger and Jankowski. Frankie was relieved to see the big men. They'd saved his ass on more than one occasion in the last year, and he knew they wouldn't let the obnoxious reporter disrespect Nessa.

Turning to the officer beside Nick, Nessa pointed toward the door leading into the back.

"Thanks for bringing Mr. Sargent in for me, Officer Eddings. Go ahead and show him to an interview room and I'll be there shortly."

Nick shook his head and banged his fist on the counter.

"Oh, no, I'm not sitting around here while my competition scoops the story at Mosquito Lake," he insisted. "Just tell me what you want and let me be on my way."

"Calm down, Mr. Sargent, or should I call you Mr. Sokolov?"

Nick's face flushed a bright pink, but his angry scowl remained.

"My professional name and my given name should be of no concern to anyone but me. Now, why did you want to speak to me?"

"I wanted to know if you have information on the whereabouts of Alexandra Marsh. She's missing, and I have reason to believe you might know where she is."

Arranging his face into an ugly smirk, Nick sighed.

"I don't know anyone named Alexandra Marsh, Chief Ainsley. Whoever your source is, they must have mistaken me for someone else. Now, if that's all, I'll be on my-"

"She goes by Lexi," Nessa said, ignoring his denial. "And she was a regular visitor at Molly Blair's house."

Nessa paused, then stepped closer to Nick.

"I hear you were, too. I also know you were a guest at the Riverview Hotel the night Portia Hart died."

Frankie thought he saw fear flash in Nick's eyes before the reporter looked away in mock disdain.

"Who have you been talking to, Chief Ainsley?" Nick's voice was ice cold. "Let me guess...*Hunter Hadley?* You know he's got a grudge against me, right?"

Nessa didn't respond. She glanced over at Frankie and raised her eyebrows. He grimaced and shook his head. He hadn't found Lexi.

Turning to Vanzinger and Jankowski, Nessa gestured to the door.

"Will you guys show Mr. Sargent back to the interview room? I just need to take care of something, then I'll join you."

The detectives hustled Nick into the back as Nessa came over to stand in front of Frankie and Barker.

"I just got a text from the crime scene lab. They found drugs at Molly's house, and the tests have confirmed large quantities of Oxytocin, Fentanyl, and heroin. It was a serious operation. I'm worried Lexi's addiction may be worse than I thought."

Her grim words gave Frankie an idea. He jumped up and began to pull Barker toward the door.

"Come on, partner," he urged. "I think I know where Lexi is."

CHAPTER FORTY

L exi ran down the dimly lit stairs, her heels clicking a frantic rhythm that matched the erratic beating of her heart as the man's footsteps grew louder, descending toward her like an avalanche rolling down from a mountain.

Jerking awake, Lexi heard the faint rumble of thunder somewhere in the distance. She tried to sit up, but her head connected with metal, and she slumped back onto the thin carpet beneath her, mind spinning as she realized she was still trapped in the car trunk.

Her throat was dry and painfully sore; she tried to draw in short, shallow breaths, but the little air that remained was thick with the putrid scent of decay. The dead body behind her was starting to rot, and the terrible heat in the car would only accelerate the process.

Refusing to give in to her panic, Lexi maneuvered her hand into her pocket and pulled out her phone, but the screen remained dark. Despair set in as she remembered the battery was dead. Letting the phone slip from her fingers, she felt her hope draining away.

No, I can't give up. Not yet. I'm still alive. I'm still here.

She forced herself to focus on the distant sound of the thunder. A storm was finally brewing, and the long, hot dry spell may be coming to an end. She imagined the feel of the cool raindrops on her face and on her skin, just like when she'd been a little girl, catching the raindrops on her tongue and splashing along in the muddy puddles.

At first the sound of a man's voice close by seemed to be part of another dream. Had she fallen asleep again? No, she definitely heard someone talking. Her blood ran cold at the thought that maybe the man who'd attacked her had returned to finish the job.

Has he come back for me? Is he out there now, preparing his final act?

Clenching her fists at her side, Lexi braced herself for whatever might come. Better to end her life fighting than to let herself just fade away into the darkness around her.

"I bet she came here looking for more pills."

The voice sounded familiar, but it wasn't the hateful voice of the man that had killed Molly. It was Frankie. She was sure of it.

"Nessa said Molly Blair had a shitload of drugs, so I'm thinking Lexi was hoping she left some in the house."

Opening her mouth, Lexi tried to call out, but her throat was too dry; only a raspy gasp escaped. Tears slid down her cheeks as she listened, desperate for Frankie to say something else, but she heard only another roll of thunder somewhere far to the east.

She attempted to lift her right arm, but it was stiff and cramped. It took all her strength to raise her fist and bang it against the trunk's metal lid. The muffled sound was pitifully weak, and Lexi knew there was little chance anyone outside the car would notice the soft noise. There had to be another way.

My legs are strong. If I can get them in the right position, maybe I can....

But her legs had fallen asleep; they were numb and heavy, and when she moved them, they exploded with excruciating pain. Fighting back a wave of dizziness, Lexi used her foot to explore the trunk, careful to avoid the dead body behind her.

Her toes pushed against a metal bar; it shifted at the pressure, and she recognized the cylindrical shape of a tire iron.

Gripping the tool with her toes, she inched her leg up, dragging it toward her hand. After several agonizing seconds, she gripped the tire iron in her hand and strained, her arm trembling with the effort.

"I was sure she was gonna be here, man," Frankie said, passing close by the car. "I mean where else could she go to get a fix?"

The disappointment in his voice puzzled her.

Why does he care? And why hasn't he given up on me? Everyone else has. My father. My mother. Even my so-called friends. Why not him?

She didn't understand Frankie's determination to help her, but she knew this might be the last chance for her to help herself. Tightening her hand around the tire iron, Lexi wrenched her hand up, angling the end of the tool toward the metal lid. A hollow *clang* sounded in the darkness.

Gritting her teeth, Lexi once again yanked the tire iron up as hard as she could. She was rewarded with another loud *clang*. She tried to lift her hand again, but the tire iron slipped from her sweaty grip, falling onto the carpet with a soft thud.

"You hear that?" Frankie asked, his voice coming closer. "I thought I heard something in the garage."

"There's nobody in there. I already looked."

Another deeper voice crushed Lexi's hope. Opening her mouth, she tried to scream, straining against the painful knot in her throat.

"Look, there's another car in here. The Jag was here yesterday, but this Toyota wasn't." Frankie sounded confused. "Who would park a car at a fucking crime scene?"

Knowing it might be her last chance, Lexi felt around beneath her, searching for the tire iron. Her frantic fingers settled over her phone.

It may not turn on, but I can still use it to call for help.

Grasping the phone in her hand she struck it against the lid again and again. The *clink, clink, clink* reverberated inside the trunk and echoed in Lexi's ears. Shaking from the exertion, she felt her grip on the phone loosen. As the phone fell away, the lid popped open, letting in a flood of light that burned her eyes.

Frankie stared in at her with wide eyes, and she glimpsed a big man standing next to him. Then strong hands were lifting her out of the trunk and lowering her onto the smooth pavement of the garage floor.

"Lexi? What the hell happened to you?" Frankie smoothed her damp hair back from her face. "Who did this to you?"

"There's another woman in here," the big man said, his voice grim. "Looks like she's been dead a few days. I'll call 911."

Lexi tried to speak, but her mouth and throat wouldn't cooperate. She finally managed to rasp out a soft moan, but Frankie shook his head, his face tight with worry.

"Don't try to talk." He smiled down at her. "The ambulance will be here soon, and everything will be okay."

She raised her eyes to his as her last bit of energy faded away, and with a final exhale, she gave in to the darkness.

CHAPTER FORTY-ONE

As the call rolled to voicemail again, Hunter slammed his phone on the desk. He'd been trying to reach Veronica for hours and she wasn't picking up. Fear kindled in his chest, and he stalked to the window to stare out at the darkening sky.

Has something happened to her? Is she in some kind of trouble again?

Finn called to him from the doorway.

"Still no word from Veronica?"

Looking back at Finn, Hunter shook his head. No use pretending he wasn't worried. Jordie's son was as smart and intuitive as his father had been, and the worry was clearly etched on his face.

"I have an idea." Finn stepped into the office and closed the door behind him. "Although Veronica would kill me for saying this."

Hunter raised his eyebrows, open to any suggestion that might take his mind off Veronica's disappearing act.

"I think we should call her mother." Finn held up his hand at Hunter's instant frown. "Hear me out. Maybe her mother knows where Veronica is, and if not...well, she can find out."

"What do you mean...she can find out?"

Finn grinned.

"Hey, mothers know everything, right?"

The playful words hit Hunter in the gut, ripping open a wound that had festered inside him ever since he'd been old enough to realize that everyone but him seemed to have a mother.

251

Hiding the unexpected jolt of pain, Hunter turned away.

"Look, if you're just fooling around, then I'd rather be alone."

"I'm serious," Finn insisted. "I mean about asking Veronica's mother for help. I overheard her complaining that her mother is always tracking her on the *Find My Phone* app."

A spark of interest ignited at the possibility that Veronica's mother may be able to tell them exactly where Veronica had gone. If nothing else, it could relieve his fear that she might have continued chasing the story and gotten in over her head.

"Okay," Hunter agreed. "It can't hurt to ask."

"Actually, if Veronica finds out what we're about to do, she'll probably go batshit," Finn conceded. "But we'll worry about that when and if the time comes. Now, who's going to make the call?"

Hunter tried to picture his old history teacher's face. Ling Lee had been a popular teacher at Willow Bay High when he'd been a student. Eventually, she'd been promoted to her current role as the school's principal, but from everything he'd heard, she was still popular with both the student and their parents.

"A lifetime ago Ms. Lee used to be my high school history teacher," he told Finn, realizing he hadn't thought about his high school years in a long while. "So, I guess it'd make more sense for me to call the school. I'm pretty sure summer school is in session."

Feeling more nervous than he'd expected, he picked up his phone and googled Willow Bay High School. Moments later he was waiting on hold for Ms. Lee to pick up.

"This is Principal Lee. Who's calling?"

The voice on the other end of the line sounded strangely familiar. Almost two decades had passed since he'd heard it, and he suddenly felt like an awkward teenager again.

"This is Hunter Hadley, Ms. Lee. Veronica's station manager. I was hoping to talk to you about your daughter."

"Oh dear, what's happened to Ronnie?" Ling's voice morphed from polite to panicked within seconds. "Is she okay?"

Startled by Ling's reaction, Hunter quickly reassured her.

"As far as I know your daughter is fine," he said, glancing at Finn, who stood over him with an expectant expression. "It's just that when she left the station this morning she was rather upset. I've been worried about her, and she won't answer her phone. I was wondering if you might know where she is."

"No, I haven't been at home," Ling replied. "And Ronnie gets mad if I call too often to check on her, especially on a big news day. So, I haven't tried to reach her."

Before Hunter could ask his next question, Ling answered it.

"I'll try her now. Hold on, please."

Cheerful music flooded through the phone, and Hunter held it away from his ear. It sounded like the marching band version of Willow Bay High's fight song. A few seconds later the music abruptly stopped, and Ling was back on the line.

"She's not picking up." Ling sounded as disappointed as Hunter felt. "But that isn't unusual. She probably thinks I'm calling to nag."

Seeing Hunter's defeated expression, Finn whispered loudly, "Ask her to use her *Find My Phone* app."

Hunter cleared his throat and waved Finn away.

"I'm sorry to cause you unnecessary worry, Ms. Lee, and I'm sure everything is fine, but with everything going on in town, I was hoping you might-"

"Get to the point, Mr. Hadley," Ling demanded. "Is there something I can do that might help my daughter?"

The principal's reprimand stung.

"Yes, Ms. Ling. You can track Veronica using the *Find My Phone* app. Just to let us all know where she is, and that she's okay."

Hunter waited for a response, hoping Ling wouldn't accuse him of stalking her daughter or invading her family's privacy. He already felt guilty of both, but instinct was telling him that something was wrong. He couldn't just let it go, could he?

He heard Ling's sharp intake of air.

"Oh, that's strange. Ronnie's heading east on the turnpike. Why would she be crossing the state?"

Thinking through the information that had come to light in the last few days, Hunter tried to imagine where Veronica was going.

Didn't Portia Hart and her brother live on Florida's east coast?

A more disturbing possibility occurred to him. He tapped the *Mute* button and looked at Finn.

"Where does Julian Hart live?"

"A little place called Hart Cove," Finn said, without hesitation. "It's a beach town just north of Palm Beach. I think the town was named for its founder, Portia's great-grandfather."

Unmuting the phone, Hunter cleared his throat.

"Ms. Lee, I think Veronica must be following up on the Portia Hart story," Hunter said. "She may be trying to get an interview with Portia's brother, who lives on the coast."

"All by herself?" Ling sounded scandalized. "Shouldn't she have taken along someone on the camera crew to film it? Ronnie told me yesterday that you'd hired a new guy. Someone much better than the last guy."

Glancing at Finn, Hunter agreed.

"Yes, we do have a new guy on the crew, and yes, Veronica should have taken at least one crew member with her. That's our policy, but I think she decided not to follow the rules this time."

He didn't want to admit to Ms. Lee, or to himself, that Veronica most likely wasn't trying to get an interview, and that she no longer considered herself to be working for Channel Ten. She was going to find Julian for more personal reasons.

Hunter's hands clenched into fists at the thought.

"But if she's on assignment, why isn't she answering her phone?" Ling asked. "You said she was upset. How upset was she?"

Suspecting Ling would see through an attempt to sugar-coat the situation, Hunter decided to tell the truth.

"She was upset enough to walk out," Hunter admitted. "And she implied she wouldn't be back."

"But she loves her job," Ling protested, "She would never quit without a good reason."

Hunter bit back the initial response that came to mind.

Maybe she wants to be with Julian. Maybe that's reason enough.

Scolding himself for being a fool, Hunter decided he'd already made a big enough fool out of himself for one day. It was time to man up and move on. Besides, he needed to get back to work. There was too much going on in Willow Bay for him to sit around feeling sorry for himself.

"I'm sure Veronica is fine. She probably wants some time alone."

The words tasted bitter in his mouth, but he wasn't sure what else there was to say. Promising Ling Lee that he would stay in touch, he disconnected the call and turned to see Finn frowning at him.

"Is that what you really think?" Finn asked. "Cause a few minutes ago you were as worried as I am. What's changed?"

Dropping his eyes, Hunter wondered how he had let himself become emotionally involved. He was no longer sure he could trust his own judgment, but he thought maybe there was someone he could trust. Someone who would help him figure out what to do next.

* * *

The lobby of the Willow Bay Police Department was quiet when Hunter and Finn walked in, with Gracie bringing up the rear. The desk sergeant held up a hand.

"No filming inside the station," the officer called out. "And the city's media relations officer is the only one that can give an official statement. All I can tell you is *no comment*."

"Good to know," Hunter replied dryly, "but I need to see Riley Odell. Her assistant said I'd find her here."

"She's in with the chief," the officer acknowledged, eyeing Gracie. "That a service dog? We only let service dogs in here."

Looking down at Gracie, Hunter decided the Lab could be considered an emotional support animal.

And I can be her emotional support human.

Glancing up at the officer, Hunter nodded.

"Yeah, she's an ESA. now can you let Ms. Odell know I'm here?"

Moments later a man opened the door to the back and stuck his head out. Hunter recognized Tucker Vanzinger's red crewcut.

"Come on back, Hadley." He stepped aside to let Hunter through. "Riley's meeting with Chief Ainsley in the briefing room."

He led them down a narrow hall, stopping in front of an open door.

"Come on in, Mr. Hadley."

Nessa Ainsley stood at the front of the room beside a whiteboard. Riley Odell sat at a long table in front of her. Both women smiled when they saw Gracie trot in.

"She looks like she's feeling better," Nessa said, offering the white Lab a smile. "And who've you got here?"

"I'm Finn Jordan." Finn stuck out a hand. "I'm a temporary crew member at Channel Ten."

Hunter shook his head and put a hand on Finn's shoulder.

"Finn's an old family friend," Hunter clarified. "He's doing me a favor by filling in on the news crew. Gracie's his dog."

"How can we help you, Mr. Hadley?" Riley asked, apparently impatient with the pleasantries. "We're in the middle of a manhunt, so I'm sure you can understand we don't have time to-"

"I understand you gave Veronica early information on a story, and that the information was leaked," he said, irritated by her patronizing tone. "Now Veronica is missing in action, and I'm trying to figure out what happened to her."

The women exchanged a long look, then Nessa gestured to the chairs across from Riley.

"Why don't you sit down and tell us what's happened."

"I don't want to sit down," he replied, stepping further into the room. "I want to know more about this Xavier Greyson character you told Veronica about. I want to know if he could be a threat to her."

Riley sat back in her chair and sighed.

"Everything we say in this room is strictly off the record."

Nodding his agreement, Hunter waited.

"Xavier Greyson is a threat to everyone he meets, Mr. Hadley. He's a con man who we believe has killed at least five people that we know of, and there are likely more victims out there."

Hunter digested the information with growing concern.

"I told Veronica about Greyson because we were planning to release a public appeal as soon as we had a sketch available," Riley explained. "Unfortunately, someone saw Veronica's notes, and the story was leaked to Channel Six. Now Greyson knows we're after him, but nobody knows what he looks like."

Moving closer, Finn cleared his throat.

"Sorry to interrupt, but we're trying to find Veronica. This guy wouldn't have any reason to go after *her*, would he?"

Riley shrugged.

"I don't see why he would. We believe Greyson's motive was money. He targeted Portia Hart for her money, and then eliminated anyone he thought was going to get in his way."

"What about Julian Hart?" Hunter asked. "Could he be in danger?"

It was Vanzinger's turn to interject.

"As Riley said, Greyson's driving motive seems to be financial. He was after Portia's billions, only she didn't have that kind of money anymore."

Vanzinger looked to Nessa as if seeking permission to continue; she gave a slight nod.

"According to Julian Hart, Portia had lost most of her inheritance," Vanzinger said. "He'd helped her get back on her feet financially, but we think Greyson may have killed Portia when he found out she didn't have the kind of money he was counting on."

"You think Greyson may still try to get that money from Portia's brother?" Finn asked.

The room was silent for a long beat. Nessa turned to Riley.

"Would Greyson go after Julian?"

"I hadn't thought about it," Riley admitted, "but I guess he might make one last play for that billion-dollar jackpot."

She turned to Hunter and Finn.

"From what we can tell, Xavier Greyson has tried to kill anyone who gets in his way. Julian Hart would be fair game."

"Then we better warn him," Nessa said, pulling out her phone.

She scrolled through her contact list and tapped on a number, then put the phone on speaker and waited. After six rings the call rolled to voice mail.

"Mr. Hart, this is Chief Ainsley in Willow Bay. I have reason to believe Xavier Greyson may be headed your way. Please return my call when you get this message. And please be careful. Greyson's a dangerous man."

Spinning on his heel, Hunter crossed to the door.

"We think Veronica's driving toward Hart Cove right now to find Julian," he said, as Finn and Gracie scrambled to follow him. "Xavier Greyson may have the same idea."

"Wait, Mr. Hadley," Riley called out. "If there's even the slightest chance Xavier Greyson is going after Julian Hart, then you need to stay away. We just told you...he kills anyone who gets in his way."

"Then I can't let Veronica get in his way," Hunter said, stepping into the hall. "I'm going after her."

Riley continued to object, following him through the lobby and to the curb where his Audi was parked. Hunter looked back to see Finn and Gracie on the sidewalk.

"You stay and take care of Gracie," he said to Finn. "I'll be back."

"Hadley, you know we can't let you go after Greyson on your own," Vanzinger insisted, reaching out a big hand to stop him.

But Hunter wasn't listening. He threw off Vanzinger's hand and hurried around to the driver's side. As he started the engine, the passenger door opened, and Riley Odell jumped in.

"What the hell are you doing?"

"I guess I'm coming with you," she said, buckling her seatbelt.

Suddenly the backdoor flew open and Tucker Vanzinger squeezed his big frame into the backseat.

"All right," he said, grinning at Hunter in the rearview mirror. "Let's do this."

CHAPTER FORTY-TWO

The darkening sky ahead reminded Veronica of her two-year stint as Channel Ten's weather girl, when she'd often wished for rainy days or inclement weather so that she'd have something exciting to report. The end to the state's record-breaking dry spell would be big news.

Forcing herself to concentrate on the road ahead, she blinked back tears. She would no longer be reporting on the weather or anything else. At least not for Channel Ten.

I can't think about that right now. First, I need to make sure Julian's okay. Then, I can decide what to do with the rest of my life.

She'd been driving for more than three hours, and she'd tried to call Julian a dozen times, growing more nervous with every call.

What if Julian already has done something stupid? What'll I do?

Seeing the exit for Hart Cove, Veronica steered the red Jeep onto the ramp and headed east toward the coast. Based on her research, she knew that the only way to reach the tiny beach town was on a two-lane highway that had seen better days.

Most of the town's residents were wealthy northerners who used Hart Cove as their winter retreat. They didn't want to make it easy for the average tourist to discover the secluded beaches.

A winding road led Veronica past large palatial estates set back from the road. These were the beachfront mansions that only a select few could ever afford, and elaborate fences had been constructed to keep unwanted riffraff away.

Rain began to patter against the Jeep's windshield as Veronica pulled up outside a sprawling, oceanfront estate. A tall wrought-iron gate blocked the path to the driveway. It was closed and locked.

Climbing down from the Jeep, Veronica studied the gate's keypad. She pressed the *Call* button and waited, feeling the rain begin to soak into her long, dark hair. Finally, she stepped back and studied the house. Was there another way in? Her eyes fell on the house number: 1001 Hart Cove Way.

Couldn't hurt to try it. Most people use something easy to remember.

She entered 1001 on the keypad, and the gate slowly swung open.

Jumping back in the Jeep, she followed the broad driveway around to the side of the house, ending up in a bricked courtyard with a four-car garage on one side and a scenic path to the beach on the other.

She surveyed the house, expecting the door next to the garage to swing open at any minute, wondering if Julian would be angry that she'd showed up uninvited.

Maybe he'll be glad someone cared enough to check on him.

Stepping onto the brick pavement, Veronica ran through the rain to the garage and peeked in a narrow window on the side of the building. A white Mercedes was parked in one of the bays.

So, he is here. At least I didn't make the trip for nothing.

She scurried to the door beside the garage, taking shelter from the rain on the little covered porch. She assumed the door led to the kitchen, or maybe to the servant's quarters, like in *Downton Abbey*.

There was a decorative window high up on the door, but Veronica couldn't see any light or hear any sound coming from within.

"Julian?" she called, raising her voice over the patter of the rain. "It's me, Veronica. Please, let me in."

Still no movement or sound came from within. Imagining Julian's limp body splayed on the kitchen floor, Veronica clutched the doorknob and turned. To her surprise, the door swung open, revealing a large, dimly lit kitchen.

"Julian? Are you in here?"

The gentle rush of air from the vent in the ceiling was the only sound she heard. Leaving the door slightly open, she moved further into the room, noticing a set of keys had been dropped on the massive kitchen island that dominated the room.

Crossing to the door leading into the hall, she stuck her head through. The house was dark. All the blinds were closed, and no lights were on. She hesitated, feeling her heart begin to thump a panicked beat in her chest.

I never should have come here alone. He could already be dead. Maybe he's upstairs in the bedroom, or in the bathroom like his sister.

Veronica heard a faint *drip, drip, drip* behind her. She spun around, certain that Julian would be standing there, but the kitchen was empty. The dripping continued, and Veronica followed the sound to a large upright freezer.

It was the kind of deluxe appliance her mother always talked about buying but never did, and a dark puddle was growing underneath it, fed by the incessant *drip drip drip* of more liquid from within.

"What is this?" Veronica whispered as she bent to touch the puddle, then recoiled at the cold, viscous texture. "Is that...*blood*?"

Jerking on the freezer's handle, Veronica wrenched the door open. At first, she couldn't register what she was seeing. A man's body had been shoved in the freezer; his face was hidden, but she recognized Julian Hart's khaki pants and long-sleeved shirt.

She reached out a trembling hand to touch his arm. It was frozen stiff and as she watched a spattering of ice crystals fell from his shirt. She looked down to see a puddle of congealing blood on the bottom of the freezer.

"Julian, no, oh my god, no!" Veronica sobbed out the words, backing away. "Why...why did you do this?"

The irrational thought that maybe Julian was still alive, that he couldn't have been in there very long, took hold. She forced herself to once again reach out. She tugged on his rigid, unyielding arm, using the cuff of his sleeve to pull his arm toward her.

The skin on his hand and wrist was as white as snow, and Veronica felt tears fall down her cheek as she held his hand, not knowing what else she could do. She'd arrived too late.

There was no point in sending an ambulance, but she'd have to call 911 anyway. The police would need to investigate. Something terrible had happened in this house, and a man was dead.

Pushing the unwieldy arm back in place, Veronica frowned.

Didn't Julian have a birthmark on his wrist?

She thought back to Saturday night. The night she'd had a drink with Julian in the Riverview Hotel bar. He'd lifted his right hand to take a drink, and she'd seen the heart-shaped mark.

Staring at the man in the freezer, Veronica backed away. She leaned her head against the wall and closed her eyes.

If that's not Julian, then who is it?

"What's wrong, Veronica?"

She screamed as a deep voice broke the silence. Julian was standing in the kitchen doorway.

"You don't...you aren't..."

Her mind reeled, trying to make sense of what was happening.

"No, I'm not dead, and I'm not in the freezer," he said, his voice silky smooth. "I'm also not Julian Hart."

An ugly smirk spread across his face.

"Julian didn't have a birthmark, of course, but I didn't think anyone would notice that I did, not with my long sleeves."

He pushed back his sleeve to reveal the heart beneath it.

"The sleeves were also handy in covering up some very inconvenient scratches," he said, holding up his arm. "Portia Hart was a real fighter."

Veronica gaped at the man who stood before her. Gone was the shy, unsure expression. A victorious sneer rested in its place.

"You're not...Julian," she whispered in shock.

"No, that's the real Julian." He pointed to the freezer. "Poor guy's been in there since Friday. I needed him out of the way while I disposed of Portia."

Veronica swallowed hard and inched backward. The pieces were beginning to fall into place. She'd fallen for this man's evil con, and now she was in terrible danger.

The man chuckled, removing his glasses, and brushing his floppy bangs back out of his eyes. He pointed to a snapshot under a magnet on the refrigerator door. In the photo, Portia Hart stood next to a young man that looked remarkably like the man in front of her.

"Of course, with my new haircut and glasses, I was sure I could fool anyone. Anyone that hadn't met him, that is."

"Then you're...Xavier Greyson?"

His face tightened, and the amused smile faltered.

"That's who I used to be. But none of that matters now that you've made it so very easy for me to *tie up the loose ends*."

His hands tightened into fists as he moved closer, and Veronica prepared to run. If he got his hands on her she'd end up like Portia Hart. He'd make it look as though she killed herself. Pain knifed through her at the thought of her mother's grief.

"From now on, I'm Julian Hart, a man so broken up over his sister's death that he has to jet off to a secluded island to heal."

Knowing it might be her only chance, Veronica jerked the freezer door wide open, smashing it into Xavier's face and leaving it swinging between them as she bolted toward the door.

With frightening speed, Xavier grabbed for her, but she dodged his hand and ran toward the beach. She didn't look back as a bolt of lightning flashed over the water, lighting up the sky.

CHAPTER FORTY-THREE

Tucker Vanzinger's legs were painfully cramped by the time the Audi skidded to a stop in front of the wrought-iron gate. He looked up at the house number to verify they were in fact outside 1001 Hart Cove Way, and then pushed himself out of the car, carefully unfolding his long legs and stretching to revive his circulation.

"I don't see Veronica's Jeep." Hunter looked through the fence toward the house. "Maybe she's already come and gone."

"Well, we're here now." Vanzinger was reluctant to get back in the car even though it had started to rain. "And we need to check on Julian Hart. We've gotta make sure he's okay and warn him about Xavier Greyson."

Hunter opened the trunk of his car and pulled out an umbrella. He popped it open and handed it to Riley.

"I'm not the Wicked Witch of the West, you know. I won't melt," she protested but held the umbrella over her head anyway.

He reached back in and pulled out a raincoat.

"Aren't you a boy scout," Vanzinger grumbled, holding up a big hand to block the rain from his eyes.

"No, I just keep an eye on the weather forecast," Hunter said with a half-smile. "It's part of the job."

"Well, I've got something that may come in even more handy if we do run into trouble." Vanzinger rested his hand on his belt, reassuring himself that his Glock was safely in his holster. "Although the place looks deserted to me."

Hunter took out his phone and began thumbing in a text message. After a few seconds, Vanzinger heard the *Ding* of a reply.

"Ms. Lee says Veronica's phone is showing she's here." Hunter looked back at the house. "The address matches what she's seeing."

Pushing the buzzer on the gate's keypad, Riley paced back and forth, her hands clenched tightly around the handle of the umbrella.

"We can't go in there without a warrant," Riley said in a low voice as if someone might be listening. "That would be illegal."

She looked up at Vanzinger. When he didn't argue, she huffed.

"And we're both outside of our districts. If we do go in, we could even be arrested."

Vanzinger rolled his eyes and put his hands on Riley's shoulders, ducking down to stand with her under the umbrella. He felt inordinately happy when she didn't pull away.

"Listen, we're not gonna get arrested, but we need to make sure Veronica and Julian are okay in there."

He stared down into Riley's dark, guarded eyes, allowing himself to remember how different it had been before he'd ruined everything.

"Wait, Hunter, where are you going?"

Shrugging off Vanzinger's hands, Riley chased after Hunter, who was striding along the gate, looking for an opening. Spotting a low hanging tree, Hunter swung his legs up and balanced on a branch, staring over the fence.

"I don't see anything from here," he called down to Riley. "I'm going over. You guys wait in the car."

"Hell, no, I'm not waiting in the car," Vanzinger boomed. "I didn't drive three hours out here to wait around in a car."

But Hunter had already disappeared. Vanzinger looked over at Riley, who shrugged and nodded.

"Okay, I'm in," she said, putting down the umbrella and scurrying over to the tree. "Give me a boost."

Wrapping his hands around her waist, Vanzinger lifted Riley up and deposited her on the tree branch. He hovered underneath her as she scooted up to the fence and grasped the edge.

"Okay, wait there," Vanzinger commanded, swinging his long legs up and over the branch, which bowed under his weight.

When he looked around, Riley was gone. Cursing under his breath, Vanzinger maneuvered himself onto the fence and looked down, relieved to see it was an easy drop onto the ground below.

He hit the ground, sending muddy water splashing all over his pants and shoes, then surveyed his surroundings. Riley and Hunter waved for him to follow them as they slipped around the house. He stopped short when he came around the corner.

Hunter opened the door to a big red Jeep that was parked in the brick courtyard and slipped inside, out of the rain. Riley jumped into the passenger seat, and Vanzinger was left to wedge himself into the Jeep's narrow backseat. Once he'd wiped the rain out of his eyes, he saw Hunter holding up an iPhone.

"It's Veronica's," he said, his eyes bleak. "So, she may not even be here anymore. Maybe she and Julian took off together."

"If they did, they left the door open."

Vanzinger pointed to the door by the garage, which was blowing back and forth in the rain and wind.

"That can't a good sign." Riley's eyes were wide. "Maybe we should call for help. Ask the local cops to provide back-up."

"We can't wait that long." Hunter's hand was already on the door handle. "Something's definitely wrong here. I've got to find Veronica before it's too late."

A loud crash of thunder sounded overhead, and a bolt of lightning illuminated the sky as Hunter opened the door, then hesitated.

"Did you hear that?"

"Yeah, I heard that. Everybody in town heard that," Vanzinger said, spooked by the lightning. "It's called a thunderstorm."

Holding up a hand, Hunter listened. A faint scream could be heard on the wind. It was coming from the beach.

"Someone's screaming, and I think it's Veronica," Hunter said, lunging out of the Jeep and slamming the door shut.

Vanzinger reached forward and put a hand on Riley's shoulder.

"Stay here and lock yourself in," he ordered. "I'll go find out what's going on and come back."

"Fuck that, Vanzinger," Riley said, opening her door, "I didn't drive three hours to sit around waiting in a car."

She took off running after Hunter as Vanzinger struggled to extricate himself from the compact backseat.

"Next time I call shotgun," Vanzinger muttered, as he started running after Riley.

Another bolt of lightning flashed directly in front of him, but he didn't stop. Riley was out there, and he had a feeling she was going to need him.

CHAPTER FORTY-FOUR

Riley watched Hunter pound down the path toward the beach, knowing she would never be able to keep up with him in her strappy sandals. She skidded to a stop at the top of the wooden stairs that led down to the sand. From her vantage point, she could see a woman in the distance running along the waterline. Wet strands of long, dark hair hung down the woman's back, confirming Riley's fear that it had to be Veronica Lee.

Lightning tore open the sky above her, and Riley cringed against the wooden rail, sure that she would be struck down at any minute. Statistics of how many people were struck by lightning each year ran through her head.

Is it forty people struck by lightning each year, or forty people killed?

All she could remember for sure was that Florida was the lightning capital of the US and that being on the beach in a thunderstorm was an extremely bad idea.

Straining to see Veronica through the downpour, Riley didn't hear the footsteps until they were right behind her. A strong hand gripped her arm, and a deep voice spoke in her ear.

"You're gonna get yourself killed out here."

Shaken by Tucker Vanzinger's sudden appearance, Riley turned to glare at him, then pointed out toward Veronica's receding figure.

"Veronica's running that way, and Hunter's going after her."

Vanzinger strained to see the figures moving down the breach.

"That's not Hunter," Vanzinger said, squinting against the rain. "The man running after Veronica looks like Julian Hart."

Riley followed his gaze toward the man sprinting across the sand. His shirt was plastered to his skin, revealing his muscular back and arms. He was gaining on Veronica with every step.

"There's Hunter," Vanzinger cried, pointing to another figure moving at top speed. "If he catches up, he's going to need help."

Riley watched as Vanzinger gripped his holster and started down the stairs. He stopped and looked back at Riley, trying to yell over the storm, but the wind carried his words away.

"What?" she yelled back, following him halfway down the stairs.

"I said go call for backup," he yelled louder. "And hurry!"

Whirling around Vanzinger charged down the remaining stairs two at a time. She watched him join in the race across the sand, then pulled out her phone and tapped 911. But when she held it to her ear, she couldn't hear anything over the crashing surf and booming thunder.

Climbing to the top of the stairs, she threw one last look at Vanzinger's retreating back, then hurried back toward the house. The back door was still open, and Riley ran inside, immediately slipping on the wet tile floor. She fell and slid against the wall, coming to rest beside a large stainless-steel freezer.

Pushing herself to her feet, she looked down at her hands in confusion. They were smeared with a dark, sticky substance.

What the hell...what is this?

She lowered her gaze to the floor; she was standing in a thick puddle of blood. Recoiling in horror, Riley backed away, banging into the freezer door, which was slightly ajar. She grasped the handle and tried to steady herself as her feet once again slipped out from underneath her.

The door swung fully open as she fell backward, landing hard on her tailbone. Bracing herself against the wall, Riley managed to rise to her feet again and her eyes followed the trail of blood. It appeared to be coming from within the freezer. Leaning forward to take a closer look, Riley heard a faint voice nearby.

She spun around, searching the shadows, just as another flash of lightning lit up the room. Riley saw that the room was empty, even though she could still hear the voice.

"What is your emergency, ma'am? You've reached 911..."

Riley stared at her phone, realizing the voice she'd heard was the 911 operator. Relaxing her shoulders, Riley raised her eyes to the open freezer. A man's body had been stuffed inside. What skin she could see was ghostly white and covered in ice crystals.

Unable to stop herself, Riley emitted a terrified scream.

"Ma'am, where are you, what is your emergency?"

The sound of the operator's calm voice reached through Riley's panic. She held the phone up to her ear with a shaky hand.

"I'm a state prosecutor at the scene of an active crime," she gasped. "There's a...a dead body here...and an officer is now in active pursuit of the...the suspected perp."

"What is your location?"

Riley tried to think. She knew the address. Finally, it came to her.

"It's 1001 Hart Cove Way," she managed to say, her voice still hoarse from screaming. "We need police backup and an ambulance."

Dropping the phone back in her pocket, Riley viewed the body again, unsure who the man was.

Could this be Julian Hart? If it is, who's the man chasing Veronica?

She took several careful steps away from the freezer, leaving smears of blood on the white tile floor, and plucked a snapshot off the refrigerator. A beautiful woman with blonde hair and a happy smile stood beside a man that looked vaguely uncomfortable. He also looked vaguely familiar.

The man looks like Julian Hart, but...he isn't. Is he?

Thinking back to the few times she'd met Julian in person, she could see the resemblance, but it wasn't the same man she was looking at in the photo. She flipped the photo over and read the scrawled names on the back: *Portia and Julian, 2018.*

The truth hit her like a punch. The man that had come to Willow Bay wasn't the real Julian Hart. She looked toward the freezer.

The real Julian Hart is the man in that freezer. And the man who came to Willow Bay is a murderer and a fake.

There was only one person that would have the audacity to pull an outrageous con using the assumed identity of a billionaire, and the willingness to kill anyone who got in the way.

Xavier Greyson had tried to run a high stakes game, and he'd almost gotten away with it. His trail of victims was stunning.

Suddenly she realized that the serial murderer and con man might manage to take a few more lives before he was through. He was out there on the beach running after Veronica Lee, perfectly willing to kill Hunter Hadley and Tucker Vanzinger if the need arose.

The bastard might even get away with it.

Shuddering at the thought of Xavier Greyson evading capture, Riley knew she had to do something. She couldn't let the heartless killer get away. Not again. Not after everyone he'd destroyed.

Moving slowly across the grimy floor, Riley reached the door and ran back into the storm. She felt the rain wash away the blood on her hands and legs, glad to get rid of the sickly-sweet stench.

As she reached the top of the stairs, she heard the wail of sirens in the distance, and looked to the west, wondering how far away they were, and how soon help would arrive.

The figures on the beach were growing smaller, but Riley could see that Veronica was still running, but she was slowing down. The man chasing her was only a few yards behind, and Riley was mesmerized as she watched the surreal scene playing out in front of her. Once again Xavier Greyson was within reach.

The ruthless con man who had stolen Miriam Feldman's money and thrown her body into the water for the fish to eat was right there on the beach in front of her after all these years, and Hunter Hadley and Tucker Vanzinger were right behind him.

After everything he's done, he can't get away this time, can he?

Her anxiety mounted as she saw Veronica stumble and fall into the crashing surf.

CHAPTER FORTY-FIVE

Veronica's heart pounded like a jackhammer in her chest as she ran through the sand. Her legs were getting heavier and weaker with every step, and exhaustion was overtaking fear as her strength began to drain away.

Glancing back in desperation, she saw that Xavier Greyson was only a few yards behind her, his handsome face twisted into a terrible grimace as he ran. Adrenaline flooded through her at the sight, fueling a momentary burst of speed.

Then the sand underneath her seemed to give way, and she stumbled and fell forward into the choppy water.

Pushing herself onto her knees, Veronica tried to stand just as Xavier grabbed a thick handful of hair and forced her further into the water, pushing her head down into the salty waves as she fought to keep her face above the surface.

Panic bloomed in her chest, and she clawed at the iron fist that held her underwater. Desperate for air, she kicked out at Xavier's legs, but the heavy pull of the water absorbed most of the force.

Struggling back to the surface, she gulped in a mouthful of saltwater and sea air. A flash of lightning lit up the sky above her, and Veronica saw the savage look of triumph on Xavier's face as he pushed her head under again. Too weak to resist, Veronica felt her body give in to the pull of the waves.

A strange calm settled over her as she let her body go limp.

So, this is it. This is how it all ends.

Her mother's face floated in the water next to her, the familiar eyes no longer worried, a gentle smile turning up the corners of her mouth as she spoke in a voice that soothed away all fear.

Everything will be all right now, Ronnie. You can let go. The pain and the struggle are behind you now.

Comforted by the gentle words, Veronica felt herself drifting freely with the tide, all resistance fading away.

Then a blinding flash of light above her opened the heavens and illuminated the water, and the hand in her hair was suddenly gone. Lifting her head out of the water, Veronica wiped saltwater out of her burning eyes and squinted up at the big man who had suddenly materialized beside her.

Hunter Hadley looked down, his face tight with anger and fear.

"Get out of here," he shouted, pointing toward the shore.

She stood on shaky legs, lifting her face to Hunter just as Xavier Greyson rose out of the water behind him.

"Watch out!" she screamed. "He's behind you!"

Spinning around, Hunter crouched in a defensive posture as Xavier Greyson sprang forward to tackle him. Veronica saw both men tumble into the water. She splashed toward the shore on trembling legs, then turned to see Xavier and Hunter still wrestling in the foaming waves.

She took a few stumbling steps up the beach, knowing she had to get help, but her stomach heaved, and she bent and retched out a mouthful of saltwater. As she wiped her mouth on her soggy sleeve, Veronica felt a big hand fall on her shoulder.

Too exhausted to scream, she twisted her head to see a muscular man looming over her. Relief flooded through her as she recognized Detective Vanzinger.

"Thank God you're here," she gasped, coughing up another mouthful of sandy water. "He's trying to kill him..."

But her relief was quickly replaced by fear as Vanzinger motioned for her to step out of the way, and she saw the big Glock in his hand. It was the same model that her mother had taught her to shoot at the gun range.

"No! Don't shoot!"

The scream ripped through her throat as she saw Hunter's broad back in clear range of Vanzinger's weapon.

"If you miss, you'll hit Hunter!"

Her words evaporated into the wind, but Vanzinger hesitated as the men continued to struggle in the water.

"Shit!"

He lowered his weapon and splashed forward, circling the men as the waves crashed over them.

Resisting the urge to collapse onto the wet sand, Veronica forced her feet to move, willing her legs to carry her back into the water.

I have to get Hunter out of the way so Vanzinger can get a clear shot.

Rain beat down in relentless fury, pelting her skin and drenching her hair, which hung in heavy, wet strands around her face.

Ignoring the water churning around her knees, she grabbed out and caught hold of Hunter's shirttail just as a wave smashed over her, tossing her toward the shore.

As she sputtered and fought to regain her feet, she realized she was still holding tight to Hunter's shirt. He erupted from the water next to her, spitting out a mouthful of saltwater as he spun to see Xavier charging toward Vanzinger.

The explosion from the big Glock echoed over the water like a clap of thunder just as a bolt of lightning lit up the cloud-darkened sky.

Xavier jerked backward. A spray of blood stained the shifting water around him a garish red, then washed away into the ocean's depths as if it had never existed. He vanished into the water, then surfaced again as a violent wave propelled his limp body onto the shore.

As the wave receded, Veronica's eyes widened in fascinated horror; a trickle of blood seeped out of a crimson hole in Xavier's forehead, soaking into the wet sand beneath him.

"Tucker!"

Startled by the anguished cry from behind her, Veronica spun around to see Riley Odell racing across the sand toward the water. The prosecutor didn't hesitate as she reached the water's edge. She plunged forward into the waves.

Only then did Veronica realize that Detective Vanzinger was gone. Before she could react, Hunter's voice sounded in her ear. She felt his strong hand grip hers as he dragged her toward the spot where Vanzinger had last been standing.

"Must have been...the...lightning," Hunter gasped. "He was holding...the gun, and then he just...went down. We've got to find him."

He dove headfirst into a breaking wave. Seconds later Riley emerged to take a long gasping breath.

"I...can't...find him," Riley panted between sobs. "He's gone!"

Sucking in a deep lungful of hot, salty air, Veronica prepared to dive under just as Hunter shot up out of the water. One arm was wrapped around Vanzinger's broad chest, the other arm was already pushing through the water toward shore.

Veronica splashed over to Vanzinger's side, taking hold of his limp arm. The big detective's water-logged body was unbelievably heavy as she helped Hunter keep his head out of the relentless waves.

Assisted by the incoming tide, they finally deposited the big detective onto the safety of the sand. Veronica's trembling legs gave out underneath her and she sank onto her knees. She felt the warmth of Hunter's body next to her and looked over as he checked Vanzinger for a pulse.

Hunter's face was grim as he gave a slight shake of his head.

"Is he breathing?" Riley asked above them in a ragged voice.

Tilting Vanzinger's head back, Hunter leaned forward and listened, his eyes resting on Vanzinger's chest, watching for the tell-tale rise and fall, but the big man was motionless.

"He's not breathing," Hunter croaked, then cleared his throat. "Let's start CPR. Veronica, you breathe. I'll do the compressions. Riley, you count us through it."

The faint wail of a siren rose over the roar of the ocean as they began working on Vanzinger's motionless body. Veronica kept up a steady stream of breaths, listening to Riley's desperate countdown.

"...and one, and two, and three, and breathe, and one, and two..."

After what seemed like hours, Veronica felt the paramedic's impatient hands on her shoulders and allowed herself to be moved to the side. She watched as they rushed forward with a defibrillator, allowing herself a small hope that the big man could be revived.

"I've got a pulse!"

When she heard the paramedic's excited shout, Veronica collapsed onto her back in the sand and looked up. A patch of blue sky peeked out through the dispersing clouds. The storm was over.

CHAPTER FORTY-SIX

Nessa straightened the stack of folders on her desk and shut down her computer. It was Friday afternoon, and for the first time in ages, she was leaving the office early. She planned to make one quick stop before heading home to spend a relaxing weekend with her family.

That is if you call doing laundry and housework relaxing.

The thought brought a wry smile. She was actually looking forward to a weekend of chores. And maybe she and Jerry would finally get a chance to take Cole and Cooper out for pizza. It would be a pleasant change to have the whole family together after everything she'd been through in the last few weeks.

The initial media circus surrounding Portia Hart's death, and the subsequent discovery of Xavier Greyson's crimes, had resulted in many late nights and working weekends for the WBPD and the prosecutor's office. And with Tucker Vanzinger still recuperating in the hospital, the workload had been unusually heavy.

But as she turned off the lights and closed the door to her office, Nessa felt proud of how her little department had handled the crime spree. Xavier Greyson had been a career con man who had committed multiple homicides over the span of a decade; her team had managed to end his final spree of murder and mayhem.

Melinda Woodhall

Walking the few blocks to Barker and Dawson Investigations, Nessa found Frankie throwing darts at a newly hung board on the wall. Barker sat behind his desk squinting at the computer screen.

"You boys look busy," Nessa teased, dropping into a chair across from Barker. "No more big insurance investigations?"

Frankie rolled his eyes as he threw another dart. It clattered against the wall then fell to the floor.

"Don't even get me started on Maxwell Snake-in-the-Grass Clay," Frankie said. "That man is on my shit list."

"Well, then you'll be happy to hear that the state prosecutor for Hart Cove has decided to charge Mr. Clay with fraud."

Looking somewhat mollified, Frankie threw another dart.

"What about that scumbag, Nick Sargent?" Frankie asked. "You got something on him that'll stick?"

Barker finally looked up from his keyboard.

"I thought you'd cleared him," Barker said, leaning back in his chair. "I mean, Lexi Marsh identified Greyson as the man who attacked her, right?"

Doubt flickered through Nessa's mind.

Is Nick Sargent in the clear? He may not have killed Portia Hart or attacked Lexi, but he's guilty of something. I'd bet my paycheck on it.

She saw Barker watching her with a suspicious frown.

"What, Sargent's not in the clear?" he asked, folding his arms over his chest. "What's he done?"

"I'm not sure," Nessa admitted. "But he was seen hanging around Molly Blair's house. And we know Molly was supplying drugs to Lexi and some of the other girls working for her."

"Oh, so he's that kind of scum," Frankie said, shaking his head. "I bet the loser tried something with Lexi."

Nessa sighed. Nick Sargent felt like a loose end, but they hadn't been able to prove he was guilty of any crime, and he'd denied having any involvement with Molly Blair.

"Lexi Marsh has identified Xavier Greyson as the man she'd seen in the stairwell and the man who attacked her at Molly Blair's house. But she refuses to say anything about Nick Sargent."

Frankie snorted.

"The poor girl's probably too scared to say anything."

He hurled another dart, this time missing the wall completely.

"She was hooked on drugs and turning tricks," he said, picking up the dart and dropping it on his desk. "So, she's gotta be thinking she'll get in trouble if she admits it."

Nessa shook her head.

"No, I don't think that's it. Riley Odell agreed to give Lexi immunity. She's not planning on prosecuting her for illegal possession of prescription drugs or prostitution."

"Okay, but if Lexi talks and you guys try to prosecute Nick Sargent, her activities will be made public." Frankie's voice had taken on a defensive tone. "She probably doesn't want her family and everybody in town finding out what she's been up to."

Barker studied Frankie with knowing eyes.

"You seem to know an awful lot about how Lexi Marsh is feeling. Maybe you can talk to her and convince her to come clean."

Waving the idea away with a skinny arm, Frankie frowned.

"Nah, man. I don't want to get into her business. She's been through enough without having to face some jerk in court."

Nessa thought that the pained expression on Frankie's face didn't match his words. Shooting a sly glance at Barker, Nessa stood and picked up a dart. She stood in front of Frankie and waved it in the air.

"How about we make a bet, Frankie. If I get a bullseye, you'll go talk to Lexi and find out what she knows about Nick Sargent."

"You? Make a bullseye?" He scratched the stubble on his chin. "Okay, but what'll I get if you miss?"

"I'll let you ride in the Charger with my emergency lights on."

Frankie's face lit up at the thought.

"Okay, deal."

Nessa winked at Barker and turned toward the board. With a swift flick of her wrist, the dart flew to the board, sinking smoothly into the bullseye.

"What?" Frankie's eyes were wide. "How'd you do that?"

Barker laughed.

"She hustled you, man. Nessa's won the WBPD's dart tournament three years in a row."

Later, as Barker walked Nessa back toward the station, his mood turned serious. He stopped at the corner and looked over at her.

"I just want you to know that I'm really impressed with how you're handling the new job," he said, holding her gaze. "And as the father of a female who lives in this town, I'm glad we have you out there chasing the bad guys."

Nessa felt her cheeks grow hot.

"You may be a little biased, but...thanks."

Barker shook his head.

"No, I'm not biased. You make a real good chief."

His words replayed in her mind as she headed home, and for the first time, Nessa felt confident that Barker was right.

I guess I do make a pretty good chief after all.

CHAPTER FORTY-SEVEN

The recreation room inside Hope House was quiet. A few residents sat around the television watching a game show, while several others drank coffee and chatted in a corner alcove. Lexi Marsh hovered in the doorway, unsure if she should go inside, or go back to her room.

"I could really use a cup of herbal tea," a voice spoke behind her. "Why don't you join me?"

She turned to see Dr. Regina Horn, the rehab center's director and the woman who had been Lexi's therapist during the two weeks she'd been at the facility.

"Okay," Lexi agreed, glad to have someone to sit with.

Once they were settled into a table by the window, Lexi sipped her tea and tried to think of something to say, but Reggie spoke first.

"You've been here a few weeks now...how are you liking it?"

"I'm getting used to it, I guess." Lexi wondered if that was strictly true. "Although I've been a little restless today."

Sipping from her mug, Reggie seemed to consider the statement.

"Well, restless can be good. That is if it prompts you to go out and make good things happen."

"I feel like I should be doing something productive." Lexi looked around the tranquil room. "And not just sitting around here doing nothing."

Reggie's laugh was infectious, and Lexi found herself smiling, even though she wasn't sure what was so funny.

"You're here building yourself a foundation for a whole new life," Reggie said, still smiling. "And you don't think that's productive?"

Lexi giggled, liking the feeling of being happy. Of not being worried, or sick, or scared.

"I guess you're right," she told Reggie. "I've got a lot of work to do right here before I go out there."

Looking through the big window, Lexi was surprised to see Frankie and his partner walking toward the building.

"That's a friend of mine," Reggie said, looking pleased. "I didn't know Peter was going to come by and see me today."

"Peter?"

"Yes, Peter Barker." Reggie grinned. "He's my *special friend*."

Lexi smiled and looked out the window again, but the men had already disappeared through the front door.

"I've met Frankie," she admitted, feeling awkward. "He's the one who...helped me. I think he's your friend's partner."

Reggie stood, motioning for Lexi to stay seated.

"I'll go see where they are. You wait here."

A sudden urge to flee took over Lexi, and she had already pushed back her chair and was preparing to rise when Reggie reappeared, followed by Frankie and Barker.

"You're not leaving on my account, are you?" Frankie asked. "Cause I promise I won't bite."

His words brought Lexi back to that last night in the Riverview Tower hotel. She'd used the same phrase with the man in Room 1025. The man that Nikolai had called Mr. Murray. The man she had tricked so that Nikolai could take a picture.

"Whoa, I was just kidding around," Frankie said. "You look like you've seen a ghost. Am I really that scary?"

Lexi shook her head, trying to erase the terrible image of the hotel room, never wanting to go back to the place she'd been before Frankie had saved her.

"Thank you," she blurted, surprising both herself and Frankie. "I'm not sure I told you that before. But if I didn't, I should have."

"You don't have to thank me," Frankie said, glancing at Reggie and Barker with an embarrassed grin. "Just being a friend."

Swallowing a lump that had formed in her throat, Lexi shrugged.

"Well, you're one of the only friends I have left now. So...thanks."

Barker slapped a big hand on Frankie's narrow back.

"Listen, Frankie. I'd like to talk to Reggie in private. You think you can sit here and entertain Lexi until we get back?"

Lexi watched Barker and Reggie leave, then turned to Frankie with narrowed eyes.

"Okay, let's skip the part where you pretend they didn't just leave so you can talk to me," she snapped. "What do you want to know?"

Holding up his hands in surrender, Frankie nodded.

"Yeah, yeah, you're right. I wanted to ask you a few questions. So, kill me why don't you."

"Questions about what?"

"About Nick Sargent."

She felt his eyes on her, watching her reaction.

"Let me ask you something first."

"Ask me anything you want," he said, dropping into a chair. "I'm an open book."

"Why'd you come looking for me?" She swallowed hard, trying to keep eye contact. "After I yelled at you and kicked you out...why did you keep trying to save me?"

He opened his mouth, then closed it again. Lifting a skinny hand, he scratched at his chin, then dug in his pocket for a stick of gum.

"Well? I thought you were an open book," she said, curious about his reaction. "I can take it, whatever it is. I mean, if you were interested in hanging out, or whatever-"

"No," he said, his voice firm. "It isn't that. I mean you're a lovely girl and all, but I'm too old, and you're...not old enough."

"Okay...then what?"

Banging his palm on the table, Frankie looked out the window.

"I had a little sister, okay? She was only a kid really when she started getting in trouble. I wasn't there to...to help her out."

Frankie's voice wavered, but his eyes were dry.

"She overdosed. Died on the bathroom floor in some shitty apartment. I mean...she was my little baby sister, you know?"

He ran a hand through his hair and raised haunted eyes to hers.

"Anyway...I was off fucking around when it happened. It still gets to me sometimes. I guess that's why I wanted to help you."

His voice softened as he dropped his eyes and stared at his hands.

"You kinda remind me of her...of my little sister."

Holding back sudden tears, Lexi put her hand on Frankie's hand and squeezed. It felt good to be comforting someone else for a change. She'd been feeling sorry for herself for way too long. It was time to grow up and own her mistakes.

"Nikolai...that's what we called Nick Sargent...he was with me at the hotel the night Portia was killed. We were...running a game on some guy. Nikolai wanted pictures. I don't know why exactly. I think blackmail or something like that."

Frankie stared at her without speaking. She couldn't tell what he was thinking, or if he was judging her. All she knew was that she had to get it all off her chest. Whatever happened, she needed to come clean. Only then would she be free to start over.

Reaching into his pocket, Frankie pulled out another stick of gum and handed it to her.

"This will help with the cravings," he said. "Now tell me the rest."

CHAPTER FORTY-EIGHT

The lobby at Willow Bay General Hospital was busy as Riley walked through the sliding doors and headed for the elevator. The doors slid open to reveal a very pregnant woman and her visibly nervous partner. Riley smiled as the woman shuffled off the elevator. Stepping inside, she pushed the button for the intensive care unit and drew in a nervous breath at the thought of finally seeing Tucker Vanzinger.

While she'd called often to check on Vanzinger's condition, using her position as a state prosecutor to get official updates on his progress, this was the first time she would see him in person since the day on the beach two weeks ago when he'd been struck by lightning.

The elevator opened onto a circular nursing station, which appeared to be deserted. Riley walked down a long, white corridor, stopping outside Room 610. She knocked softly on the door, then pushed it open and peered inside.

Straining to see into the dimly lit room, Riley could make out Vanzinger's red hair on the pillow, and his broad shoulders under the thin white sheet. His eyes were closed, and he appeared to be sleeping peacefully.

Before she could move further into the room, a soft hand clutched her arm. She turned to see a pretty woman in blue scrubs.

"I'm sorry, but we need you to check in at the nursing station before you enter a room," the nurse said, guiding Riley back into the hall. "Are you a family member of the patient?"

Riley hesitated, unsure what exactly she was to Vanzinger.

A work colleague? An old flame? An acquaintance?

Seeing the nurse's expectant stare, Riley took out her ID badge and flashed it at the woman.

"I'm a state prosecutor, and I'm working on a case that involved Detective Vanzinger. I'm here to check on him."

The nurse frowned.

"Mr. Vanzinger's not well enough to answer any questions," she said, her back stiffening. "So, if you're trying to interrogate him, I suggest you-"

"No, I'm not going to interrogate him," Riley protested, her voice wavering. "I just want to make sure...he's okay. I was with him when he was on the beach and...well, I'm worried about him."

The nurse studied Riley's wan face, then relented. She relaxed her shoulders and motioned for Riley to follow her.

"He has been doing much better lately," the nurse said, entering Riley's name in her log. "I'm sure he'll be happy to have a visitor."

"Last time I called to check they said his injuries were neurological in nature. What does that mean exactly?"

Handing her a visitor's badge, the nurse began walking back toward Vanzinger's room.

"Well, it's hard to say what the long-term effects will be, but right now he's still suffering some memory loss, and has bouts of pain and dizziness. Hopefully, those symptoms will abate in time."

Pushing the door open, the nurse waved Riley in.

"There's a call button by the bed if you need anything."

Riley looked back but the nurse was gone. She turned to the bed and saw that Vanzinger's eyes were open.

"Hi." Her voice came out as a soft croak. "How are you?"

"I'm in the hospital, so I guess I'm not doing that great," Vanzinger replied. "And I've been awful lonely. Where've you been?"

The hurt in his voice surprised her.

"I called to check on you almost every day."

She stepped closer, clutching her purse against her body as if shielding herself from his judgment.

"I wasn't sure you'd be up for visitors."

Keeping his eyes fixed on her, he shook his head in disbelief.

"I died out there. Did you know that? My heart stopped beating, and I wasn't breathing. I was dead."

Riley gasped, stunned by the pain she saw in his eyes.

"You know the first thing I thought of when I came back to life?"

His voice shook with emotion, but his gaze was steady.

"I thought about you. I wanted to see you. But you weren't here."

"I'm...sorry."

Riley's voice cracked as she reached for his hand.

"I should have come sooner. I wanted to but..."

Clasping her hand in his, Vanzinger pulled her closer.

"But you're still holding a grudge," he finished for her. "You wrote me that letter. After I left. Told me when I left that you'd hate me until the day I die."

Riley had forgotten about that letter. It had come from a dark place. She cringed as she thought of everything she'd written.

"Well, guess what?" Vanzinger continued, his voice softening. "That day has come and gone, Riley. I died out there, and now I'm back. And it's time to let that old grudge go."

His words sliced through her, cutting her free from the past.

"You're right," she whispered. "I've been scared, and I've been punishing us both. I'm sorry."

She opened her purse and pulled out the book she'd read from front to back the night before. The corner of one page was folded, and she opened the book, then looked up at Vanzinger.

"For every decision you have to make, don't choose hate, don't choose greed, don't choose fear. It's simple...choose love."

Holding up the book, she showed Vanzinger the cover.

"That's from *Simply Portia*, the book Portia Hart wrote. I read it last night, and...well, I started thinking about my choices. It seems I've been making all the wrong ones. I don't want to do that anymore."

Hope sprang into Vanzinger's eyes.

"You know I would never have hurt you like that if I hadn't thought I was saving you, right?"

Vanzinger gripped her hand as if his life depended on her answer.

She nodded, clearing her throat.

"Nessa explained what happened. She said Chief Kramer and Detective Reinhart were dirty. They threatened to kill you if you exposed them, forced you to leave the WBPD."

Vanzinger nodded, his hands shaking with the memory.

"They wanted to destroy me. The only thing I cared about then was my work as a detective...and you. I couldn't risk being with you. I knew they would use you against me. Try to hurt you or...worse."

Riley thought back to the day on the beach. The day she'd seen Vanzinger's dead body lying on the sand.

"I think I finally understand," she said, realizing it was true. "When I thought you were dead...I would have done anything..."

Pulling her tighter against him, Vanzinger whispered in her ear.

"The hardest thing I've ever done is to walk away from you."

A knock sounded on the door, causing Riley to stand up and try to move away from the bed. Vanzinger grabbed her wrist and tugged her back as Jankowski strolled into the room, his broad shoulders making the room feel small.

"You still laying around in bed, partner?"

His eyes flicked to Vanzinger's hand on Riley's arm, and a wide smile spread over his face.

"You pulled this whole stunt just to get her back, didn't you, Tucker?" Jankowski teased. "But hey, whatever it takes."

Riley rolled her eyes, feeling as if she'd gone back in time a dozen years. Back to her days as a law intern. Back to the days when she and Vanzinger used to hang out with Jankowski and his wife, Gabby. The thought of Gabby wiped the smile off Riley's face.

Death is real, and it can come for any of us, at any time.

She squeezed Vanzinger's hand, reminded again that she should be grateful he was still with her, and that they'd found their way back to each other.

"So, I guess you're the new town hero, Tucker."

Jankowski nodded his approval.

"You took down a serial killer and survived a lightning strike on the same day. You're a legend around here."

Blushing at the effusive praise, Vanzinger met Riley's eyes.

"I had a little help you know," he said. "Riley, and Hunter Hadley, and Veronica Lee. It took all of us to figure out what the hell was going on and stop Xavier Greyson."

Jankowski studied the two of them together, and Riley saw a flash of sadness in his eyes. Maybe he was thinking of Gabby, too.

"You guys make a good team," Jankowski finally said. "Tucker, you can bring the bad guys in, and Riley, you can send them to jail."

"Sounds good to me," Vanzinger agreed. "Just as soon as I get out of here, I'll get started."

Thinking of the call she'd gotten from Nessa on the way over, Riley figured she'd have the opportunity to lock up another bad guy sooner than she'd expected.

No matter how many criminals she prosecuted, there were always more just waiting to come out of the woodwork. At least now she had a partner in her fight against crime, and no matter how bad things got, she wouldn't be alone anymore.

CHAPTER FORTY-NINE

Hunter opened the cardboard box and began piling in the books from his shelves. The sale of the station wouldn't be final for a few more weeks, but he didn't see any reason to delay the inevitable. Once the new owners came in, he knew he would surely be replaced with someone else.

They'll want to bring in someone they know. Someone they trust.

And he couldn't blame them. If it was his station, he'd do the same. Although he wasn't sure he'd hire himself. At least not as the station manager.

I'm better as a reporter. That's my calling. Not pushing paperwork and kissing up to fickle advertisers.

His phone buzzed in his pocket; Hunter was tempted to ignore it. He wasn't in the mood to talk. But the slight chance that Veronica might be calling prompted him to dig his phone out and check the display. He raised his eyebrows when he saw that the caller was Frankie Dawson.

"Mr. Dawson, how can I help you?"

"Well, you can start by calling me Frankie."

Smiling in spite of his sour mood, Hunter tried again.

"Okay, Frankie, how can I help you?"

"I have a new acquaintance I think you're gonna want to talk to." Frankie sounded unusually smug. "If you've got time to come to my office, I'll introduce you."

Intrigued, Hunter decided he could use an excuse to get out of the office. Besides, it would give him a chance to take Gracie for a walk.

"Okay, I'll be there shortly," Hunter agreed.

Dropping the phone back in his pocket, he opened the door to his office and called out to Gracie, who was lounging by Finn's desk.

"You want to go for a walk, girl?"

Finn looked over and nodded.

"Sure, I do."

He grabbed his phone and Gracie's leash.

"Where are we going?"

Hunter sighed, knowing it would useless to argue. Finn had been sticking to him like glue for the last two weeks, perhaps sensing that his time at the station would soon be coming to an end.

Walking toward the door, Hunter passed Veronica's desk, but he refused to torture himself by looking at her empty chair. He had no choice but to let her have the space and time she needed to heal.

Which was why he hadn't reached out to her after the traumatic events in Hart Cove. She'd gone through hell, and Hunter knew from experience, it would take time to recover.

He'd suffered from PTSD for years after the explosion in Kabul. The shattered bodies of the women and girls that died in the explosion still haunted his dreams and had caused him a lot of pain and soul searching during the years since.

How could he expect Veronica to react any differently? How could she not be scarred? She wouldn't be human if it didn't bother her.

She found a dead body stuffed in a freezer and saw a man shot dead right in front of her. Of course, she's bound to be traumatized.

Besides, what did he have to offer her now that the station was being sold? It was best to let her have time to figure out what she wanted. And if he was honest with himself, he needed to do the same.

* * *

Frankie was waiting at the door when the trio arrived. He waved Hunter, Finn, and Gracie into the little office and pointed to a couple of folding chairs across from his desk.

"Have a seat, gentlemen. Our guest will be joining us shortly."

Hunter cocked an eyebrow at Frankie's exaggerated hospitality, noting a self-satisfied gleam in his eyes.

"What's going on, Frankie," he asked, dropping onto a chair, and folding his arms over his chest. "You've obviously got something up your sleeve."

"It's called payback, my friend."

A knock on the door sent Frankie scurrying over. He opened the door to reveal a heavyset man with thinning gray hair and thick, busy eyebrows. The man stormed into the room, his face was red and sweaty, and his shirt collar was too tight.

"What's the meaning of this?"

He waved a piece of paper in his hand as he looked around the room. Seeing the three men and the dog, his anger turned to confusion.

"What is this? Some kind of shakedown?"

Frankie laughed, then shrugged.

"You could call it that I guess, Mr. Murray. But it's not the type you're probably used to."

He turned to Hunter and smiled.

"Mr. Hadley, I'd like you to meet Mr. Lloyd Murray."

Hunter stared at the man in shock.

"You're Lloyd Murray? The man who's buying Channel Ten?"

Murray's broad face grew even redder.

"Who are you...what do you know about that?"

"I'm the current station manager at Channel Ten," Hunter said, looking toward Frankie. "And I'm not sure what is going on here."

Frankie held up his hands as if to quiet a crowd.

"That's where I come in. You see, Mr. Murray is being blackmailed into buying Channel Ten. There were some... how do I phrase this ... *compromising* photos taken at the Riverview Hotel a few weeks ago."

Pacing the room as if he were a lawyer in a courtroom drama, Frankie turned his gaze on Murray, who stood frozen in place.

"The blackmailer kept his identity secret, isn't that right, Murray? But he told you to use all that money you've got to buy Channel Ten. Otherwise, your wife and kids would receive copies of the pics. Am I right?"

Murray blinked, but he didn't say anything. Hunter could see the wheels spinning frantically in his head.

"Do you know who the blackmailer is?" Hunter asked, trying to calculate what the information might mean to him. "And why they'd want Mr. Murray to buy the station?"

"Yes, and yes," Frankie said in triumph. "I know the answer to both of those questions. You see, I have a source who knows who took the photos. In fact, that source is at the WBPD right now giving a statement."

Panic bloomed in Murray's face as he absorbed Frankie's words.

"So, the good news, Mr. Murray, is that you no longer have to spend millions on a station you don't want to buy."

Frankie paused for dramatic effect before he continued.

"The bad news is, your fucked-up attempt to screw around with a girl half your age might be exposed."

Raising a fist, Murray seemed prepared to lunge at Frankie, but both Hunter and Finn stood up at the same time, glaring at the man. When Gracie began to growl low in her throat, Murray spun on his heel and banged through the door.

Hunter watched the door swing shut behind him, then turned to Frankie with angry eyes.

"Who blackmailed Murray?" he demanded. "And why make him buy the station?"

"You're the one who put me on to it."

Frankie leaned against his desk and crossed his skinny arms over his chest. He smiled at Hunter's puzzled frown.

"You asked Nessa about Nick Sargent's involvement with Molly Blair. Turns out the loser was involved in a few different rackets. Drugs, prostitution, and blackmail."

Frankie scratched at the stubble on his chin.

"Although why he targeted the station...I'm not so sure about that. Which is why I called you over here."

Shaking his head, Hunter tried to process what he had learned.

"I was aware Nick that had been trying to damage Channel Ten. I mean, he was stealing our employees and advertisers every chance he got, but...this? He must have been out to completely destroy the station."

Finn put a hand on Hunter's arm.

"I hate to tell you this, but I think it was personal."

Hunter frowned, not quite understanding.

"I think he wanted to destroy *you*, Hunter. Or at least your career. I'm not sure why, but some people just want to ruin anything good they see. They don't like to see people getting ahead."

Thinking back to everything that had happened in the last few months, Hunter could see that Finn was right.

"Well, whatever reason Sargent had, at least now the station isn't being sold," Finn said, sounding happy.

"No, not as soon as we thought," Hunter agreed. "But the board is still determined to sell. So, eventually, it will happen. Unless..."

Hunter hesitated. His idea of buying the station himself wasn't feasible. Putting it out there would only give Finn and the rest of the crew false hope.

"Unless what?" Finn asked. "Come on, Hadley, don't leave me in suspense. If you know of something that could save the station, you gotta try."

Exhaling, Hunter sank back into the folding chair.

"It's just...I've been thinking about buying the station myself."

He kept his eyes down as he explained why it wouldn't work.

"I've been through the financials a million times, and I just don't have enough to pull it off. I even thought of asking my father for a loan, but I don't want to spend the rest of my life under his thumb."

Reaching down to scratch Gracie's neck, Hunter tried to explain.

"You see, Finn. My father isn't the kind of man your dad was. Your dad was good, and he was honest."

Hunter struggled to find the right words.

"My father...the mayor...well, he's more interested in protecting himself and his position than in doing good. I've made the decision that I don't want that kind of energy in my life anymore, and I can't go back on it now."

"I wouldn't want you to," Finn said, reaching out to put a hand on Hunter's arm. "And I know Dad wouldn't want that either. Which is why I have another solution for you to consider."

Looking up in surprise, Hunter saw that Finn was smiling.

"I may actually know someone who could be your partner. You guys could go in fifty-fifty or something."

"Okay, who is it? Someone I know?"

Finn nodded and raised his eyebrows.

"It's me," he laughed. "Who'd you think I meant...Gracie?"

The Lab looked up expectantly at her name, but Finn was staring at Hunter, waiting for his reaction.

"You?" He finally managed. "But..."

"Yes, me...that is if you don't mind a partner that is twice as good-looking as you and half your age."

"I'm only thirty-six, smartass," Hunter said, beginning to smile. "Do you have the money to invest?"

"My dad left me a trust fund," Finn said, his eyes shining with pride. "He was a smart man, you know. He made some early investments in technology, and he lived a simple life."

Swallowing hard, Finn held Hunter's gaze.

"I know Dad would be happy his money's going to good use. And I have some great ideas for taking our online operations to a whole new level. That is...if you'd be up for making some changes."

Hunter nodded, feeling as if a weight had been removed from his shoulders. This idea might actually work out. It might be his chance to start again.

"I think it's definitely time for some changes," Hunter agreed. "And the first change I want to make is the station manager."

Finn blinked.

"What do you mean, change station managers?"

"I mean I want to be out in the field again," Hunter said.

He had the feeling if he didn't make the leap now, he might never get another chance to do what he'd been born to do.

"I want to go out and report on stories that matter. I want to investigate the world again. I don't want to sit in my office and watch other people live out my dream. I don't want to let the fear control me anymore."

"That's deep, man. But I gotta few things to take care of."

Hunter had almost forgotten that Frankie was in the room. He laughed, glad to have finally admitted to himself what he needed.

"Besides, I'm sure you guys need to get busy on your new story."

When Hunter looked at him blankly, Frankie shook his head.

"Come on man, I thought you were a reporter. I've just handed you a mega scoop on slimy Nick Sargent and that dirtbag Murray. You tellin' me you aren't gonna jump on that?"

Frankie slapped his palm on his desk for emphasis.

"Especially seeing how Nick was the one that screwed you guys over on the initial Xavier Greyson story."

The comment caused Hunter's stomach to drop.

"From what I hear he paid some bartender to steal the information so your station would get blamed for the leak."

Hunter looked at Finn, wondering if he'd known this, but the young man looked as blindsided as he felt.

"Nessa told me that fucked up mess caused Veronica Lee to quit." Frankie scowled. "Man, she was your best damn reporter."

Crossing to the door, Hunter turned to see that Finn and Gracie were right behind him. They needed to get back to the station. They had a story to produce.

If I do this right, it could be my one chance to win back Veronica's trust.

CHAPTER FIFTY

Veronica sat up in bed with a start, gasping for air. She'd had another nightmare about Xavier Greyson. This time she'd been back under the waves, gasping for breath, as her mother's voice told her to let go. But in the nightmare, the words didn't bring peace, they brought anger.

Why did Ma tell me to give up? Shouldn't she have encouraged her only daughter to fight for her life? Or is my life not worth fighting for?

The irrational anger at her mother remained as Veronica made her way downstairs. It was a Saturday, and her mother was in the kitchen making breakfast as Veronica shuffled in. Winston lounged in a patch of sunlight, and Veronica bent to scoop him up.

"I'm glad you slept in," Ling Lee said, giving her daughter an assessing stare. "You've been working too hard."

Ignoring the comment, Veronica hugged the big tabby cat against her and took down a mug. She would have a cup of tea and some toast and then head out again. Her research in Hart Cove was almost done. One more day and she'd be ready to write the final report.

"Listen, Ronnie, I need to tell you something."

Ling stood at the sink, her back turned to Veronica.

"And it is something that is not easy for me to say."

Veronica heard the tremor in her mother's voice and hesitated. What would make her mother sound so scared? Was she sick? Did she have cancer?

"I know I should have told you before...about your father."

Heart pounding, Veronica set Winston on the floor and crossed to stand beside her mother. She waited, not wanting to interrupt, not wanting to give her mother any reason to stop talking.

"I know you've been going to see Dr. Horn lately, and...I made an appointment, too. I figured if you were brave enough to go..."

Questions rose in Veronica's head, but she forced herself to remain quiet. This was her mother's story to tell.

"Dr. Horn said I should tell whatever feels right when I'm ready. But I think that day might not ever come, so...I'll tell you now."

Drawing in a deep breath, Ling looked out the window, keeping her eyes on the garden beyond.

"When I met your father, I thought he was a wonderful man. I was so young, and I loved him...very much."

Ling choked on the words, and Veronica reached out and put a hand on her thin shoulder.

"Or, I should say, I loved the man he *pretended* to be. But he had lied to me. About everything. His name, his background, and the way he made his money."

A sick ache started up in Veronica's stomach as Ling spoke. Somehow, she'd known the truth would be ugly. But she'd always held out hope she was wrong.

"Eventually, I found out enough to be scared, and I decided to leave. I was young and...well, I thought it would be best."

She paused as if building her courage, and when she continued, her voice was thick with pain.

"Your father went...mad. He did things I cannot bring myself to speak of. But I've written it down. If you choose to read what your father has done...what your mother has suffered, then I'll show you."

Ling turned and looked into Veronica's eyes.

"But if you want to let it go, then I'll burn the paper, and you and I can move on with our lives. It is your decision."

The pain in Ling's eyes was more than Veronica could bear. She pulled her mother to her, feeling Ling's thin shoulders shaking with emotion.

"Don't worry about that now," Veronica soothed, murmuring the words Ling had always used to comfort her as a child. "Everything will be okay. Whatever happens, and whatever I decide, we'll always have each other. That will never change."

But as she finished making her tea, Veronica wondered what her decision would be. She thought of the book on her dresser, and the new story she'd been working on, and wondered if fate was trying to tell her something.

* * *

Veronica steered the Jeep toward the highway, knowing she had a lot of thinking to do in the three-hour drive ahead of her. Her phone buzzed in her purse, and she reached in to pull it out. The number on the display made her heart stop.

Hunter Hadley hadn't tried to contact her since the day on the beach two weeks ago, and she hadn't called him.

She'd needed time to come to terms with everything that had happened, and she had assumed he was busy moving on with his life.

But she had missed him, and she had planned to reach out to him once she'd completed her story. Hunter may not be her boss anymore, but she respected his judgment as a reporter, and he'd be honest enough to tell her if her piece was good or not.

"Veronica? How are you?"

His familiar voice sent a pleasant shiver down her spine.

"I'm good, thanks."

She forced a cheerful tone.

"Just heading out to finish up a report I've been working on."

"A report? That's great," he said, clearing his throat. "I was wondering if you could stop by the station. It won't take long."

Hesitating, her eyes fell on the corner of the book sticking out of her bag. She drew in a deep breath and made a decision.

"Okay, I can be there in ten minutes, but I can't stay long."

She steered the Jeep toward Channel Ten and tried to calm her nerves. She'd hear what he had to say, and then she'd be off.

As she stepped into the station, she saw Hunter and Finn standing with the crew under the big screen on the wall. Hunter called her over with a smile, pointing to the screen.

"This is the special report I wanted you to see. It's almost done. Just needs a few finishing touches."

Hunter moved closer as the segment began, whispering in her ear.

"We put this together for you."

Puzzled, Veronica watched as the exposé on Nick Sargent unfolded, revealing a long list of illegal and unethical activities he was accused of committing.

She was stunned to see they'd even included his role in obtaining her notes about the Xavier case and leaking the story before the WBPD was ready. Nick's actions had prompted Greyson to leave town and had ultimately led to his attack on Veronica.

At the end of the report, she saw footage of Detective Jankowski walking Nick into the police station. Riley Odell was smiling in the background.

"Well, what do you think?" Hunter asked after the segment had ended. "Of course, we need a reporter to introduce the story to the rest of the world. Someone who knows what she's talking about."

"I can't believe Nick did all that."

Veronica shivered at the thought of the harm he'd caused.

"How'd you and Finn pull it all together?"

"Well, that's a trade secret," Hunter teased, "and we can only tell the secret to employees of our station."

Standing in front of the crew, Finn held up his hands.

"Can I have your attention? I want to make an announcement."

The room grew silent as all eyes turned to Finn.

"The pending sale of Channel Ten has been canceled," he called out, catching Veronica's eye, and smiling. "The buyer backed out, which is good news because that means Hunter and I have put a bid in for the station ourselves."

As the crew began to cheer, Hunter held up a hand.

"It's not official yet, but if things work out, we'll all be able to keep on doing our work. Finn and I will keep you all posted."

Veronica felt a rush of relief. She hadn't caused the station to go under, and Hunter and the crew were going to be all right.

"I hope you'll come back. Your job's still waiting for you," Hunter said in a low voice as the crew began to disperse. "Unless you've got another job. You said you're working on a new story?"

Feeling suddenly shy, Veronica nodded.

"Yes, I mean...I haven't gotten a new job, but I am working on a new story." She bit her lip and looked up at him. "In fact, I was just on my way to finish up my investigation."

She looked at her watch.

"And I've got to leave now if I'm going to make it on time."

Hunter's face fell, but he nodded.

"Okay, I understand."

"But, if you're up for a road trip, you can come along with me."

A smile lit up his face, and he called out to Gracie.

"Come on girl, we're going for a ride."

* * *

Hart Cove Cemetery sat in the afternoon sun. Its neat rows of gravestones and the mourners gathered around the newly dug graves, shaded by a family of sprawling oak trees.

Veronica lifted her face to the east, imagining she could feel the breeze from the ocean half a mile away. The service had been emotional, with several friends and neighbors offering touching tributes to the siblings who were being laid to rest side to side next to their parents' well-tended graves.

As people began to move back toward their cars, Veronica greeted several of them and waved to others.

"You met all these people when you were working on your story?" Hunter's eyes were curious as he watched her.

"Well, I tried to talk to everyone around here who knew Portia or Julian," she said, pulling out her notebook. "You'd be amazed at how much people around here admired them."

Scanning through her notes, Veronica thought about the impact the Harts' had made on the little town.

"Xavier Greyson lied to me, and to the police about Portia," she said. "He told us that Portia had lost her money to bad investments. But that's not true. She gave away most of it to help others."

Pulling her copy of *Simply Portia* out of her purse, Veronica opened it to the last page.

"It's right here in her book. I guess Xavier Greyson never read it." Veronica cleared her throat and read aloud in a clear, soft voice.

"I want to spread my good fortune to others before I go. That's why I make it a point to donate to as many worthy causes as I can. It'd be a shame to die holding on to money that could've helped someone else."

Hunter smiled at the words, his eyes lingering on her face. She blushed and looked down at her notebook again.

"And Julian's paintings are incredible. He was truly talented. They both were. I wish I'd had the chance to meet them."

305

"I guess you have, in a way," Hunter said, gesturing to the people who were getting into their cars in the little unpaved lot. "You met the people they helped, and felt the impact they had, and now you can tell their story."

Veronica felt her eyes tear up, and she looked away, not wanting him to see how much she was still hurting.

"I just didn't want them to end up being a horror story on the news. I didn't want them to only be remembered for the terrible way they died."

She lifted her eyes and tried to smile.

"Maybe my story will remind people that it isn't how we die...it's how we live that matters."

"Is that in Portia's book, too?" Hunter teased, reaching for her hand. "Because I think it makes a lot of sense. And I also think I've been focusing on the wrong things for too long."

Squeezing his hand in hers, Veronica stepped closer, intoxicated by the heat of his skin and the longing she saw in his eyes.

"I have, too," Veronica said, lifting her face to his. "But I'm making the decision here and now, to focus on what's important."

Hunter smiled, his mouth only inches from hers.

"And what is it that's important to you?" he murmured.

"It's simple," she said, pulling him closer. "The only thing that really matters...love."

Read the Next Book in the Veronica Lee Thriller Series
By Melinda Woodhall
Read Her Final Fall: A Veronica Lee Thriller, Book Two Now

ACKNOWLEDGEMENTS

IT'S EXCITING TO BE INTRODUCING a new thriller series to my readers, and I first want to thank everyone who has read the Mercy Harbor series and provided me with feedback and encouragement. I was truly grateful for their kind support as I was writing this book.

I wrote this book during the winter holidays and spent many nights and weekends to get it finished on time. I'm incredibly lucky that my wonderful husband, Giles, and five amazing children, Michael, Joey, Linda, Owen, and Juliet, give me the time and support I need to write.

I give thanks every day that I have such a supportive extended family, including Melissa Romero, Leopoldo Romero, Melanie Arvin Kutz, David Woodhall, and Tessa Woodhall.

My mother's love of reading stays with me as I write each book, and I know without her early encouragement, I never would have found the courage to write my stories and share them with the world. Thanks, Mom!

If you enjoyed this book, please
Leave a review for Her Last Summer

ABOUT THE AUTHOR

Melinda Woodhall is the author of the new *Veronica Lee Thriller* series, as well as the page-turning *Mercy Harbor Thriller* series. In addition to writing romantic thrillers and police procedurals, Melinda also writes women's contemporary fiction as M.M. Arvin.

When she's not writing, Melinda can be found reading, gardening, chauffeuring her children around town, and updating her vegetarian lifestyle website.

Melinda is a native Floridian and the proud mother of five children. She lives with her family in Orlando.

Visit Melinda's website at www.melindawoodhall.com

Other Books by Melinda Woodhall

The River Girls
Girl Eight
Catch the Girl
Girls Who Lie
Her Final Fall
Her Winter of Darkness
Her Silent Spring

Made in United States
North Haven, CT
24 March 2025

67190862R00186